Terry

after 55 years

a friend

K. B. Pell[illegible]

aka Kall[illegible]

# MARY LOU

## Oh, What Did She Do?

K. B. PELLEGRINO

This is a work of fiction. All of the characters, names, incidents, organizations, and dialogue in this novel are either the products of the author's imagination or are used fictitiously.

LifeRich Publishing is a registered trademark of The Reader's Digest Association, Inc.

LifeRich Publishing books may be ordered through booksellers or by contacting:

LifeRich Publishing
1663 Liberty Drive
Bloomington, IN 47403
www.liferichpublishing.com
1 (888) 238-8637



ISBN: 978-1-4897-1881-5 (sc)
ISBN: 978-1-4897-1882-2 (hc)
ISBN: 978-1-4897-1880-8 (e)

Library of Congress Control Number: 2018909155

Print information available on the last page.

LifeRich Publishing rev. date: 08/31/2018

**Sung by Ronnie Hawkins and the Hawks**

## "Mary Lou"

I'm going to tell you a story about Mary Lou
I mean the kind of a woman who makes a fool of you
She makes a young man groan and an old man pain
The way she took my money was a crying shame.

(Mary Lou, Mary Lou) She took my diamond ring
(Mary Lou, Mary Lou) She took my watch and chain
(Mary Lou, Mary Lou) She took the keys to my Cadillac car
Jumped in my Kitty and she drove-a-far ...

Apex (3) – 9-76561, Canada. Released in 1959. Genre: Rock

# Contents


CHAPTER 1 The Fire, 1963 ........ 1
CHAPTER 2 Church, 2017 ........ 12
CHAPTER 3 Beauregard Reviews the Accident Report ........ 21
CHAPTER 4 Loss of Family, Lake Placid, New York, 1975 ........ 29
CHAPTER 5 Church, West Side Country Club, 2017 ........ 38
CHAPTER 6 San Francisco, 1981 ........ 46
CHAPTER 7 A Georgia Visitor from the Past ........ 53
CHAPTER 8 Detectives Deliberate ........ 63
CHAPTER 9 Nashville and Memphis, 1982 ........ 70
CHAPTER 10 Dinner at the Club ........ 81
CHAPTER 11 Police Focus on the Non-open Case ........ 87
CHAPTER 12 Gar Lonergan Retains an Attorney ........ 99
CHAPTER 13 Brooklyn, New York, 1996 ........ 107
CHAPTER 14 Gar Lonergan Reveals ........ 119
CHAPTER 15 Detective Jim Locke ........ 125
CHAPTER 16 Hunt and Find, Private Investigators ........ 130
CHAPTER 17 The Wedding ........ 134
CHAPTER 18 Silverstein Detectives ........ 140
CHAPTER 19 Opening the Leana Lonergan Case ........ 150
CHAPTER 20 Mary Lou's First Love, 1976 ........ 163
CHAPTER 21 Collaborating at the Station ........ 169
CHAPTER 22 Attorney and Client ........ 175
CHAPTER 23 Detective Ashton Lent ........ 180
CHAPTER 24 Attorneys Search the Lonergan Home ........ 186
CHAPTER 25 Surprises, New York City, 1996 ........ 191

CHAPTER 26 Inventory Control....197
CHAPTER 27 The Detectives at Work.... 203
CHAPTER 28 Potential Defense Investigation....213
CHAPTER 29 Who Could Have Killed Her?....222
CHAPTER 30 A Visit Home, 2014....226
CHAPTER 31 MCU Reviews and Reviews Data....232
CHAPTER 32 Beauregard and Norbie Confer.... 240
CHAPTER 33 New Evidence Emerges.... 248
CHAPTER 34 The Devil's in the Details....253
CHAPTER 35 What Suffices for Justice?.... 260
CHAPTER 36 Protecting the Almost but Not Innocent Victim.... 264
Acknowledgments....271
Care to Review My Book?
(or "Honest Reviews Don't Kill")....272
More Books by K. B. Pellegrino....273
Preview: "Brothers of Another Mother –
All for one – Always?"....274
BONUS....275

# 1

# The Fire, 1963

THE EXPLOSION ERUPTED IN the early morning hours, on the top two floors of a three-story house that sat on the crest of a hill. The home's location in a rundown and congested area near Windsor, Connecticut, brought a surge of activity, including firefighters, paramedics, police officers, neighbors, Red Cross volunteers, fire stalkers, and church ladies. Two children, Mary Lou and Timothy, sat quietly in their pajamas and watched the flaming chaos in front of them. Mary Lou calmly watched the flames and thought, *How strange! The first floor isn't burning up.*

Some neighbor ladies had wrapped Timothy and her in blankets. Mary Lou thought, *They think that they can get us to come with them. No way are we going with them. We're watching the fire. Timothy is only five years old, and if they try to take him, he will go on a screaming tear. He won't let anyone touch him. If they try to talk with him ... well, they won't understand that he will just scream and kick and bite. I'm only eight years old, but I know what he needs and wants. Just look at him grasping that plastic game piece; he still wants to play the game. They'll find out that I'm the only one who is able to calm him.*

The good ladies let the children watch the fire. It went on for hours. The first professional attempt to talk with the children did result in some information. Mary Lou said, "The house exploded, and we ran outside because we were afraid."

When asked who else was in the house, Mary Lou (not Timothy) answered, "Our mother, father, and Austin, our other brother. I'm sure they're dead because they were upstairs in bed."

Mary Lou saw that one of the firemen, who was listening to her, ran to inform the others that there were three unaccounted for people. Despite their quick actions, they were unable to save the rest of the family.

The firefighters, police officers, and fire investigator, as well as a lady from social services, asked Mary Lou why she and Timothy were on the first floor at three in the morning and were not in bed.

Mary Lou was quite clear. "Timothy wanted to play Chutes and Ladders before bedtime, like he was promised, but Daddy was drunk and sent us to bed instead. We decided to get up in the middle of the night and play. It was only fair, because Timothy was promised he could play before bed."

The fire investigator asked Mary Lou why Timothy wouldn't talk to them. Mary Lou said, "Timothy is autistic and only talks to some people, but he'll always talk to me."

Several neighbors confirmed Timothy's autism and quickly stated that the children's parents were constantly in an inebriated state. Mary Lou was asked about her brother Austin.

"Austin used to be a really good brother, but when he became a teenager, he started threatening Timothy and me. He was no longer nice."

Mary Lou heard a policeman, a fireman, and the important lady say that the children should not be questioned anymore until there was a child psychologist to assist in the task.

She thought, *Timothy has a psychologist. They always want to know what's in his mind. Well, Timothy never tells anyone but me anything at all. I'll be careful.*

With a great deal of effort made by many people, and aided by next-door neighbors Mrs. Mabel Baker and her son Burt, who was in the same grade at school as Mary Lou, the children agreed to go with the lady from social services. The lady said that she had found a good temporary home for them with truly sympathetic people.

Mary Lou thought, *We have to sleep somewhere. Maybe the bed will have clean sheets. Timothy is going to get really tired, and when that happens, he's not easy to keep quiet.*

Mary Lou overheard Mrs. Baker, who speaks loudly all the time, assuring the lady who said she was from social services that there were no other relatives. Mrs. Cora Court, Mary Lou's mother, had told Mrs. Baker at one time that both she and her husband, Cal, were only children and had only a distant cousin who was not worth nuthin'. She further stated that the older brother, Austin, had turned into a juvenile delinquent who respected nobody in the neighborhood, adding that the younger kids had probably been saved from such a fate by the fire. "God works in strange ways," she said.

Mary Lou was upset that Mrs. Baker continued to rant on about what happens in a neighborhood when low-level alcoholics move in. Mrs. Baker railed that the only nice things about this family were the two younger children, who were never given a bit of attention. "I know personally they were getting money from the state for Austin and Timothy. Austin is supposed to be depressed, but for a depressed boy, he certainly gets in a lot of trouble teasing kids and hurting animals. But I never saw him hurting himself like depressed people do. And as far as Timothy's autism, well, maybe he has it or maybe he doesn't. I wouldn't talk to anyone in that family but Mary Lou, if I had a choice. My Burt really likes her, although she's not too friendly with him. She's lucky anyone talks to her, coming from that family. They got state money, so they could sit around all day, drink, and get rowdy with their friends. They had a coupla bikers in there all the time. God forgive me, but I'm telling you those kids are better off without the parents and brother."

Mary Lou had difficulty controlling her feelings. *No one on the street thinks that Mrs. Baker is nice. They all call her a busybody, and her son constantly bothers me and follows me around. I'm not lucky that he tries to be friendly. He's not a friend. He's a bullying little bug—one who probably bites.*

Mary Lou and Timothy arrived early in the morning at what was called their new foster parents' home. Ernestine and Lester Prior were lauded as good people, known throughout the area for their success in raising (along with their one biological son) six foster children, and five of those for more than twelve years. There'd be no fooling around with the children's rights under Ernestine's protective umbrella.

A psychologist specializing in victims of trauma and a police detective visited the children at their foster family's home much later in the day.

Ernestine greeted them at the door, and when asked if she had questioned the children about the day's events, she replied that she knew better than to look for information so soon or to question the children. Mary Lou was quite satisfied with Ernestine, especially when she heard Mrs. Prior say, "That's your job, Detective. Get it right, and don't put any thoughts in their heads, please. They have to carry on from here. I don't want any additional ideas floating around their brains. And no guilt. Do you understand me?"

Dr. Metas, the psychologist, questioned the children, but only Mary Lou responded. She noted that Mary Lou's answers to practically all questions were devoid of emotional overlay to the point of total detachment. Mary Lou's only instance of any type of connection to other human beings—and she questioned her own judgment on this—was her obvious protective efforts on her brother Timothy's behalf.

Before Dr. Metas could initiate a conversation, Mary Lou asked, "What will happen to Timothy? You just can't put him in one of those homes; he's very smart, you know. He knows all his letters and numbers and can read, and he's only five. I've taught him everything. He just needs special help, and he's a good little boy."

Mary Lou thought that Dr. Metas was trying to make her feel better when she asked, "Do you think that Timothy will be happy staying with the Priors?"

Mary Lou did think that it would work for Timothy but asked, "How old are Mr. and Mrs. Prior? They look old to me. I need to know how old they are. I can't have them dying too, before Timothy is through school and has a job and an apartment. He'll be all right then."

Dr. Metas looked to Mary Lou as if she were uncertain about what Mary Lou had said. Mary Lou heard her whisper to the detective, "Do you think that Mary Lou is showing emotional involvement with Timothy, or just undertaking the sisterly job of Timothy's caretaker? You know, Detective, for all the trauma of the previous day, Mary Lou appears untouched and terrifically poised for an eight-year-old child." The detective nodded in agreement.

Mary Lou watched Dr. Metas studying her. The doctor thought, *She is pretty, with that blunt-cut hairstyle, almost platinum hair, and brilliant blue eyes. Mary Lou will be a showstopper someday. And Timothy is the typical blond, tousled-haired, little boy who tickles your heart just looking at him. They could have a future. But I must get back to the present—collect a fuller picture of the Court family. That is the important item on my agenda.*

Mary Lou was quite objective in her analysis of her dead family. She told Dr. Metas and the Detective that Mom and Dad were mean and drank all the time. They never cooked dinner. Her brother Austin used to cook spaghetti and beans for them and canned fruit salad, before he became what her mother called "a motherfuckin' teenager." Austin had grown bigger than their dad by then, and nobody gave him a hard time anymore, even when the school called about his constant fighting.

Mary Lou said, "Austin started to be mean to me and Timothy. He wouldn't feed us unless we told him that he was in charge. He wouldn't give Mom and Dad their cigarettes when they were drunk unless they gave him money and thanked him over and over. Timothy and I hoped that he would stop, because it took forever, but Mom and Dad gave in to whatever he wanted. Austin also got rid of the sleazy guy, Biker, who came over whenever Dad was gone and would get in bed with Mom. Austin said that he would cut his little dingy off if he came back, and Biker never came back again."

A fuller picture of the everyday life of the Court family emerged.

Mary Lou said, "Our parents were grouchy in the morning, saying that they needed to clear their heads and drink their coffee. After that, they would give orders to us. Only Timothy and I obeyed orders to clear the dishes, make the beds, sweep the floor, and put the laundry in the wash. I would bring Timothy to a day care center for the handicapped, located on the way to my school; and then go to school. Mom wouldn't let the handicapped transporter take Timothy because she didn't want the neighbors to talk."

"Austin would go to school if he felt like it. By the time we returned from school each day, Mom and Dad were happily imbibing. That's what they called it. They used to say, 'Imbibing is enjoying the fruits of life in your own home. Drinking is low-class.' The remains of takeout lunch were always on the table, and Dad would start talking and acting dirty. He would say to Austin, 'Big boy like you probably getting lots of cunt out there. Take my word for it: It's free for the taking. Just don't get anyone pregnant, or you'll be stuck with a family to take care of me.'

"Mom would get mad and show her fanny—she never wears underpants like me—and tell Dad to kiss it like he always wants to do, but he can't get it up. Then Dad would start on me, telling me I'm almost to the point of interest. In another year or two, he might be interested, or maybe Austin could be the first. He would laugh. Mom would get a little mad but never told him to stop talking dirty. They normally left Timothy alone, except when they called him Dumb Nuts."

Mary Lou said that if she talked to anyone on the street, or that if anyone should take an interest in her, her mother would forbid her to speak to the person.

Dr. Metas asked what she would do then, and her response was, "I would never let my mother see me talking with neighbors. But sometimes the neighbors would say good things about me to my mom or dad, or to Austin, and my parents would punish me for being a traitor to the family. Dad used to get into fistfights with all the men in the neighborhood, until one man knocked him down. Then Dad didn't go out very often after that, and mostly at night."

Mary Lou heard Dr. Metas talking to Ernestine. "I've received all the children's school reports, and they are almost glowing. Mary Lou is at the top of her class but rarely speaks in class. Her teachers said that she is an organized child who does what is expected of her. She does not make much of an effort to have friends, but all the children want to be friends with her. Timothy has been diagnosed with autism but is very bright. He does well one-to-one with an aide, but the confusion around a large group makes him rock back and forth with his hands over his ears. If he is very upset, he screeches in a high octave that sets your teeth on fire.

"When I asked Mary Lou if Timothy would screech at home, she became very angry. She answered 'Yes, he would screech when they were mean to him, but mostly they left him alone. When he screeched, Mom would lock him in the closet. I'd go in there with him or else he would hurt himself, banging away until he could make himself quiet.' How often this punishment happened is difficult to know. Mary Lou figured maybe twice a week.

"I also asked Mary Lou what her favorite games were. What games did she like to play? Mary Lou seemed confused with the question and said that they only had Timothy's Chutes and Ladders game, which was a gift he won at school. She wasn't allowed to play ball in the street with the other kids. Her mother said, 'That's for lowlifes, not little girls."

The detective called for the children to focus on the subject of the fire. He noticed that neither child demonstrated any reaction, which surprised all three adults present, as did Mary Lou saying, "I know how the fire started. Mom and Dad couldn't fill the cigarette lighter with fluid. Their hands shake all the time. They can't do lots of things. Normally I do it for them, and sometimes Timothy does too because he's really good at things like that. But Austin wouldn't let us do it.

He made Mom and Dad do it. He said, 'If you're old enough to drink and smoke, then you have to do it yourself.' They tried their hardest but kept spilling the fluid on the tablecloth. Austin finally let us refill the lighters. He said that they were helpless and would cause a fire, because Mom always had candles lit. She said they gave the dump atmosphere."

The detective asked what time this had all happened. Mary Lou answered, "Around nine thirty at night."

The detective questioned, "Mary Lou the fire started at three o'clock the next morning, so how could this be the start of the fire?"

Mary Lou said without a moment's thought, "My mom and dad started fighting and then yelling at me and Timothy. Timothy started screeching, and we both ended up in the closet while Mom and Austin blamed Dad for setting off Timothy. Mom said, 'You stupid fool, you know how he gets, and now we have to listen to him. I should put him in a home like the social worker wants.' Dad and Austin both protested because they wouldn't have any support for Timothy, if he didn't live with us. Mom said that it was just a matter of time before he would be put away. Mom said, 'He's too weird for normal living. You all know that. Might be better for him to leave while he's young. Austin, you can get a job when you're sixteen. You don't like school, anyway.'"

Mary Lou said that Austin got mad at that and started throwing things around. "I heard them drinking all night with Austin, and they let us out of the closet at midnight. The house was a mess. Timothy protested again and wanted to play Chutes and Ladders because earlier they had promised him. Instead, we were sent to bed. I made a deal with Timothy that when the others were in bed, we would go down to the first floor, where we wouldn't be heard, and play the game. That was how I got Timothy to go to bed without howling again."

Mary Lou said that she then fell asleep and awoke when the bedroom clock read 2:35. "I woke Timothy, and we went down to the first floor to play. We normally slept on the third floor, and when we went past the television room on the second floor, I saw that Mom had left the candles burning. That's why I believe that the candles burned downed to the tablecloth that had the lighter fluid on it."

The detective asked, "Mary Lou, were there holders under the candles?"

"Mom had small plastic plates she would put under the candles that always smelled terrible when they burned."

Dr. Metas asked when Mary Lou had seen the first evidence of a fire. Timothy, who had not talked at all, suddenly said, "Bang, bang, woof—gone, gone!" He then repeated himself, put his hands over his ears, and repeated himself.

Mary Lou made Timothy face her, took his hands off his ears, and said, "It's all right. There's no more big bang—no more fire. Timothy, we're safe."

Dr. Metas asked if Timothy was saying that there was an explosion first or smoke first. Mary Lou said, "We heard some noise on the second floor, and so we tried to be very quiet so that nobody would hear us downstairs. Then I heard a bottle drop, and then an explosion, which made Timothy go into his screeching. Timothy is really strong when he's in a tantrum, but I knew that we had to get out of there, and so I dragged him, screaming for his game, out of the house. When he saw all the flames from the fire, he calmed down and watched with me. That's all I know."

Later, the fire investigator met with the psychologist and the detective, and using the children's interviews, they attempted to determine the cause of the blaze. Based on centers of intense heat and what could be garnered from the victims' remains, it was determined that the father could have come down to the second floor, if in fact he had been sleeping on the third floor. He may have knocked over a bottle of booze onto a burning candle, tried to pull it back, and maybe slipped, pushing the candle onto the kerosene stove. It was decided that a small flame from the lighter fluid, candle, and bottle came first, and when he tried to move the burning mess, it hit the stove and exploded.

The other two bodies were found in the second-floor bedrooms, one in each. Unexplained was the reason that there was a tight metal guide wire above and across the bottom step going from the second to the third floor. The wire didn't burn, and they could think of no reason to have a wire in that place.

Investigators from both police and fire reviewed the scene many times, and although their logic for the fire start was reasonably clear and supported by evidence, there also existed the distinct possibility that the father had tripped on the wire coming down the stairs with a bottle in his hand, landing on the table with the candle and the remains of the lighter fluid, and knocked the candle over. That started the fire, which then hit the kerosene stove. In this scenario, he may have been hurt in the fall and unable to stop the carnage. Relying on this theory, the fire's start went from accident to potential murder. The wire was wrapped around nails on either side of the stairs. The installation was deliberate. Who would do that? They needed an answer.

After much negotiation with Mrs. Prior, Dr. Metas, the detective, and the fire investigator again met with the children, accompanied by an attorney for the children. Mrs. Prior requested a lawyer for the children, saying, "If they were my own children, I wouldn't let you near them without an attorney. I have a duty to protect these children, and they truly have suffered more than most of us in their short lives."

All in all, there were seven people in the room with the children. Mary Lou and Timothy sat together with Mrs. Prior, and their attorney sat opposite them. The others sat on a separate couch and chairs. The detective asked Mary Lou if she knew that there was a wire across the stairs going from the second to the third floor. Surprisingly, Mary Lou said, "I knew about the wire. Dad once caught Timothy and me going down to the first floor to get food in the middle of the night. He put the wire in to trip us up so he could catch us, but we know where the wire is, and we just climb over it. He's never caught us since."

Dr. Metas asked, "Mary Lou, does your father sleep on the third floor or the second floor?"

Mary Lou answered, "Sometimes he sleeps on the third floor,

if Mom kicks him out of bed, but not too often. Their room is on the second floor, and it's the biggest room. Austin's room is also on the second floor, and there's a television room and another storage room. Timothy and I sleep in one room on the third floor, and there is another bedroom."

The detective asked Mary Lou how she got the front door unlocked, enabling her and Timothy getting out so quickly.

Her answer was, "It's never locked. Dad gets package deliveries in the middle of the night on Tuesdays and Thursdays. He leaves money in an envelope for the man who comes." The fire occurred on Wednesday in the early morning.

The arson case was left open for three months while investigators pursued the "deliveries" and their origin. Despite a lot of noise concerning drug deliveries done this way in or near this neighborhood, authorities never found the delivery person. After a long delay, the case was closed as an accidental fire.

# 2

# Church, 2017

THE NEW AND FABULOUS country club called Lone Horse was located in a town in Massachusetts adjacent to Connecticut, near the city of Springfield. It was filled tonight, and its wealthy, high-class patrons were acting quite rowdy. It was the second year after the club's opening, and the private owners had invested over forty-five million dollars in the facilities. They had drawn the high rollers of society and the wannabes for the 2017 four ball golf tournament. Tonight after the banquet dinner, some well-known business owners, lawyers, doctors, and politicians, all male, had formed into a little group to discuss some pressing matters. Edgar Lonergan, normally called Gar, joined them, causing a bit of a stir.

"Where the hell have you been, Gar?" said Ed Loughlin. Ed was not known for his discretion, and he felt there was no reason to be discreet because his profession was in waste management. Ed was noted by the community for the many overly large homes he owned in several areas of the country. All were in famous vacation areas such as West Palm Beach, Chatham on Cape Cod, a condo in New York City, and one on the short Alabama Gulf Coast. "It's been two fucking years, and you disappear from society. Well, I mean our society."

Jake Lemanski tried shushing him but Ed was not to be shushed, as his three ex-wives would have told anyone who would listen. Ed said that Gar had been mourning long enough. "After all, it's been two long years since Leana died. Now, I know it was an awful tragedy, but two years, and we haven't seen hide or hair of you. Buddy, come back to the living."

Norberto Cull, or Norbie, was a well-known defense attorney who had won cases not just locally but also nationally. He had a reputation as a haberdasher's delight. His favorite shopping mecca was in Montreal, where he was fitted properly by a French tailor specializing in tapering, nipping, and making a suit look fabulous—all at a price. Norbie's fashion sense was in keeping with his high-class courtroom presence; it was noted by a local judge unhappy with the current dress codes in his courtroom, who remarked, "Thank God someone is showing respect in this court and dressing well."

Norbie skillfully guided the conversation. "God, I'm happy to see you, Gar. We've just been discussing Trump and his tweets. I'm so pleased to change the subject. I didn't see your name, so I'm guessing you didn't play. Of course you didn't play. You would have won if you had. Have you joined this club, or are you still in the one in West Side?"

Norbie listened as Gar slowly answered minimally with, "To answer one question, I still belong to West Side Country Club, and now I've joined this icon to conspicuous consumption. To answer the other question, it takes time to recover. And it hasn't been two years, only about twenty-one months, since October 2015. Leana died in a horrible way, and I still have nightmares thinking about it. It's taken me a couple of years to regroup with my children and grandchildren. That's not too long. Now, enough is enough on this subject. What's been going on in western Massachusetts during my little hiatus?"

Norbie thought, *Thankfully we've moved on. Moved on to men and golf, and I suppose even women and golf. Well, let's say golf aficionados. They can talk and talk about the difficult green, the lay of the grass, dampness, loud noises, sun in their eyes, and their personal stress as an explanation for the ball in the woods, water, sand, or whatever. And this group of men is no different.*

In the midst of a discussion of a great hit made by Ed that gave him a birdie, business gossip that could end up being the basis of the next deal prevailed. All the while, as the men dissed a food meal with snide remarks, Norbie thought, *Just another day on the links for the guys.*

Norbie always enjoyed these meetings of the group because they were more than meetings. The men were members of a certain kind of informal club often called church. He thought that it was as if they'd modernized the old European men's clubs of the 1800s. Over really good bourbon or wine and smokes—and there was no shortage of wine and cigar connoisseurs in this club—deals were made, information was garnered, and some self-aggrandizing prevailed.

Norbie loved the camaraderie, as did the other six to twelve who would get together both at this new over-the-top country club or the staple club in West Side. The West Side Country Club had recently been purchased by a group of partners while Gar was gone. Gar had been missed. If he had been around, he surely would have been part of the partnership that had purchased the West Side Country Club. WSCC had been the group's harmonious home escape from home for at least fifteen years. However, Lone Horse had some little pleasures that were new, one of which was the opportunity to store in its controlled environment members' own vintage wine, to be taken out for an important client—or in this case, to compete with a fellow member of the church.

The origin of the name *church* came from one of the Catholic members of the club, who told his wife that he would no longer be going to Sunday morning mass because he would be attending church on Saturday afternoons and then going to dinner with his friends once a month; the first Saturday of the month. It was a great strategy for him, but his Protestant and Jewish friends had more difficulty using church as an excuse. Norbie had heard that the more current description for their church was that it was a mnemonic for the Committee for Hosting Upcoming Remedy Choices for Holistic Health, but he did not believe that. No, that was a Republican's idea of humor, and it fell flat for two reasons. First, no spouse would ever believe it, and second, every spouse knew that the husbands looked too damn happy about attending church for it to be legitimate.

Norbie liked attending church, but he had no problem calling it what it was. He knew that he was keeping up with all the business and interests that any red-blooded male in business would need to understand. He was quite happy to see Gar return to the fold. Bringing him aside to allow for private conversation between them, he filled Gar in on his last two years with the hope that Gar would discuss his life during his absence from the area.

Gar did not take too long before bringing Norbie up to date. Norbie listened carefully as Gar reported on his travels, listing visits to Europe, South America, some Asian countries, and all over the North American continent. His experience in Paris with his daughter Paige was important to him. Paige had just broken her engagement to Larry Albridge and was smarting over what she considered his lack of appreciation of her.

Norbie was confused and said, "I read that she married him recently. In fact, that's how I knew you were in town. It was a destination wedding in the Dominican, wasn't it?"

Gar smiled his famous smile and said with great sincerity, "I finally did a good thing, Norbie—first in a long time. Paige is a bit cynical for a beautiful twenty-seven-year-old woman with an MFA in design and a good job. She doesn't trust easily for many reasons. She was particularly not endeared to Leana despite the fact that Leana was very good to her. She never wanted me to marry Leana. Her reasons were all a bit fuzzy—nothing cut-and-dried, just her feeling that Leana was not all that she seemed to be, that Leana had secrets. Anyway, Larry told Paige that he was going to Philadelphia on business and had a return flight on a Friday at 3:00 p.m. to Bradley on a certain date. To surprise him, Paige took an Uber to Bradley and waited for the flight. He was not on it. She called his cell but didn't tell him that she was at the airport. He said that he had just landed and would pick her up for dinner at seven. She's feisty and said, 'Don't bother. I won't have dinner with a liar.' She refused to speak to him again."

Norbie thought *Larry is a really stand-up guy. I can't even imagine him lying to Paige. He's a methodical corporate lawyer who likes things organized and logical. I've had work with him, and frankly, I've always found him honorable. Nice-looking guy who doesn't screw around.*

Instead he said, "I think Paige should have asked for an explanation."

Gar laughed, agreed, and said that in order to take the heat out of the equation, he offered Paige a trip to Paris. "You know, Norbie, I was hurting, and Paige was hurting. Paris did its magic after a couple of days of 'How could he lie to me?' When she started to laugh again, I reminded her of all her lies to me as a teenager, and that it never stopped me from loving her.

"That's when she told me that she hadn't stopped loving Larry. I gave her some great advice that my dad once told me when I was dating Madeleine, my first wife and truly the love of my life. She was about twenty, I was twenty-three at the time, and she was seeing several other guys. My nose was out of joint, and I was thinking about not calling her again. I was ranting about her to my dad. and he said, 'Gar, if she marries someone else and you never tried to marry her, how would you feel then? If your answer is regret, well, don't be a fool. Go after her. If she refuses you, you tried your best. You may be hurt, but you'll have no regrets for your own inaction.'"

Gar stated that Paige gave him an argument, saying that the analogy wasn't perfect. "After all, Dad, Mom didn't directly lie to you. She was just a twenty-year-old having fun. Larry lied to me. He's a lawyer, and he knows the implications of a lie."

Gar said that he let Paige fester for a couple of days, and she finally called Larry. "Next thing I know, it was all lovey-dovey. His lie was that he went to his grandmother's in Atlanta to get a family engagement ring to offer to Paige with a wedding proposal. The ring is two hundred years old and has about ten carats of diamonds in it. Paige is lucky that he didn't hold her temper fit against her. Talk about a lack of trust. He lied because if he told her he was seeing his grandmother without bringing her, she would be unhappy. Guess it's just another case of damned if you do, damned if you don't. At least Paige and I were able to sort things out. The last few years have been difficult for my children."

Norbie, who normally didn't intrude with an unsolicited personal question, asked, "Gar, you said that Madeleine was the love of your life. I notice that you didn't disappear for two years after Madeleine died, as you did after Leana died. Never mind—none of my business!"

Gar let out a deep, almost guttural sigh. "Life is complicated, Norbie. I can't talk any more tonight. I trust you—most importantly, because you're represented me in a couple of cases, and you've earned my trust. To me, you've got some of the trappings of a confessor. I just need some time before I take that step. Instead, tell me about what's been going on in the area. I read about the kid who murdered all those other kids, and you represented the kid's mother who gave a false confession. Tell me about that."

Norbie detailed as much as he could about the child who was a serial murderer, as well as her mother, who was willing to go to jail to prevent the prosecution of her twelve-year-old daughter.

Norbie tried to answer Gar's interest in how a kid could be a sociopath at the age of twelve. Norbie's answer did not satisfy him; in fact, he was aghast when told that Norbie thought there were many sociopaths in any normal population distribution, and he even promised that Gar was dealing with some of them on an everyday basis.

Norbie responded to Gar's two new questions, "Wouldn't you know? I mean wouldn't you be able to see the problem if you saw them in action every day?"

Norbie tried to explain his understanding on the subject while reminding Gar that he was not a sociologist or a psychologist, but just an experienced lawyer who dealt with human problems. "Gar, I'm not a priest, but I do think that a strong moral upbringing may protect society from the negative actions of many individuals who qualify as sociopaths based on their biology. Some of the social factors that we can measure in humans who may be sociopaths include their being narcissistic, lacking in empathy, and lacking in feeling guilt. You normally realize someone is a sociopath only when you have witnessed the evidence of the damage they've inflicted on others."

"Look around you at our club members; there may be one or two who fill the bill. Good old boys that we have a lot of fun with, but you find yourself unwilling to get too close to them. Your self-protection radar is at work when you find yourself avoiding close contact. However, sometimes when we experience the sophisticated ones who are bright, good looking, and charming, it's difficult to assess their danger because they tend to give perfect responses to our deepest desires. They almost mirror our thoughts as if they are a perfect companion."

Norbie watched as Gar's complexion paled while he listened, leaving him unsurprised when Gar quickly looked at his watch, saying that he was late for a business call and left without a goodbye to the other members of the church.

Norbie rejoined the group that now included Ed Loughlin, Jake Lemanski, Carlo Morelli, JR Randall, and JR's brother-in-law Rudy Beauregard, who was JR's guest. JR, which stood for Randall Junior (backward because his dad was RJ), was the only son of a farmer and nurseryman with land and several garden stands in both Connecticut and western Massachusetts. Known for the fortune he had made as the heir to a small farming business, JR could talk plants, soil, and landscaping with the best in the business. He had developed a national e-commerce segment of the business that sent unusual plant specimens anywhere in the country. Norbie used his service when his wife insisted that she needed white forsythias for the yard, and she could not find them in the regular garden centers.

Norbie greeted JR's brother-in-law, Rudy Beauregard, who was the captain of detectives in the Major Crimes Unit in West Side. Norbie and Beauregard went back in time, mostly on opposite sides of the professional legal fence. Beauregard was built for football defense:

solid but not fat. He was what Norbie's wife Sheri called, "Trustworthy with a good face and not bad looking."

The churchgoers all liked Beauregard, who occasionally joined them at both country clubs as someone's guest. He was an avid golfer when he was able to play, but he was not into fancy wines; he was more of a steak and beer kind of guy.

Carlo, Jake, and Beauregard were conversing quietly, and Norbie overheard Gar's name mentioned. Their conversation focused on Leana's tragic death. Carlo asked Beauregard if he knew how the accident happened and whether there were any questions about it. Beauregard did not answer immediately. Finally he said, "There were questions. I can give you a summary of what is generally known from the press. Leana went over a cliff at midnight that normally had a guard rail in front of it with bright yellow florescent strips adhered. However, there had been recent road work, and the guard rail was being replaced. As a result of the repairs being made, there were temporary brightly lit signs in place. In fact, there was a backhoe loader left on-site over the weekend. Leana died on a Sunday night. Her car went through the temporary barrier, totally avoiding the backhoe. The temporary lights were broken, and further, there was broken glass that did not match the temporary lights, but there was no damage to the backhoe. The source of the broken glass was unknown, but forensics said it was from construction lighting and could have been from before the accident. The accident was questioned. There were skidmarks where Leana tried to bear to the right to avoid the backhoe. Her alcohol level was just below the legal limit. The accident was investigated at the time; even to the point of police asking her doctors if she had cataracts because she was at the right age. Her doctor said that she did, but they weren't mature; she was probably a year or two away from having surgery, and she never complained about driving at night. The car, a 2015 Maserati Ghibli, tested out okay. It was some gray color."

Ed broke in. "God it was a pretty sedan. Gar paid a lot for it. I heard that she insisted that it be a Maserati, and my oh my, she looked good in it. Probably she'd look good in a Ford pickup."

Beauregard continued after the interruption. "We closed the case but still found it strange that if she missed the curve, she should have hit the backhoe, not go right over the cliff. We wondered for a bit if it was a drive suicide, but there was absolutely no evidence that Leana lacked a zest for life."

Jake, who was a car aficionado and a well-known stud for all his fifty-eight years, moaned the loss of two examples of the best of breeds. With little consideration to appropriateness, he said, "Great little chassis on both her and her ride. Too bad!"

There was a spot of silence. Norbie reminded them all, "Gar has truly suffered from Leana's loss. Maybe more respect is due, don't you think?"

The gentlemen all agreed, but Jake said, "Don't be too harsh on me, Norbie. The lady maybe wasn't always a lady. That's all I can say."

At that time, the upstairs event flowed into the downstairs pub, encroaching on their private conversations; and so the church service ended.

# 3

# Beauregard Reviews the Accident Report

CAPTAIN BEAUREGARD ASKED MILLIE Banks, the single admin staffer for the Major Crimes Unit, to pull the Leana Lonergan file from closed files. He could see that she was not surprised as she quickly pulled the file box from her desk for the second time in a month; the first had been during the previous week. She knew he had a bee in his bonnet about this case. He simply couldn't put aside the several notes sent to the station from different unknown sources concerning the case. He was on the prowl, and it didn't take a detective to spot the captain of detectives going into full sniffing mode.

Beauregard had not shared all that he knew with the guys at church about the supposedly closed Leana Lonergan case; he stated only what was publicly known and could be discovered by anyone reading or listening to the press. He had become involved with the case after the state police had been brought in for accident reconstruction. The West Side captain on traffic called MCU because he wasn't satisfied with the traffic department's own computer reconstruction. He again wasn't satisfied after they had finished with the case, and he requested that Beauregard give it a look-see.

Beauregard reviewed their conclusions and didn't like the facts cited in this investigation. There was a call from a neighbor who lived just below the accident scene that concerned him. Enough so, he had Jim Locke, a detective noted for his interview style, meet with the neighbor woman. Beauregard knew he was not alone in his questioning the interpretation of the facts in this case, because the captain in charge of traffic and accident division had also questioned the facts. Beauregard wondered what could be the source of the extra construction glass found at the scene. The neighbor talked about sudden bright lights. Where could they have come from? Because the accident resulted in a fatality, there had been multiple reviews on the known contributing facts to the accident. Also, much attention was given because the Lonergan family was a well-known and respected family in West Side, a small suburban city in western Massachusetts.

He looked again at the notes received in the last two months. All had different post marks. All had different writing, and two had letters cut from newspapers and magazines. There was also the one bit of information that they had received immediately after the accident and that did not quite fit in with the facts. Beauregard carried the box into the conference room and did what he could do better than any of the detectives. He spread the info out on the table. Beauregard chided himself, thinking *No one could make an organized mess on a table as quickly as I can. After all, this isn't a murder, so there is no murder board, just this table.*

He looked at the call from the resident who lived near the accident scene. He recalled the steep road that took a ninety-degree uphill to the left or downhill to the right, with the guard rail in the middle to protect the houses situated about one hundred feet beyond the road and guard rail —a *Y* separation from the main road. The guard rail had been removed after being damaged by several previous accidents, in order to repair the road and install a larger and heavier guard rail. An oversized jersey barrier had been temporarily put in place. The backhoe was also there and should have stopped a car that went through the large, lit signs. It would have for certain if the car was trying to go left, but it did leave room if the auto went slightly to the right.

The problem in understanding the accident lay in the fact that if the driver was attempting to go to the right, then the accident could not have happened that way. Experts projected that she would have maybe scraped the signs, scraped the temporary jersey barrier that was to the left, and gone over some bumpy turf, but then she would have straightened out. Leana did not have that much booze in her, and from all accounts she was an excellent driver. The temporary signs had large neon blinking arrows pointing left and right. Left was a more difficult turn, and she should have been turning left if she was headed for home. Instead, she went to the right but not on the road. She went over the cliff at a high speed, bypassing but scraping the edge of the Jersey barrier enough to have moved it. That part fit his analysis. Everyone said that Leana had a heavy foot on the gas pedal.

Detective Jim Locke's interview with Patricia Hegarty, the neighbor whose house was located nearest the accident scene, did not enlighten them; rather, she created a cloud. Additionally, Beauregard thought from the notes that she was an intelligent, observant, and helpful person devoid of being overly emotional. She was the type of witness the department's detectives normally would like, but in this case her story opened up possibilities that Chief of Police Coyne really did not want to explore.

Beauregard read that Patricia could not sleep on the night of the accident. Her house was located in the dingle below the road barrier, and in fact the auto ended up about ten feet from the decorative fencing and shrubs bordering her house lot. She had a house built on one and a half acres, and her kitchen faced the hill with the barrier on it. The report said that Patricia had an early morning meeting with a child's parents, at which time she, as the school psychologist, was going to suggest family counseling. She knew that it would be a difficult interview, and she was going over it in her mind regarding how to approach some pretty caring parents about the fact that she had concluded that their son's actions bordered on manic depressive without saying that.

Patricia had poured some chamomile tea, hoping to stop her mind from running amuck, when she saw large broad range lights, like construction lights, facing toward her house. She wondered whether the city was installing the new barriers in the middle of the night for the next morning. She had seen that kind for work done on the highway, but never in an area like hers. They were so bright that they made her wake up completely despite the chamomile tea. Detective Locke questioned how long the lights were on, and she said from about five minutes before the accident; they became less bright and then shut down immediately after the accident.

Patricia figured that maybe the car took out the construction lights. She said that she grabbed some jeans, a sweater, and boots, but by the time she got around her fence to the accident site, there were police cars and fire trucks there.

Beauregard read a direct quote from Patricia in the report, in which she said, "I knew immediately that the driver was dead. The police were talking to some people, and I thought that they were witnesses, so I didn't push what I knew. I called later when I read the papers and no one had talked about bright lights. I know what I saw, and they looked like bright construction lights to me. I think that they may have been the cause of the accident. The temporary arrows have been up for almost a week, and they did a good job directing me to my home. The papers did not say she was driving under the influence."

Beauregard knew that there were no construction lights put up by the city, but there seemed to be some evidence of movement of soil at the site, maybe for equipment. However, the city's Department of Public Works and its subcontractors showed no evidence of records or orders for construction lighting. There had been a lot of digging and patching in the area, but because new asphalt had not yet been put in place, the area was messy at best.

Beauregard did have other witness interviews, including one from a man who lived on the lower, left-hand side and who insisted that he saw a truck leaving within seconds after the crash. Unfortunately, on a Sunday night there was no other known traffic around that time.

Beauregard looked again at the reports. Leana had been at the West Side Country Club until about eleven thirty. She was not with her husband but had attended a big function and dinner there with friends. Her whereabouts from eleven thirty onward were unknown. Her husband had stayed at home with their dog, which had been bitten by a coyote in their yard. Earlier, he had taken the Weimaraner, Dagmar, to the vet and believed that he couldn't leave her alone all evening. Dagmar had been seriously attacked and was having trouble walking. Gar's son, Paul, was visiting from San Diego without his wife, Marsha, and they were happy to have some alone time as father and son. Beauregard thought, *Great alone time it turned out to be. We found nothing suspicious in Gar or Paul's reactions to the news of Leana's death, but family alibis are always looked at carefully.*

It might have just been left at that but for the four letters. Beauregard deduced that maybe two of them were from the same person because they were the two with pasted news and magazine letters printed. He looked at them on the table. Naturally, the notes had no signatures.

Note 1 was dated March 2, 2016. It was postmarked from San Diego. There were no fingerprints, and it was printed on plain copy paper off a HP DeskJet.

> Dear investigator in the death of Leana Lonergan in a road accident:
>
> *Please be advised that there are many who would want her dead. I, for one, want to give the murderer a prize for removing that manipulative, evil beauty queen from the earth. If you ever find out who did it, please advertise so that I can be a character witness for his good name. Justice has prevailed.*

Note 2 was dated April 30, 2016. It was postmarked from Florida with no fingerprints. It was written on a brown paper bag in a cheap white envelope.

> Police—the bitch deserved to die. I'm sorry I didn't do it. Look to where she's been and who she's hurt. Finally she's in hell!

Note 3 was dated February 7, 2017, postmarked from Chicago. No fingerprints, and it was pasted on lined paper in a cheap white envelope.

> Leana has done evil to many. Check her history.

Note 4 was dated March 20, 2017, postmarked from Brooklyn. There were no fingerprints, and it was printed on plain paper in a cheap white envelope.

> Haven't you read my letter? Check Leana's history. I'm sick of waiting for you to see the truth.

Beauregard believed that something was not quite right. Normally his gut would direct him toward a piece of evidence to explore, and he could at least get started. Here, he had a problem: there was no officially open case. Chief Coyne did not want to open this case. Chief Coyne would only authorize an open case if there was a significant piece of evidence to explore. The chief was aware that there were letters but refused to look at them or talk about them. After all, they were anonymous, and the trail was cold and didn't warrant the money for further investigation.

Beauregard could not forget Jake's remark from the other night, gossip it may be, but Jake's gossip was normally right on. Leana had a reputation, apparently, but Beauregard had not heard that before. Mona, Beauregard's wife, did not like Leana, but Mona's sixth sense about people was not a basis for inquiry. But he quoted his eldest son's favorite saying when Mona wasn't around, "What the fuck?" and called in the team. *Closed case or not, MCU Detectives Smith, Locke, and Aylewood will work with me and my hunches. I know that!*

The other detectives in Major Crimes were pleased to escape the day's tedium of writing reports, which was what their day presently had on the agenda. Nothing major was on for work this day despite the bureau's name. Their current efforts involved reviewing detail for court cases, filing, looking at some referrals from vice for possible problems, and taking calls.

The detectives were coming off a serial murder case of six children and everything looked like small potatoes to them after that hyper-adrenalin, fever-pitch investigation. Detectives Jim Locke, Mason Smith, and Petra Aylewood gathered in the large conference room and with interest viewed the accident case spread out before them.

Petra, always quick to react and nicknamed Bolt, said, "Captain, an accident case? Are you kidding? Are things really that quiet, huh?"

Beauregard said, "No, we can't investigate this case. It's not open to investigation. But things are quiet for us now, and I hoped that you would look at what's before you. You are not being called into an investigation, but what you do on your own time on the phones or computers to clear up some misgivings I might have would be appreciated."

Now four sets of eyes reviewed the notes, the file, and the Hegarty interview. Mason Smith, the cool, African American IT specialist detective, was the first to react. "Love this kind of work. I have connections with police IT, and in case you computer-ignorant folks don't know, we're a special division of police answerable only to ourselves as to how to get certain kinds of info. I think this lady Leana has some ghosts from her past. No reason why I can't do a callout for background check. I'll start with info on her marriage records and go from there."

Jim Locke, the resident psychologist detective, remarked, "If there is any work history on Leana, then I should be the one to follow through on that. After all, I can get info from an Egyptian 5,000-year-old mummy."

All sighed and nodded while Petra said, "We know that, Jim. We have all partnered with you on interviews; most of which lasted about three times longer than normal. Although I suppose they often do result in more information than expected."

Beauregard said, "Enough is enough. Bolt, I know that you have friends who are members of the WS Country Club. Because you are our only connection there, see what some of the members are saying."

"Sure, Captain. I'll get my friend Margie to invite me to lunch. Margie knows everything about every woman in West Side who has any money at all. It is Margie's life work to know who has what, goes where, and wears what. I'll get some background on this Leana."

With that, Beauregard thanked them and reminded them that this was not an open investigation. He additionally told Mason to hit police forces in the areas from which letters were postmarked. "I know that the postmark may not be where they live, but just in case, check the police there. By the way, here is a picture of Leana, her stats, and her last job before marriage. She worked for Liam O'Neil Public Relations Firm as a publicist. That's how she met Gar Lonergan, her husband."

Beauregard had some concerns about his actions in this closed case and the possible ramifications. He thought, *Using social security numbers is not part of the discussion, and I know in my heart that Mason will somehow connect through that number. Therein lay a potential hazard for me if anyone ever questioned why we're using protected information for background on a woman killed in an accident. Hopefully they will find nothing suspicious and nobody will ever know. I can't believe the ridiculousness of how carefully I live my life, only to occasionally do something really stupid and probably unnecessary. This is just an example of actions I take that risk my way of life. But I have to do this. I just have to.*

# 4

# Loss of Family, Lake Placid, New York, 1975

MARY LOU DID NOT cry at her adopted mother's funeral. She sat next to Timothy and her older stepbrother Jason as the minister extolled her mother's virtues. She agreed completely with the minister about her mother's goodness. Ernestine Prior died suddenly of a massive coronary only eighteen months after her husband had passed. Lester's death wasn't sudden like Ernestine's; it took two years for him to pass, filled with regular bouts of chemotherapy for his lung cancer. Mary Lou's dad had only one fault that she could see, and that was his history of chronic smoking.

Lester and Ernestine had taken in her and Timothy as foster children after their birth parents and brother were killed in the family home house fire. They quickly adopted the children, and Timothy had done very well. He was now in community college a year early because he was breathtakingly facile in mastering math, accounting, and finance principles. His focus on accounting would, she knew, give him a viable work future. He received not only disability income but all kinds of services for which Ernestine had diligently worked the system to obtain for him. His ability to finish college would not be thwarted by lack of finances.

Mary Lou was angry. She knew when her adoptive parents had taken them, that they were too old to finish the job. Here she was, at age twenty, not finished with college, and both her parents were dead. Her stepbrother Jason, her adoptive parents' natural child, was thirty-five and was not interested in his parents' other children. In fact, many neighbors believed that he resented them. Dad's friend Al Bronsen, who was the family lawyer, explained to all the children the estate that was left to them.

For the past ten years, Lester had been chief maintenance director of three large hotels in Lake Placid, New York. He was lured from his maintenance engineering job with the state of Connecticut by a group of Lake Placid resort owners who needed expertise in maintenance oversight for their large complexes. It was a great deal more work but paid very well.

Ernestine loved Lake Placid and the people there. She was a born do-gooder and volunteered for just about every church, political, and social need or function. Her volunteering included volunteering her children's services. Jason said that was why he got away right after college and went to California. "I've had enough of this giveaway to the community," he would often say. Mary Lou believed that Jason's do-good training hadn't taken. Jason considered only himself at all times.

Her mother told her that the family had taken six foster children before the Court children. However, when she and Lester saw Mary Lou and Timothy, they had known that they were meant to be their own children, telling Mary Lou, "You children are special, and we love you so."

Mary Lou sometimes believed that Jason felt she and Timothy meant too much to his parents, and he deeply resented them. *Well, that's not my problem, is it?* she'd mused many times.

She remembered Burt Butler, her supposed playmate in Connecticut. He'd stalked her at school and at home until she'd gone to live with Ernestine and Lester. His mother, Mrs. Butler, often said to her, "Young lady, Burt is a fine boy. You'd better be nicer to him. After all, we know your family history, and fortunately Burt doesn't mind." She would say these things in front of Burt, who would give her a stupid grin. Burt had the nerve to tell her that he knew how really bad she and Timothy had been. She was pleased to go live in Lake Placid.

Mary Lou couldn't fault her new parents' training, but there were necessary adjustments, and the children adjusted. Ernestine was particularly persistent in instilling good manners in the children, along with good posture. Mary Lou remembered how lazy Mr. and Mrs. Court and Austin were. She really didn't like thinking of her birth parents as her parents; instead, she called them Mr. and Mrs. Court, and she never referred to Austin. Ernestine taught the children to socialize, mainly to help Timothy, whose desire to stay to himself was considered to be counterproductive to a socially integrative and good life; at least according to Ernestine. She refused to think of Autism as limiting but would rather point out substantial differences that Timothy had compared to what she called mainstream children. She said Timothy had wonderful strengths not shared by most people, adding that she would make sure that those strengths were developed.

Ernestine insisted that the children listen carefully to others, even if they didn't like what others said, and that they greet all whom they met with a happy face. They were to always dress appropriately for the occasion. It was understood that the children should treat everyone with kindness and good manners.

Ernestine even gave the children lessons at the dinner table on how to use a fork, spoon, or knife; how to set the table; and what kind of conversation was acceptable at the dinner table. She also insisted that they take ballroom dancing lessons, which she said were gender neutral and would assist them in developing graceful movements in their bodies.

Mary Lou had pointed out to her mother that there was nothing gender neutral about ballroom dancing because the guy always took the lead. Her mother quietly told her, "Go along with those small things and understand that it may look like the man is taking the lead, but look carefully, and you'll see in most cases it's really the woman who is leading?" Needless to say, the children were loved by all their friends' parents, who regarded them as the most mannerly children in all of Lake Placid.

Mary Lou personally considered all this training to be helpful, and she agreed with Ernestine that it was just as important for Timothy as it was for her. After coming to live with the Priors, she quickly realized that she had no understanding of what the world at large respected or expected. Mr. and Mrs. Court had only taught her what they'd expected, and it was always about meeting their needs. Well, they had taught her well. Mary Lou thought, *I'll never forget the lesson of the importance of having my needs met. I'm not spending my life meeting someone else's insane needs.*

The funeral service ended, and the church ladies were holding a luncheon for Ernestine's family and friends in the church hall. Considering the small population size of the town, with the number of full-year residents at about 2,500 in Lake Placid, it was a good thing that the people tended to involve themselves in community service. Mary Lou thought, *How could anything get done if people only worked for pay? There isn't enough money to go round, other than for necessaries.* Most every full-time resident in Lake Placid and the surrounding areas worked in the tourist industry, which was a three-season industry; business dropped down in April and May. Additionally, she thought, *If we had stayed in Connecticut, then I would never have become a good skier or made friends with so many from New York City and Montreal.* Mary Lou often heard Ernestine proudly telling her friends that her daughter was able to talk with anyone and hold her own. That was a compliment that Mary Lou valued because she believed it to be true.

Her attention was suddenly drawn to a conversation between her stepbrother Jason and the family lawyer, Al Bronsen. Jason wanted to know how much cash he could get immediately. Mr. Bronsen said that the home was a big asset, and it would take a bit of time before it was sold. He stated with certainty that the home could bring over ninety thousand dollars because its location and condition were pretty nice. There was also a condo worth twenty-five thousand dollars. Lester had worked diligently to keep all his assets in good shape.

She heard Bronsen say that there was a decent investment account in the amount of $150,000, some cash, a $150,000 insurance policy, two cars and a truck, furniture, and a little bit of jewelry. The will stipulated that because Jason was in their lives much longer than the other children, he would get 55 percent of the residual estate.

Al Bronsen told Jason that Ernestine believed his receiving the largest share of the estate was fair because Jason was their first child. Mary Lou would get 40 percent of the residual estate, and the remaining 5 percent would go to the church. There were a few specific requests. Timothy would get title to the condo that the Priors had purchased just before Lester's death, and he would also receive the three-year-old Toyota Tundra truck with extended cab because he loved it. Mary Lou would get the one-year-old Honda SUV, leaving Jason with the five-year-old Honda sedan. It made sense because Ernestine had recently purchased a new sports car for Jason.

Also, a specific request was made of thirty thousand dollars for Mary Lou's education. There was none made for Timothy's education because the state would pay for that, and in fact Timothy was left out of the rest of the estate because it would simply go to the state of New York.

Bronsen said, "Ernestine explained that she could trust Mary Lou to attend to Timothy's needs, and that the estate was too small to take a chance on the state of New York going after it for Timothy's needs."

Jason was unhappy with the litany of bequests and said, "How much to me, and how soon? I want to get out of here. Tell me where to sign to sell the house and the stupid car, and I will take my split of the investment account and cash up front."

Mr. Bronsen answered, "I can't easily tell you that. I must value the whole estate and see how much of it is easily convertible to cash.

There are expenses for filing, there may be some associated taxes, there is a need for a trustee and the resultant fee, and there is the cost of the real estate agent's fee. Distributions can't be made until I file the estate, a trustee is in place, and cash after expected expenses is calculated. Then I can disclose that there are sufficient funds to allow for specific distributions. At that time, the remainder will be available to be split among the heirs. The condo is already in both Ernestine's and Timothy's names, and until Timothy is in full majority by age, I am his appointed guardian, as well as Mary Lou's until she is twenty-one years of age. I will put the home up for sale immediately. I promise you that I will work diligently to settle this estate and take a small fee."

Bronsen continued. "Ernestine has asked that her friend Phyllis at the church act as trustee. She is an accountant, and Ernestine trusted her and felt that she would protect the assets not only based on her personal relationship but also to protect the 5 percent going to the church. It's a good plan, Jason, but you must be patient."

The lawyer went on again to point out that as soon as they filed and he was assured of enough money to pay estate and income taxes for Ernestine and her estate, then specific requests would be honored first.

Mary Lou had joined them and was by now fully apprised of the financial details. She said, "Al, I'm transferring to SUNY Albany for the fall semester. How will I pay for it if the bequest is not free by then?"

Al assured her that something could be done by then, and he would also try to free the cars and truck for immediate use. He said, "Before you leave, please speak with me about this issue."

Jason was angry. "It's bad enough that she gets almost as much as me, and maybe more if there's not enough cash. But you're worried about getting her thirty thousand for college when I have a family to support and need the money? I'd better get reports from you soon, Al. She's not even blood, and she gets maybe more than me in the end. And the state of New York pays for 'poor' Timothy. My parents may have found goodness in these two, but I have never approved of my parents recycling human trash as a good deed. I wouldn't sleep well with them in the same house as me. Well, fuck all this bullshit." He stormed off.

Bronsen sighed and said to Mary Lou, "Please don't let him upset you. He has been lost for a long time. Jason has only one of his parents' wonderful traits, which is that he is a hard worker. The rest are lost on him. He really can't see value in his parents and their commitment to society and those in need. It's lost on him. Try to understand him and keep in contact. He will see the error of his ways. After all you and Timothy are his only family left."

"Al, thank you, but I don't think that Jason thinks of us as family, and he won't allow contact. You have a good heart like Mom and Dad, but I see him for what he is, and he wants control over us and is ashamed of Timothy."

Al was astonished at that remark. "Why, Timothy is wonderful. He's ahead educationally and very nice. Is it because of his autism? That's crazy. Timothy is doing an internship for a friend of mine this summer and I know it will result in a job for him when he finishes his associate's degree. Furthermore, I know that the firm will support him in his pursuit of getting a BS in accounting. What's to be ashamed of?"

Mary Lou did the right thing: she simply hugged Al and said goodbye. Before she left him, she asked how soon she had to be out of the house and was told that she could stay until the end of the month. She could then move in with Timothy until she went to SUNY in the fall; he explained that Jason wanted him to charge her rent after the end of the month. She thanked him and said that she would stay with Timothy and get him settled. She would move to Albany in early July.

Mary Lou said her goodbyes to the church ladies and her parents' friends. She was about to get Timothy to return home when Al motioned her over, checking to be certain that Jason had left.

"Mary Lou, your mother was contacted by your birth mother's family, informing her that your maternal grandfather had died. The insurance company and the estate attorney have been searching for quite a while to find you. You are one of five cousins, including

Timothy, who have inherited one-fifth of his estate, each for over $750,000. His share will be put in a trust for him, if you agree; it will interfere with any assistance he's able to get in the future from the state, but that assistance will no longer be needed. He's going to be financially independent from his work alone. He's a good kid. I'll call you for signatures. You know, your mother didn't have the time to implement her desire that this be done before she died, but it was what she wanted for Timothy. I hope you agree with me. You will have a check for your share by next week, so don't worry about the tuition and money for a dorm or apartment. Just send the bills to me. I said nothing about this to Jason because it's not his business and would further inflame him. I hope that this softens the sorrow you've had to bear."

"That can't be, Al. Mrs. Court was an only child. I've heard her say it over and over. She told everyone that both she and Mr. Court had no relatives. How could I have three cousins? Where was Mrs. Court from? She always said that she was from the South and that it wasn't a place anyone would want to visit, let alone live."

"The attorney is from Jonesboro, Tennessee, which is most famous for its annual national storytelling fair. I will talk to him and ask about the family for you. It might be important for you to contact some of them and discover some family history."

Mary Lou stiffened up and shook her head. "No, Al, I'm not going down that path. I know that there is nothing there for me other than this money. I'll take that, and I'll never turn back. It can't be good there—that I know." She shook his hand, fetched Timothy, and headed to the only home she knew, now knowing it was no longer home. She had played her role. She had been the good little girl. It did her some good, but that life was all gone now. She laughed and muttered almost silently, "Good is not a virtue helpful to me, other than as a pretense to misdirect others. I will never again wait on others to direct my life."

Mary Lou could see that Timothy was concerned by her facial anger. She was remorseful that she had not hidden her feelings.

He said, "Mary Lou, you're not mad at me, are you? I haven't done anything really bad, so don't worry."

Mary Lou reassured Timothy, but then she wondered how she would tell him she was leaving for good in July. Perhaps she could promise to see him for his birthday each year, which was a week before Christmas, on the eighteenth. That would be enough for him. Timothy didn't require a lot of emotional investment. *Yes, that will be enough.*

Al Bronsen approached Mary Lou as she was leaving and, was clearly upset with himself. He wanted reassurance that she would be okay with today's news. He told Mary Lou that he hoped the money would help assuage any resistance she might have had related to her birth parents. The Jonesboro attorney who'd called had inferred that Mrs. Court, Mary Lou and Timothy's birth mother, was the young daughter who'd run off with a ne'er-do-well bum who worked on the family farm. Mrs. Court's parents had searched for her but never heard a word about her. There was some talk that she was pregnant and that her brother had threatened to kill the boyfriend, but the attorney said that was just "good ol' boy" talk. "After all, this is Tennessee," he said in his explanation.

Al said to Mary Lou, "Before you leave, maybe you should think about some blood relatives you have who may want to know you and Timothy. The Tennessee attorney said that they were good people. In the South, Mary Lou, that is a sterling recommendation."

Mary Lou answered, "I'm not interested in them, Al. I'm not interested in anyone connected to them other than Timothy."

# 5

# Church, West Side Country Club, 2017

BEAUREGARD WAS SUFFERING FROM the blistering heat; the sun sent shafts of light into his eyes every time he took a shot. Well, golf was not his or his companions' game today. Beauregard had been invited to join one of the foursomes. Although known for his unflappable ability to ignore weather while playing a game he had learned to love, Beauregard was dripping with sweat and was listing with fatigue as they left the eighteenth hole. He thought, *It's only six o'clock in the evening, but we look frumpy and sad. Time to get to the pub for a beer.*

Their companion foursome, already cooled down and on their second drink, welcomed the newcomers with, "Christ you look like old men crumbled by the game."

"Paris and Dingle, and by God Sicily, have better weather than this in July," Gar said. "And I should have stayed away longer."

"Today was a bitch. Although I did beat Norbie, and so for that the day is not lost," said Beauregard as he ordered some kind of Mexican beer, for which the other players ranked him as an international 007 type sitting down with the "poor folks."

Beauregard's brother–in-law, JR, who had a low-key sense of humor dripping with sarcasm, told the group, "Beauregard, have you taken lessons from Gar's long sabbatical and started ordering internationally now?"

"Nah, I'm pretending to be a high-class defense lawyer, like Norbie. You know, consorting with criminals on a daily basis. Poor Norbie—earning a $200,000 fee probably required twenty hours of work this week. And think of some of his clientele! He's represented all of you. God, the guy suffers. Norbie, I think you should buy the next round, and the one after that. My support is worth something, and I don't get any perks being on the other side of the criminal justice table."

The bullshit continued until they moved over to eat and had to sit at two separate but adjacent tables of four. The pub was packed tonight, and the guys were not dressed for the upstairs dining area unless they sat on the porch. Unfortunately, there was some kind of ladies shower going on up there, and no seats were open for them.

Jake Lemanski and Ed Loughlin were at one table with the two doctors, Samir Chaya (called Sam) and Gautam Suri (called Tom). The former was Lebanese American, and the latter was born in Indian but raised in California. They were the answer to the church's desire for diversity inclusion. Not one member of the group had any reservations about race—maybe gender, but not race. Beauregard's wife expressed concerns that many of the club members were misogynists who thought they were for equal rights until some lady came in with a short skirt, and then the good old boys were back in the saddle. Some at-large members of the country club perceived that the church members were truly diverse and hoped to be included in the group; the church took in occasional guests for services as long as the guests were equally filled with political and social rage against whatever was going on in the world, loved golf, were filled with offbeat humor, were family men, and were generally of good moral character (other than the occasional extra wife).

Ed Loughlin was eager to reprise the conversation from a week ago, saying to Jake, "So what have you heard about Leana? Gar and Norbie can't hear. Their table's away from us. If Leana was easily available, I never heard about it. Surprising to me—I'm in the know."

Jake laughed along with Sam, both of who were born lady charmers. Sam said, “In Lebanese culture, if you want to know who is a woman of easy virtue, don’t ask the men—ask the women. They always know, but they gossip among themselves and don’t necessarily let us in on what they have learned. My wife is Italian American, and she’s as bad as my sisters. She knows who’s getting a divorce six months before the couple has made the decision.”

Tom, not to be excluded from the wisdom expressed at the table, agreed with Sam. “Indian culture traditionally gives a woman a protected status, which surely doesn’t allow her the freedom that the West allows women. But within its protection, men know nothing about what’s going on. So, Jake, what do you know? Don’t keep us waiting.”

Jake was eager to share. “Now, you guys know it is a well-advertised fact that we men don’t gossip; we only discuss important issues. In this case, what kind of woman was Gar’s wife, the beautiful and cultivated Leana? Well, I met a guy through business—the owner of Buy-iCloud, Inc., Don Turtolo. Don has spent his professional life in computers, and a few years ago he transitioned into this entrepreneurial endeavor for iCloud data storage systems for printing pictures off a person’s cloud. He developed a system for selling an automatic picture or data album that could be sent to the customer within a few days. The customer could choose, click, and receive an album. He had early entry in the game and sold out for an astronomical number to the now leading iCloud company. Turtolo now owns a personal software company, which is really a training company for other companies, leaving him in a semiretirement position.”

Tom said, “I want the gist of it, Jake, not the history of business. Get with it.”

Jake continued. “Don is a good-looking guy who spreads money around. Likes to impress, and he does. The first time I saw him and Leana together was in one of those hokey little roadside restaurants near Palmer on one late afternoon. You know, where you can get a steak, onion rings, and a beer for fourteen bucks. Leana and Don were in there, and they sure were enjoying each other's company. Not touching each other, but definitely a twosome."

Ed said, "Look, I've tried to flirt with Leana and wasn't successful. Are you sure they were a perfect couple? Leana did some public relations work even after she married Gar, and Gar's got a lot of money. It could have been work related. I don't see Leana as the 'love means more than everything' type. Why would she leave a cushy life with a nice guy, and for what? Actually, I don't see Leana in love—ever. I've never understood Gar's marrying her. I think he was on the rebound after his wife's death. Now, that was an example of two people in love."

Beauregard was known for his excellent hearing, and today he listened as Sam attempted to give insight into Gar's marriage choice. "Not all marriages are founded in love. Comfort and respect are also good foundations for marriage. But I personally know Don, and I find what you said interesting. I have never seen Don and Leana together, but Don went into a deep depression about the time that Leana died, and I know he was looking for a psychiatrist. He didn't ask me for a referral because I wouldn't tell you this if he did, but my wife told me, and you can take that information to the bank. Don't know how she knows, because she's not even in the medical field, but she knows. But Jake, you said 'the first time' was there. You saw them together another time?"

"Not me, but my wife, who never liked Leana. She told me she saw them at the Natick Mall shopping together, and they looked quite involved. And believe me, Betty has met them both and would never make an identity mistake. She'd be the perfect court witness: she sees everything in a flash."

Beauregard strained to listen carefully as the guys moved on to discuss whether Don had been stupid to sell his company early. The debate ensued and included the group carefully counting the number of companies started in western Massachusetts that had later been sold early to big-time corporations not located in the area. Their collective opinion included an expectation that this was the norm given western Massachusetts' many educational resources and its small-business entrepreneurial history.

Beauregard smiled as Tom discoursed. "We from western Massachusetts are inventive because this area is semi-urban and has allowed us more personal freedom to look around and see the big picture, but we're also able to be part urban sprawl and be enriched by the tech and medical revolution." The guys nodded at Tom's wisdom.

Beauregard, always with one ear open to other conversations, heard the barely winning foursome discussing Gar and how he found himself back in West Side after years of work in the Boston area and New York City.

JR was asking Gar, "Didn't you go to Boston University? Is that why you worked in Boston, staying on after graduation? You did graduate?"

"Well, I did go to BU, and I majored in finance in the business school. And yes, wise guy, I did graduate. We unmarried guys were still under the shadow of the draft at the time I was in college. I think my 1952 birth date was the last birth date for conscription, and somehow I missed that. I think it was Nixon who wanted the all-volunteer army, and it was Kennedy who put married men with children at the bottom of the conscription list and married men next to the bottom. So I guess I can thank Nixon, because I was not married then and would have been called on the next list."

Beauregard heard JR say, "We did live under that cloud, always wondering when we'd be called."

Gar said, "Right you are, JR. I never even thought about exploring the world before I settled down. I never considered the concept of settling down. Both my children used that term. I wanted and moved toward developing a good life, a productive life, one that would make my parents proud. Anyway, I started working in grocery stores in high school and continued doing that in college. I also worked as a runner for a big law firm, and that was an eye-opener. This was before all this faxing and digital stuff, when materials had to be shifted quickly, and the post office was the biggest conveyor of paper. Runners who were reliable were important."

JR prompted Gar with a go-on gesture, and he did. "I also did a gig one whole summer in warehousing, where I was introduced to a different concept of production and inventory. In my senior year, I worked on a research paper for one of my professors who worked with a team from Harvard and MIT on the grocery store industry, which was a pretty important service industry then. New kinds of grocery stores were emerging nationally. Locally, we were used to A&P and First National grocery stores, but suddenly there was Jumbo's, DeMoulas (the predecessor to Market Basket), Big Y in Springfield, and many more. In the early seventies, the Curtis Brothers started a new concept of store called the supermarket. Also, it was at the beginning of the trend to specialty grocery stores that now are so important, such as Whole Foods, Trader Joe's, and many low-cost stores like Shop Rite.

"I think I became interested in the industry because working on the research paper allowed me to see the big picture of the industry. I'd had experience working in the various individual stores, and so I understood their purchasing, delivery, stocking, cashiering, security, and management concerns when I was pretty young. So goes the start of my career."

JR was fascinated but confused. "Gar, I didn't even know you were in the grocery industry. I always understood that you were a broker."

"Well, I was. I still am. I started in grocery store management. Changed jobs five times in four years, which at that time was suspicious—not like today, where that's normal. I got a chance to work for a food broker in Boston whose specialty was dealing with Italian food imports. Once I understood the concept of connections between what was needed and where to get what was needed, I found a partner who was in his own business for general but less common products, and we set off to grow big. My partner was a wonderful guy, experienced and twenty years older than me with a family, and he was willing to let me do all the searching for contacts and attending all the trade shows.

JR said, "How did you go from there to your success?"

Gar answered, "That was my education. We grew because we were reliable. I did that for twenty years, and when my partner retired, I bought him out. A few years later, I sold the business. However, now I consult for all types of businesses in the food industries. I put together companies. I have international contacts. So I guess I'm still brokering. It's been very good to me, the grocery industry."

By this time, the two tables in the bar had merged to one. Beauregard spoke up. "How'd you manage married life with a career filled with trade shows and international travel? I just do short investigative trips and find the pressure on my home life difficult—catching up after a couple days away."

Gar said, "In my day, Beauregard, the guy was responsible for making a living. When I met Madeleine at BU, she was in the school of education. She wanted to teach English, and let me tell you, her best student was me. Hell, I was not a writer. A salesman, yes, but not a writer! I still can't spell, but I had Madeleine. What else did I need? We lived on Hillside Avenue in Wollaston, a section of Quincy that was really nice and at that time affordable. The area was on the other side of Furnace Brook Parkway; it was a great area. Madeleine taught English at Broad Meadow Junior High School for several years until we had our son Paul. The school at that time covered kids from the Hough's Neck, German Town, and Marymount sections of Quincy. She loved it. We were busy, but all our friends were busy. We never asked our parents for assistance, but they were good to us. They would deliver frozen steaks from Omaha to us until they realized that I could always get food. Then they would send department store gift cards. My mother-in-law liked Remick's Department Store in Quincy, especially when she realized that they were owned by Lee Remick, the actress's family. The gifts came in handy. Life was good. I worked long hours and traveled, and Madeleine worked long hours. She never once complained."

JR said, "Madeleine was special; of course. She would never complain."

Gar continued. "Then I started to make big money at about the time that technology made life really easy for me. My mom had died, and my dad needed us. Madeleine's folks are from Ludlow, and so we were happy to come home. It was great for a long while. Then it was not great: Madeleine got sick, and you know the routine. Back and forth to Dana Farber in Boston, week after week. We were never certain, but in our hearts we probably knew that she was not going to make it. You know, there's a terrible punishment for having great love, and that's in the fact that one of you will die first."

Beauregard had not expected such a love story. He had not really known Gar and only learned what he'd heard during the occasional golf game or in the media. He would read about Gar and Leana attending public events with their pictures in the paper, or on MassLive, or whipping around West Side in some fancy foreign convertible. They were not in his league. But the love story Gar had just recalled? That was in Beauregard's league.

JR said, "I'm sorry to have opened a wound. She sounds wonderful. Good marriages are always taken for granted. Good wives are so missed."

Norbie broke the ice by complaining that the appetizers were taking too long. JR took that bait and complained to the other table of the merged tables. "Who do you know? You got your calamari before us. Not fair—we won the match."

# 6

# San Francisco, 1981

LEANA REVIEWED HER SITUATION. *How the fuck did I end up here? How could I have let this happen to me? I've grown bigger than Mary Lou. That was the old me. I should have seen what George was. Am I so stupid that I need a road map? Didn't the Courts teach me anything? It was all that damn Christian charity that Ernestine espoused. I let my guard down. Well, it will never happen again.* The pain had been bad, but the screaming of the other girls was something she couldn't easily block out.

"Mrs. Haylor." The excuse for a nurse in this backwater clinic was speaking to her. "You may leave now. I will give you a number of a doctor to call if you find you're bleeding excessively. You are to rest for a few days. We will not be at this location tomorrow. Try not to let this happen again; after all, you have a husband, and our program focuses on single women." She let Leana out through a labyrinth of about six small rooms, all occupied by young women.

Leana could not help thinking how women were the garbage disposals of society, always taking care of the mess that men did not want to deal with. *Where is George Haylor III, the important scion of a famous family, now?* She'd read that word *scion* in the newspaper account of their marriage. *Well, he's now home crying, that's where he is, saying, "Leana, a baby will be good for us. You can work for a few more months while I try to get a good job. My parents will come around."*

*Yeah*, she thought. *I passed all the tests. The parents love me. It's their darling Georgie in whom they're disappointed. Well, so am I. He's so clingy.* Leana couldn't believe how fast her dream fulfilled became not only unfulfilled but a disaster. She remembered how his classy, well-dressed looks first turned her on. She'd met Georgie at a party in a Brooklyn loft right after she had moved from Albany to New York City for work. One of her colleagues wanted her to meet Georgie, who was considered the perfect guy. His family was part of the elite living in Summit, New Jersey, who made their millions on Wall Street.

Mary Lou, as Leana had been called then, had won a coveted internship at a small, high-end boutique marketing firm in the city the summer before her senior year at SUNY Albany, and she was promised a position after graduation. The firm kept its word. It wasn't difficult work; however, she had much to learn. Management enthused over her presentations, telling her that she was on the right career path and had a future with them. She knew that she was good on her feet; she was resourceful and always prepared. She'd discovered early that the best way to move ahead was to offer to do all the reports and research required, often for her boss while he took credit for it. That was okay for now, she had believed, but she would change all that in the future.

Leana didn't know many people in the city, and she craved recognition where there was none. She could hear Ernestine say, "Never miss an opportunity to grow." When she was invited to a party at a loft, and the loft was not far from her Brownstone in Brooklyn, she jumped on it, looking forward to meeting new people.

She was overwhelmed by Georgie when she met him. He was such a gentleman. She was reminded of Ernestine continually insisting that she and Timothy had good manners, telling them that good manners often hid any negatives they may possess. In this case, she was surely right. Georgie had perfect manners, and they hid his drug addiction and his weak character. His parents considered themselves so moral, so above the masses, and their only son George, a graduate of Columbia, was a living legend for the family's future. Well, Georgie's only morality was to himself and how to keep himself high enough to be not quite out of it but playing along without making any effort. She thought for the hundredth time, *How the hell did I get conned by Georgie?*

Georgie had told her that she was a ray of sunshine and that she should change her name to Leana because it meant sun ray. She'd agreed that it was a much fancier name than Mary Lou, and so when they married, she chose Leana Haylor as her given name. They were married in San Francisco a year after they had met. His family had connected him to a great management job in a big engineering firm out there, and she moved there to marry him.

A month after their wedding, they ran into a skaggy junky who ran up and jumped on Georgie with a, "Big man, where have you been? You look really good." Georgie introduced Leana to Sun Ray, who proceeded to inform Georgie that she had a really good connection for coke and heroin. Leana thought, *Christ. I left a good job and moved across the country because this guy convinced me that I was the ray of sun in his life. I changed my name to Leana, and for what? He wanted to remember this burned-out hippie piece of dirty hair from his college days in New York. I'll fix this somehow!*

Leana walked with pain and nausea out of the seedy apartment slash commercial complex on a dark side street of old San Francisco. She had to walk two blocks away for her car. She was so tired. Her only energy lay in her desire to right her life. She thought that with some rest, she would be okay.

There would be no hospital for her. Earlier, she had investigated the name of a clinic where the doctors don't ask questions about their patients and don't report to the police. She learned then what the down-and-outs knew about how to meet their needs. If she started to bleed, she'd go there, not to the doctor she was told about.

She drove her car two city blocks to a pay phone that was in a very dark area and phoned the police. "I want to report an abortion clinic."

She gave the address in the Tenderloin section. "There are patients in there now. You must act quietly and quickly." She wondered how arrogant that nurse would be now. She got back in her car and drove home. She felt better now and laughed, thinking, *One job done.* Now she would address exiting herself out of this bad deal into which she had negotiated herself.

When she pulled up to the row house in Noe Valley, she was truly exhausted. It had been such a nice start for them when they'd first arrived. Under her guidance, the house took on a spectacular look with only a modest investment of dollars. They both had good taste, at least in the beginning of their marriage. Their wedding was attended by some important business movers and shakers, attorneys, doctors, and politicians. Sylvia, her mother-in-law, hugged her at the wedding in a grand moment, telling all the guests that she was the luckiest women to be able to welcome Leana into the Haylor family. "Leana has such grace and is adept at moving conversations where they ought to be. We are so lucky. My George is so smart to have found her."

And then it all fell apart. She could see now that she should have walked earlier or not taken Georgie's side against the Haylors. Georgie's sister Martha warned her that it would be better to face the music with her parents. But no, she could control the situation. At least, that was what she'd believed then.

Leana let herself into her home, dragging herself against her fatigue. Georgie was in a drugged stupor on the bed. At least he wasn't still on the couch crying. She saw the paraphernalia on the night stand; he was injecting again. A year and a half ago, his parents had sent him to a dry-out hospital in Kentucky, and when he'd come home, he'd been reasonable and gone to work for about two months. She had hoped that the situation could be saved. She'd had that hope for another month, and then ... Well, it was strange to see someone's soul and body disintegrate in front of you.

Leana had felt contempt when Georgie had lost his job. His boss had had quite enough of Georgie, his promises, and his no-shows for client appointments. The last no-show was a really important client who'd raised hell with the firm at being stood up. What had made the real situation clear to her was that Georgie's boss was his father's best friend and a really decent man. He'd not fired Georgie on a whim; he'd told Georgie that no one could help him but himself. True that may be, but where did that leave her? She was left supporting the drug addict and hiding her money, bank accounts, and car keys.

Still she stayed, and then she would come home to Georgie feeding all these low-level addicts dinner in exchange for drugs. One day she found the junky Sun Ray in her house, high and wearing her fur coat. Sun Ray raised a ruckus as Leana threw her out on the steps perhaps a little harder than was needed. Georgie simply smiled with a drugged-out grin. The world was wonderful when he was high.

Then her things started to disappear. His parents had recently cut off Georgie from his monthly stipend and apologized to her, saying, "We were told by the alcohol counselor that we can't be codependent. Please see what you can do to make him understand that life will get brutal if he doesn't come around." *Well, what about life for me?* she asked herself.

*And then the pregnancy. How the hell did that happen*? She was vigilant about taking her birth control pills. At first, she thought, *It would be nice to have something of me in the world besides myself and Timothy.* Then after visions of raising another weak-willed kiss-up to Mother and Father Haylor, waiting for money—or worse yet, another drug addict—she knew what she had to do. It surprised her how difficult it was for her to make the decision. But it was done now, and for the best.

She undressed, got into bed, and surprisingly fell asleep quickly. At four in the morning, Leana woke to find Georgie on top of her in an attempt to have sex. She screamed, "You insensitive scumbag! I just had an abortion. I could bleed to death. Get off me now!"

Georgie wasn't too disturbed and said, "I've found a solution. I told Mother about your getting an abortion, and she was furious, but I explained that you couldn't keep working to get me through this problem if you had a baby now. It wasn't the right time now. So she reinstated our monthly allowance. We'll be okay, baby." He tried to hug her, but her twisted facial expression stopped him in his tracks.

Leana reacted with, "You're fuckin' nuts. You're out of here in the morning. I'm not supporting you anymore. You can take your parents' stipend and shove it. Do you understand what I mean? I mean divorce—never to see your drug-addled face again."

"You cunt! You don't own this house. It's in the family trust's name. Remember that we didn't have enough credit history for a mortgage. So you can get the fuck out yourself. My mother was horrified that you aborted a Haylor baby. She'll be happy that I threw you out."

It had been a long time since Leana had felt such rage, but she had history with controlling the expression of her feelings. *No, I will ditch at my own speed, but this matter must be reasoned out.*

Like a snake, she was suddenly slithering with consoling tears to her husband. "Georgie, you have to stop taking drugs. Let's get you dried out again. Maybe you need a longer time in rehab. You go, and I'll wait for you. We'll have a baby and be a family. My God, I love you. Please, let's forget all this. I'm certain that we can make our life perfect."

As she knew he would, he said, "Okay, baby. I just need another hit. Tomorrow we'll make plans."

Georgie was now dead. The fix he'd made her inject was too much. She called Father Haylor and told him that Georgie had overdosed while she was sleeping. Mother Haylor started screaming, "It's because you aborted our grandchild! He couldn't take the guilt."

Leana started crying and stammered, "Mother Haylor, he made me get an abortion. I told him we could talk to you for help with the baby, and he said he wasn't having kids. He hit me and arranged everything. He said I could just get out and carry the brat by myself. I'm so sorry." The conversation ended with Father Haylor giving her instructions.

Barely ninety minutes later, doctor, attorney, ambulance, and a cleaning service arrived at the house on Alvarado Street. Father Haylor was conducting business for the good name of the family again. Georgie was taken to a funeral home with a properly signed doctor's death certificate. Cause of death stated was acute myocardial infarction from severe chronic rheumatic heart disease.

The attorney had Leana sign papers and gave her a check for fifty thousand dollars. The papers essentially paid Leana to squelch any story she may think about telling in the future; instead, the signed paper was an acknowledgment that her loss from Georgie's sad death from heart disease motivated the family to make this payment to help her go to graduate school, to help her recover. The cleaners went through the apartment, cleaning all drug-related materials and taking any paper with Georgie's name on it with them. By nine o'clock in the morning, they were all gone. The attorney gave instructions for Leana not to come east for the funeral in consideration of her recovering from an early miscarriage of their baby and her grieving.

She truly believed that the Haylor family was probably relieved that Georgie had died. There was no more embarrassment, and they could eulogize his good traits, which as far as she knew only included his stunning good looks and manners.

Leana, who had taken a few days off from work, started packing her things. She had a plan for where to go next. She would stay three months in a monthly rental and figure out where her skills as a political and public relations consultant were needed.

One thing was for sure: she was adamant that her next situation would allow her to build a substantial monetary base for herself, knowing that no one could be trusted to take care of her but herself.

It was just another situation that tried to defeat her, but she concluded, *Thankfully it is just another easily closed chapter in my life. Not for the first time, I've had to protect myself. I have only myself to take care of me and Timothy.*

# 7

# A Georgia Visitor from the Past

Beauregard looked at the overweight, but beautifully dressed and handsome woman whom Millie escorted to his office with a big smile on her face. The woman's card stated that she was Myra Kortiac, President, Public Relations: Public/Private Interface, 200 Peach Tree Center, Savannah, Georgia. Beauregard was knocked away by her wit and her manners, as he later explained to his wife, Mona.

Myra didn't even wait for him to ask what she wanted. "That Millie, well, I just knew she was a southern gal—all smiles and 'glad y'all came to visit.' It's just heartwarming to see someone from home up in this bastion of pilgrims. I mean, it's not that folks up here aren't polite and even friendly, but they don't normally smile with their eyes unless they know you. Well, Captain—I believe I heard Millie call you Captain—my, you must be a very good detective to be captain. I've met many lieutenants, but you're the first captain I've met from the police. I mean, I have met captains in uniform in the services at these big military balls and socials, but normally I don't see too many police at these functions other than police chiefs, sheriffs, and commissioners—you know, the bigwigs.

"Stop me talking, Captain, because sometimes I do go on. I'm here about the death of my dear friend Leana Fraine Chisholm, who I understand upped and married some guy named Lonergan, so I guess you'd know her as Leana Lonergan. I'm really happy that she married, if he was an honorable man. Please tell me about her death. From what I've been told, it was in an automobile accident."

She took a breath for a moment, and Beauregard jumped in, asking her how she'd found out about the accident given that Savannah was such a distance from West Side. He hoped that each answer would not take quite such a long time to finish, but he immediately knew that there was no shutting Myra down once she got started. He'd seen this type before, but he also acknowledged that he rather liked Myra.

"Well, now, when Leana left Savannah, she left in a hurry. I thought that one of the many men who were enthralled with her kidnapped her, but that wasn't true. I know that because I checked her bank, the country club, and a few other places, and she paid everything off from a bank in Pennsylvania. They all said that she was relocating to Pittsburgh, where she had found a wonderful position in the mayor's office. Well, that wasn't true either, because I checked that out. Now, you all probably think that I'm just nosy, but Leana was a good friend, and I'd want someone to worry about me if I left town suddenly and didn't come back. Wouldn't you?"

"Myra, do you have any idea why Leana left Savannah? I mean, was she having boyfriend or work problems? Where did the surname Fraine come from? Was that her married name?" Beauregard was hopeful that Myra could perhaps give a complete picture of Leana's past.

Myra proceeded with a review of her relationship with Leana. "Leana moved to Atlanta after the loss of her husband Fred. She said that she didn't know how to grieve, and you all know that Americans try to stuff it down—all those hurting pains. I myself was a basket case when my mama died. I finally went to grief counseling. That's where I met my darlin' Mishel. So I encouraged her. In fact, I took that little gal right under my wing.

"I met her originally at a Chamber of Commerce breakfast. She had been hired by Peaches Associates, LLC. Don't you just love that name? Y'all know that it's located in Georgia; everything of importance has peach in its name in Georgia. Peaches Associates has several offices in the state, including one in Savannah. Just sent her resume in with a picture, and she was hired after only one interview. Well, that just isn't done normally in my business, but I understand why she was hired so easily. She is a beauty, and I don't say that easily—not only good looking but smooth, you know? She knows when to be quiet and when to say something.

"Leana also has a lovely, throaty voice that you want to hear. Well, by golly, it wasn't a few weeks before we were best friends. She was so successful at Peaches Associates that other firms tried poaching her. She used her gifts to lure clients into her inner circle. and that was her entrée into their hiring her firm—probably just to get her affirmation and good will."

Myra went on to say that Leana didn't really like Peaches Associates. She said it was too big; too many hurdles to jump even to bring on a new client. "Well, I'm not a people poacher, but I did offer her a vice president of sales position at my public relations firm with a salary 10 percent over her current position and a 20 percent increase in commissions on new clients. Hell, I practically made her a non-investment partner. And it paid off. She increased my client base by 90 percent in the first three months, and it got better from there. We were quite a pair."

Myra helped Leana join the country club near Forsyth Park after Leana had explained that it was a good business decision. "I'm telling you, that gal was a Houdini at picking situations that support meeting big clients."

Myra explained that Leana saved money, found herself a good financial advisor, and invested. Within a year, she bought a gardener's cottage that used to be attached to one of the swanky homes on Ardsley Park. The original estate was broken up by the heirs into four parcels, three with two acre lots and one with four acres. The cottage was not a cottage like a cottage; it was a ten-room home that was lovely. To top that off, Leana was great at interior design, and her efforts were the source of a major article about the little cottage appearing in the magazine *Southern Interiors*. She entertained regularly with little soirees—that was what she called them. Normally about thirty people were invited, mostly couples.

"Leana believed that in business, men, women, and whatever must be included in all social happenings. She would say, 'Myra, women know as much or more than men. They all hint in different directions. Knit all those hints together, and you have a nice map of what's going on.' It was at one of these soirees that Leana met her husband, R. William Chisholm. He was the CEO of Georgia Research Group, one of the top ten successful private enterprises in the state, and certainly in Savannah.

"Now, I did warn Leana that R. William Chisholm was a player. He had recently divorced his second wife, and it was generally known that Chissie—that's what we all called him—had an eye for the ladies. Not that I think either of his wives were what I call wife material. No, both were just lazy layabouts who shopped massages, plastic surgeons, and designer clothes as their daily work. I guess they were diligent at shopping, as if it was real work; I give them that."

Beauregard jumped in. "Myra, you said *was* when you referred to R. William Chisholm. Why is that?"

"See, Captain, that's kind of the problem—why I think Leana took off. Just too much happened in such a short time. Chissie died in an accident at their second house. It happened just six months before she left Savannah."

Beauregard asked if Leana was with him when he died.

Myra said, "Leana was home in Savannah. Further, things between them were problematic. Chissie was originally so taken up with Leana's beauty that he really gave her the old 'Chissie rush.' I did warn her that he was not known for his faithfulness. She wasn't concerned. They had a prenuptial agreement that in many ways was good for her. If Chissie decided to divorce her for anything other than her unfaithfulness in the first three years of marriage, or if he died, then she would get five million in cash outright. If the marriage lasted three years and there was divorce for any reason, Leana would get an additional two million in cash for each year after the fifth year until the fifteenth. After that, upon divorce, she would get a thirty-million-dollar settlement. If he died after the fifth year then, she would split his estate with his children, with a third each."

"So let me get this right. Leana was married less than five years and would get five million in cash whether Chissie lived or died?" That kind of money was big money, and so he stated that these terms were pretty generous; that Chissie must have thought he loved Leana and maybe anticipated an extended marriage.

Her response took a moment and added a detail that Beauregard hadn't considered. "Chissie was nobody's fool. First of all, the prenup was silent on the fourth to fifth year, and so it would probably need the court's interpretation whether she would get anything at all if she left for his unfaithfulness after the end of year three and before the beginning of year five. The man was no soft touch. Also he'd dragged his first two wives through the courts for much smaller amounts, making them spend 20 percent on lawyers before either got a penny—and they each had a child with him. Those biggity ladies hated him, and rightly so; he could be mean. He would have done the same to Leana and maybe a whole lot worse because there was no child and therefore no guilt involved."

Beauregard then asked Myra when the marriage had started to fail, when Chissie had died, and whether there were questions around his death. Myra sighed and rolled her eyes, and then she started to cry. Not at his best when women cried, Beauregard asked Detective Jim Locke to bring in a box of tissues. When Jim arrived, Beauregard introduced him to Myra and asked him to stay. If ever there was the need for a patient inquiry for which Jim Locke was known, it was now. Beauregard could feel his own patience fading.

Beauregard summed up Myra's interview for Jim. He thought, *I can sum up in ten minutes what took Myra two hours to say.*

Jim told Myra to take her time and cry it out. He said, "Sometime we bottle up our feelings, and the bottle gets overfilled and needs release. Don't you feel one bit of embarrassment, Myra. It's obvious that you cared a great deal for Leana." It didn't take too long after that before Myra was ready to go on.

"Detectives, Chissie was so proud of Leana at first. He couldn't find enough venues to have her attend with him. She was so smart and dressed perfectly for each occasion. You would think that she was brought up in the South, but she said she wasn't. She never drank too much and never said too much; in fact, she may have been too perfect. Now, y'all, I say that because there came a time when everyone greeted her first and wanted to be her friend—even the women, now that she was married. She could talk politics and business with the best of them without ever making enemies.

"I think that Chissie got jealous. It was no longer, 'Chissie, you have a mighty nice filly there.' No, it became more, 'I just love that gal of yours. You can stay home.' Chissie was no longer the big alligator, no sir. Leana inadvertently demoted him to husband. It's a mistake we Southern gals don't normally make. We use *sugahh* all the time with our husbands, even when we're on a tear. A Southern boy expects to be looked up to, not to have his wife be the star. She may reflect his golden star, but by golly, she can never be the star, especially for a man like Chissie. It was the first mistake I ever saw her make, and it was a big one."

Jim asked when Myra noticed the change in Chissie's attitude toward Leana.

"Well, it was about two years into their marriage that I noticed Chissie spending more time at his man house over on the Ogeechee Marsh. Now, y'all have to understand that his man house was grand, not some little cave. In the past, he used to take his ladies who were only worthy of his time for one night over there. Out by the river was his favorite place to feel sorry for himself. I did mention to Leana that it wasn't a good sign that Chissie was by himself over at the river, but she said a marriage works best when both partners have their own interests."

Myra continued. "I told her that maybe Northern men could be alone and stay out of trouble, but by golly, that didn't work for most

Southern men. For a smart gal, she was making a big mistake here. Well, less than a year after that, the rumors started flying. Chissie was seeing a young widow who worked for his company. This was not like Chissie to mix work with home life. He was religious about his work being his domain. I think that in the marital war for who's on base, as my darlin' Mishel would say, Chissie was taking a stand. I don't really think he wanted a divorce from Leana. I could see that he was still entranced by her, but his ego was busted. I'm tellin' you, anyone could see that. I heard that he was drinking more, and Leana would leave an event or the club separately after Chissie got drunk or maybe high as a kite on something."

Myra said, "About two weeks before Chissie died, Leana and I had a girls' talk about her situation. Funny—she said that she wasn't hurt because you can't be upset if a bee stings you when you get in its way. She was a long way from letting a sting get her down. When I asked her what she was going to do, she said she was uncertain, but the end of her third year of marriage was coming up, and maybe it was time to get out. She said that she could try to hold it together for a few more years. Leana believed that in many ways, she and Chissie were a matched pair—if he just wasn't such a narcissist and imbiber."

Beauregard wanted to move the conversation forward. "Myra, what happened the night Chissie died?"

"Y'all want to know about that night Chissie died? Well, I was with Leana at her house in Ardsley, which she had finally sold that week. It took a long time to get her price. It was a darlin' show piece, and she was having a party for her friends, giving them first options on buying some of her antique pieces that decorated the home. Chissie wouldn't attend the party. He said that he didn't approve of commercialism in personal space, which was such a hoot. Chissie would sell anything for a profit. Eyebrows went up when the guests realized that Chissie wouldn't be there because he was at the river place. It didn't bother Leana at all. We were having a grand old time; in fact, she called Chissie to tell him what a gala he was missing. I heard her talking, and she was just *sugahh* all over. I remember that she didn't like that he was going out in his pontoon boat in the dark, and she asked him to be careful. I remember saying to her that Chissie was really good at boating and not to worry. I was so wrong."

Beauregard abruptly said, "Myra, just how did Chissie die?"

Myra tearfully answered, "Well, if you read the papers, it says that his blood was over the alcohol limit and that he hit something that capsized the boat. He fell in the murky water and died. Leana told me that the coroner said that he had a faulty heart valve, and that, combined with his asthma and the stress of swimming at night in the dark, was too much for him. Now, my Misha says that the pontoon boat Chissie had was made of three thick aluminum tubes, round and chambered. You'd have to puncture all the chambers to sink the boat, which is highly unlikely. But a brutal hit by something could capsize the boat. It wouldn't sink. Misha simply couldn't imagine what would hit the boat over there and not leave evidence. They're almost impossible to destroy. That's why we get them; they let us feel that the pontoon is safe, especially in lakes, rivers, and swamps. I mean, that's the reason you have a pontoon boat and not a speed boat: safety."

Jim asked, "Did the police investigate the accident?"

She told him, "There were three weeks of stories on the investigation in the papers. The police were there at the funeral, which was truly very sad. Leana was quite distressed—unusual for Leana, who normally didn't show a lot of emotion. The whole county turned out, with politicians and big business CEOs. It was a parade of the rich and powerful in Savannah; and from much of Georgia. She cried, which was normal, but she upheld well, as my mama would say. The previous wives were there with their sons, who were only interested in Chissie's estate. Leana had a good relationship with Chissie's attorneys, who often stated that she was the classiest of his wives. However, there was a holdup in the settlement for Leana. First of all, cause of death couldn't be established until the investigation was finished. Second, the estate had to wait for various insurance policies to be paid out that were to fund any shortfall in business and estate expenses and Leana's settlement. It took about five months, which my hubby says is pretty damn quick."

Beauregard asked, “Is that when Leana left Savannah, Myra?

She responded, “Leana left shortly after the settlement was signed over. I do remember her last words to me. ‘Myra, I believed that you and I would grow old together. I’m disappointed that I have to leave Savanna, but I am too overwhelmed by what might have been to stay. I do love it here. I promise that I’ll call you when I’m settled. Remember that we were special together.’”

Myra further explained, “They never did find what the pontoon boat hit. It had to be substantial. Chissie’s death was finally ruled as accidental.”

Beauregard asked Myra, “Did Leana get along with Chissie’s ex-wives and children?”

Myra smiled. “Leana adored his children, and they adored her. The ex-wives did not think too much of Leana, which Myra considered normal. Both of Chissie’s children were young men who were blown over by Leana’s style. I don’t know why she told everyone she was moving to Pittsburg when she came here to West Side. I would have been much happier to visit the Berkshires than go to Pittsburgh. I know that she did say that she had to visit a brother. Well, by golly, that was news to me. She didn’t have a brother at her wedding. I asked her, and all she would say was that he doesn’t like to travel. I asked his name, and she took a long time before she said it was Timothy. She was weird about anyone asking her about her childhood or anything, so I didn’t push it. Y’all know that everyone’s entitled to their privacy; it’s just some are more private than others. Misha and I, well, our lives are an open book. We’ve nothing to hide. But maybe Leana did have something to hide.”

Beauregard and Jim questioned Myra further about the type of work that Leana did.

Myra said with pride in her friend, “Leana’s ability to sell probably any kind of personal service, from finance to public relations to computer interface, was superior. Leana’s leaving cost me 30 percent of my clients within a year. It was a big hit for me. I’d gotten used to the good life. Leana worked part time after she married, but that was enough to keep my firm's clients. She was magic. I'm truly sorry that she's gone."

Myra then asked again about how Leana had died. Jim asked her why that was important to her. She was hesitant before answering. "Leana was a Northern gal, and occasionally she could be flip with certain people. In normal situations, it'd not be a problem, but you have to understand that when she was flip to someone in our crowd, it would appear to be a major insult because it was so removed from her ordinary way of conversing. One of the men at our club actually confronted her when she was fresh, and she reacted with tremendous rage. She said, "Your manners for your level in society deserve disrespect, and that's what you got from me, so shape up." That's why I wondered if the accident I heard about was maybe questionable—maybe she picked the wrong guy to be flip with. After all, you Northerners have a rep for being sensitive and using actions rather than words to address your difficulties."

Beauregard had to smile but said, "Myra, it has been determined to be an accident, but it certainly presented a rare set of facts. Although the case is not open, it is under review."

Myra, right to the punch, said, "Has the insurance company paid benefits? I always say that if those boys pay, it's a signal that it was truly an accident."

Jim Locke could not stop himself from smiling. "Well, insurance payoffs to the beneficiaries only speak that the beneficiaries were not deemed involved in the cause of death."

Beauregard hoped that Jim regretted opening his mouth. He thought, *Too much information, Jim.*

Myra asked if they thought it was appropriate for her to visit Leana's husband, Mr. Lonergan, to pay her respects.

Beauregard said, "It is not our policy to give out telephone numbers or e-mail, but Millie will give your card to Mr. Lonergan. If he is in town, he may be willing to contact you."

"Not to worry, Captain. I have all of Gar Lonergan's specifics. Thank you for your time." She left in a swirl of clothing and musky perfume.

# 8

# Detectives Deliberate

BEAUREGARD ASKED DETECTIVES PETRA Aylewood and Mason Smith to join him in the conference room.

Mason was carrying a folder and greeted them with a big smile. "Wait till you guys hear this. I don't think Gar Lonergan knew whom he was marrying, I'll tell you that. I got their marriage certificate, and it shows that she was a widow and had one marriage to a guy in Georgia. Her name was Chisholm, and after checking in Georgia, I was told that her husband, R. William Chisholm, was a bigwig down there. He died in a boating accident that was investigated for three weeks. The detective down in Savannah sent me copies of news reports on the death.

"Her Georgia marriage certificate had her maiden name as Prior, and she had one marriage to Frederick Fraine of Mirror Lake, New Hampshire. The police in Wolfeboro, New Hampshire, told me that Fred Fraine, a major real estate investor in property around Lake Winnipesauke, was an uncontrolled diabetic; one of them called it brittle diabetes. He died at age sixty-two in his boat, in a diabetic coma. Everyone up there was devastated, as was Leana. The chief in Wolfeboro remarked that Leana was a wonderful wife, and it was a sad day when Fred died. He was the salt of the earth and was born right up there in Tuftonboro. Her marriage to Fraine showed one previous marriage in 1996 to Aaron Goldberg of New York City, and it said that she was a widow. I have not heard yet from those folks, but it's only been two days; I'll call again. Both marriage certificates show her parents as Ernestine and Lester Prior, from Lake Placid, New York. Well the Priors were considered really good people by the Lake Placid attorney for the Prior estate. Even the chief of police up there remarked over and over about what a great family the Priors were. Ernestine was the last remaining parent and died in 1975, leaving three children, Jason, Mary Lou, and Timothy. Apparently, Leana (or Mary Lou) and Timothy were adopted. Some said it was after their biological parents and brother were killed in a fire somewhere in New England.

"I then used her name, Leana Prior, and found that a woman named Mary Lou Prior had married a socialite called George Haylor III, who was from a wealthy family from Summit, New Jersey. They were married in San Francisco at a big fracas with all the high mucky-mucks attending. At her marriage, Mary Lou changed her name to Leana Haylor. Then guess what? Within a couple of years, he died. Imagine, a young, healthy guy dying in his twenties from a heart attack caused by chronic rheumatic heart damage. Didn't that kind of stuff go out in the 1950s? I also received all the press on the death and the funeral, which took place back in New Jersey. I've sent out the name Leana Haylor to my police contacts to see where she surfaces next, and I'm waiting for a response. I love this stuff. I can't wait to find out more about Miss Leana—she's quite a piece."

Captain Beauregard took this opportunity to apprise both Mason and Petra about Myra, the visitor from Georgia.

Having worked diligently making a timeline for Leana's marriages, adoption, and birth, Bolt was the first to say, "Uh-uh. This lady's got missing time. How many more could she have married—and dare I say, how many more husbands died? Also, let's look at our letters and their postmarks. Do any of them give us a clue about other areas in which she may have lived? Can we access her social security number, since this isn't really an open case and the system will keep a record? Right now, we only have phone calls and e-mails—nothing that will raise a flag that we're involved in an investigation."

## Time Line—Event Date History for Leana

| | |
|---|---|
| January 15, 1955 | Birth? Connecticut |
| March 23, 1975 | Death of Ernestine Prior, Leana's adoptive mother |
| May, 1977 | Graduation: BA from SUNY Albany |
| May 28. 1978 | Marriage to George Smith Haylor III, San Francisco. Leana's first husband (her name had been Mary Lou Prior) |
| April 30, 1981 | Death of George Haylor III, heart attack, age 29 |
| 1996 | Marriage to Aaron Goldberg (waiting for the marriage certificate copy) |
| June 20, 2001 | Marriage to Frederick Fraine, Wolfeboro, New Hampshire; widower (her name: Goldberg) |
| September 16, 2005 | Death of Frederick Fraine, Leana's husband, age 62, of diabetes in a boat in the middle of Lake Winnipesauke, alone |
| November 15, 2007 | Marriage to R. William Chisholm, Savannah, Georgia (her name: Fraine) |
| October, 10, 2010 | Death of R. William Chisholm, age 65, in boating accident |
| May 20, 2012 | Marriage to Edgar Lonergan, age 65, West Side, Massachusetts (her name: Chisholm) |
| October 12, 2015 | Death of Leana Lonergan, age 60, in single-car auto accident |

When they were finished with the timeline, it clearly showed that Leana was hopping all over the country.

Beauregard said that social security access, although faster, would take an open investigation, approval from the chief, and maybe legal warrants from the courts. He asked whether they already had her social security number from the Priors, and Mason said that he did. Beauregard then questioned if it was from a public document, and he said it was from the estate filed in New York. "Wouldn't be allowed today, but sometimes it was used in those days to identify someone. Maybe it was because Leana and Timothy were both adopted," responded Mason.

Mason then said, "I was told by the Prior estate attorney that Mr. and Mrs. Prior were originally from Connecticut before they moved to Lake Placid for Mr. Prior's job. I have calls out for birth certificates for Timothy and Leana in that state. For some reason, he wouldn't give me her birth name—said Leana wanted nothing to do with her birth parents, and he was never to discuss the issue with anyone. He said that telling me about Connecticut was independent of his discussions with Leana. I have Leana's birth date, which is consistent for both marriage certificates and the estate documents, but I think that we are looking for Mary Lou Prior. I'm using her birth date and Timothy's birth date as good dates to find out about the birth parents. Soon as this stuff's in, it will be on your desk, Captain!"

Beauregard said, "There is a problem here. We have about fifteen years, from 1981 to 1996, unaccounted for. God, how many husbands could she fit in that space? Mason, get her name for when she married Goldberg."

"Captain, I have to check marriage records. I'll do that shortly," responded Mason.

Petra said, "I don't know, Captain. Just look at this history. So far we see three to four husbands here, and not one divorce. She's certainly able to get husbands with money. The first husband left her with very little that we know of, and she got money from Chisholm, but we don't know about Fraine. Mason, can you follow up on that when you go after the marriage certificate? We know she got some money from Ernestine, her mother. But what funds kept her afloat from 1981 to 1996? Maybe she has more husbands. Also, what about her brother Timothy? He maybe knows where she's been."

Mason said that the brother was autistic but supposedly well-to-do and well employed. He had a woman companion but was not married. "I'll call him and see what I can find out. I'd loved to go to Lake Placid for a couple of days, if the department pays."

Beauregard replied, "So would I, but this is not an open case."

Jim offered to go, saying, "I was planning to go to the Finger Lakes for the weekend and could just as easily go there. No need to charge expenses to the department. This trip would be gratis."

Beauregard knew that Jim was about two months from leaving the department. He'd watched as Jim had struggled, only to discover that there was a side of police work that just wasn't for him. But more important, he and Petra had a pretty serious relationship going, and if it continued, they could not both be in Major Crimes.

Jim had said many times, "Petra is born to be police, whereas I was born to ferret out information."

Beauregard heard through the grapevine that Jim would shortly receive his private investigator's license and would be partnering with a computer nerd private investigator in Springfield called Hunt, who was the owner of Hunt and Find, Private Investigators. He wrote a recommendation for Jim. At that time, Jim formally told him about his plans. He said that at first he was troubled about leaving, but now he was excited about his new career, or possibly two careers. Beauregard thought, *I'm not so excited.*

The firm Hunt and Find already had a book of clients for commercial work. The current owner's name was Jeffrey Hunt. There was no Find.

Beauregard told Jim, "Well, it looks as if you're the Find. Congratulations on your new partnership."

Beauregard knew that Jim had negotiated a contract with two of the neighboring police forces for outside investigations. He was pleased knowing that Jim could make a good living at what he liked to do, and that the police would not completely lose Jim's talents. Jim was also a licensed psychologist, and Beauregard knew that he was developing a clinical practice as well. He would see which one he liked better.

No one spoke for a minute because their brains were focused on the fact that Petra had put in for three days' vacation at the same time, which may not have been authorized before with two detectives out at the same time but surely would be authorized now. Beauregard told Jim to go ahead, and then he quietly told Petra that her vacation time had been authorized.

Beauregard saw Mason suppress a snicker but ignored it. Instead, he said, "Jim, maybe if we don't get all we need from the Wolfeboro area on Leana, you can take a day or two more and go over to find out about any of Fred Fraine's finances that may not be on the filed estate."

Millie brought a message to Mason, who delivered the news that Leana was married to a Harry Bergerdemaine from Memphis, Tennessee. Her name was Haylor before she was married, and she was a widow. Then the meeting was over.

# 9

# Nashville and Memphis, 1982

LEANA HAYLOR FOUND THE good ol' boy network in Tennessee helpful to her. She was just what employers wanted. Her short platinum hair and her slightly upscale good looks, supplemented by good manners and a high IQ, set her apart from her peers. Her accent was not really much of an accent, and it still needed some adaptations with a few of the more necessary quirks of the Southern language tradition. She had read about the music industry and was drawn to Nashville, Knoxville, and Memphis.

With a little ground digging, Leana found work with a public relations firm in Tennessee. The search was made easy by the 1982 World's Fair happening. It was known as the Knoxville International Energy Exposition, and Ronald Reagan opened the event on May first. It was exciting despite the fact that it had to be one of the poorest run events she had ever worked. But a blessing was given her when she met some very important people at the fair.

Music people were everywhere, and Leana soon learned a great deal about the industry. About halfway through the fair, money stopped flowing, and her firm was cut from further promised work. Her manager encouraged her move to their main office in Nashville, which pleased her to no end. She met some of the new traditionalists in country music, including the Judds, the band Alabama, and Dottie

West. She also met Amy Grant, who was into Christian music and making it pay. Leana thought, *This is what America gives us: opportunity to make something out of what may appear ordinary.* She was energized and did her best for her firm. She gained more clients from the industry for the firm, and her paycheck increased quickly, plus the perks: free tickets to just about anything. Leana was not about to spend her inheritance and lived on her salary. She used only a small portion of the inherited money, just enough to establish a home and buy a car.

Leana thought, *I'll not waste money. Big money is for investment, for growth, for use only on extraordinary investments or needs.*

Elvis Presley's mansion was opened to the public on June 2, 1982, and her firm sent her to Memphis to develop clients in the industry who were rallying around what looked to be an ongoing and successful venture. She loved Memphis as much as she loved Nashville, and the mysteries circling around Elvis, his death, his manager, Priscilla, his ex-wife, and his posse fascinated her. She added a few up-and-coming musicians to the firm's roster and reaped some work for the Presley venture.

Then she met Harry. Well, she didn't exactly meet Harry. She ran into Harry several times on Beale Street. He wasn't handsome but was manly looking and well kept. She watched him and saw no indication that he was a hard drinker or a druggie. He appeared to like the company of ladies but was never with the same lady twice, and so she fancied that he was avoiding being a twosome. She thought, *That's all right with me. It means that he is thoughtful about getting tied down.*

One day, Leana was managing a luncheon for the Memphis music industry at the Peabody Hotel. It involved waiting for the famous duck march through the hotel with the duck master in charge, which normally took place twice daily around 11:00 a.m. and 5:00 p.m., but today the eleven o'clock march was delayed. The Peabody Hotel ducks had marched through the hotel to drink from the fountain twice a day since the 1930s, making their march a local, and later national and international, cultural phenomenon. No tourists traveling to

Memphis were satisfied until the duck march was witnessed, and then they often stayed for lunch or a drink. The restaurant management wanted Leana's large group of guests in the dining room by noon with at least one drink already imbibed in the bar. She was going to have a problem herding her group of seventy-five to the dining room if the ducks didn't get here soon.

There he stood in front of her: Harry! "Well, my beautiful angel from Beale Street. You look more at home here at the Peabody than there over on Beale Street. What are y'all doing with that frown showing between your pretty little eyebrows?"

Just as quickly as a little Southern gal, Leana said, "I bet y'all say that to just about any lady." And without another word, she moved away as the ducks marched into the lobby to a Sousa march.

Harry apparently liked a cat-and-mouse game, which Leana later told a friend, and that alone should have been an early warning to her. He followed her and whispered in her ear, "I'm one of your luncheon guests, if y'all are handlin' the music luncheon. Look on your list; I'm Harry Bergerdemaine. May I make your acquaintance, Miss Leana Haylor of San Francisco?"

Although she was startled at his reference to San Francisco, she replied, "So pleased to meet you. You're the agent for at least five of the bands who are represented here, and you're from Nashville." She hoped that this would demonstrate that she wasn't afraid that he knew her background, and as a man, he would probably want to know how she knew so much about him.

"Rumors are that the little lady gets high grades for her work, but I'm from Memphis, sometimes Nashville. Is that why you spend so much time down at Beale Street? Now, I notice you wearing cowboy boots on those shapely legs, but I bet you yearn for three-inch heels."

Because he didn't take the bait and didn't search for knowledge about her info on him, but because he did show continuing interest, she looked straight into his baby blues and said, "Big cowboy like you, I bet you could help bring in all the strays for lunch. How 'bout it?"

"With a caveat," Harry said. "I get to sit with you. Nod your head if you agree." The applause for the ducks was loud, and she nodded her head. In fact, she looked forward to sitting next to Harry.

She and Harry shortly became a number. She never called him, even if she didn't hear from him in a week. He wasn't used to that, she was sure, but she knew how to play the possum game—yes, she did!

One evening six months after they had met, when he had been absent for a week, Harry asked her for the first time if she had missed him. Her answer was, "Well, I'd hoped you'd call, because I'm moving back to Nashville next Monday. You should know so that you'll be able to find another escort when I leave."

Harry's face turned a deep shade of crimson, while he sat quietly for what appeared to be a long time but was probably only a minute. Finally he said, "I've been courtin' you for six months. Have you noticed we've had no sex? Have you noticed that we are the only young people in Memphis to have no sex?" He touched her face and said, "I don't want you to go, Leana. I don't want you to go."

Leana was, for her, emotionally moved by Harry. She said, "I really don't know a thing about you. I've never been to your home. I've never met any of your friends except in passing. I don't even know if you have a family. I just can't stay for you. You understand that I can't stay as things stand."

Harry's response was immediate. "Let's get out of here. I will give it all up—let you know about my life, my real life." And with that, they took a ride around Memphis, ending up in a recently built home on Ardvale Road. He told her that it had over three thousand square feet—not huge, but enough for his two kids. He explained that he'd been married for ten years to Luanne, a gal who lived near his childhood home, and whom he'd divorced.

"I'm telling you, Leana, she left her mark on me. She had about every vice you could think of, and I spent ten years drying her out, paying her gambling debts, and wondering whether the children were really mine. I was brought up Southern Baptist, and I believed at that time, even more than Catholics, that I should stay the course. But the kids were suffering. I divorced. She disappeared right after I filed for the divorce and couldn't be located, so I got full custody of the kids. Thank God there was no custody battle, because the mother is important to the state's courts.

"You never saw me with one woman for long because I wouldn't take a chance on bringing some lady home and having a neighbor call child services on me—and they would, I tell you! I pay my bills, save a lot of money, and take care of my life. I firmly believed that after the kids were out of college, I could then search for a better life for myself, possibly with a partner. I was wrong. I can't wait that long now."

Leana did not break her tradition with Harry. She did not bite as to what he meant about being wrong. Instead she said, "Harry, how old are the children, and what are their names? Are they good children? What else can you tell me?"

Harry talked glowingly about Harry III and Luella, whom he called Tres and El, respectively. He said that Tres was sixteen, full of himself, but good in school. El was 14. "El is like my mother in her ways, but she looks like her mother, which is fortunate for her. My mom, bless her soul, is not a beauty outside, only inside. El is beautiful inside and out. Tres looks like me and acts like my daddy. He's sensible and not easily fooled by his peers. It's a trait I think he got from watching his mother manipulate others. I dearly love them. Do children turn you off, Leana?"

Leana answered, "No, Harry. I like children and am quite good at keeping them on the right track. No, they do not interfere with possibilities for you and me."

With that said, Harry made an offer. He had checked on her background and explained that he could not let someone who wasn't honest into his children's lives. He said, "When I discovered that you lost your husband at such a young age, I was full of sorrow for you. Your being a young widow explained why you moved and ended up here. I figure you just had to close that door. I'm really happy you chose Tennessee. Can you tell me why?"

Leana did some fast thinking. "Perhaps God showed me the job notice looking for public relations managers. It may have been a directive to you." She further informed him that she would have no problem with the children. She thought, *Unlike some women, who insist that their stepchildren should love them, I have no such expectations. I'll teach them manners, treat them kindly, and ignore any lack of goodwill they might have toward me.* She rationalized that she could hug them appropriately at the right moments, and their daddy could do the rest of that huggy-kissy bit. No, her problem was how to keep her assets separate from his, and how to ensure that she be fairly treated financially. She had done some research on his finances and him, and she already knew all that he'd told her. His worth was estimated at over five million in hard assets, and he also had substantial liquid assets. He had a modest mortgage on his home and a commercial loan for some other property he held. He paid his taxes and was quite well considered by all. The situation was comfortable, and she rather liked Harry. She thought that they could do well together. When he asked her, she said yes.

Harry and Leana Bergerdemaine did well together. The children thrived. Harry's business boomed, and Leana's public relations demeanor added to their success. They went everywhere together, and if Leana appeared just a bit distant from the children, well, she *was* a stepmom and from the North. What could one expect? Also, the ladies in town theorized that although she was extraordinarily pretty and had such nice ways for a Northerner, it was reasonable to expect she should have some failings. She was an excellent golfer and was great at tennis. She loved boating with Harry. She was a terrific cook and would have dinners for eight friends or Harry's business colleagues every other week.

The ladies in town waited for news that there would be a new Bergerdemaine, but after two years with no news, people figured there was a reason. Some ladies had the nerve to bring up the subject to Leana. Her reply was, "Some are blessed and some are not." That answer forestalled additional questioning.

Then there were the problems. Tres enrolled in Vanderbilt University, majoring in music and math. He did well. At the end of his sophomore year, he won an internship with a New York musical touring company that performed in various cities in New York and New Jersey. Harry asked Leana if she could call her former in-laws and ask them to perhaps visit Tres, if he got lonely.

Her reaction was not measured. It was unusual for her, and it was a mistake because Harry noticed it. She recovered quickly and said that her in-laws had never recovered from their son's death and thought that if he had stayed in New York City, they would have noticed his failing health and he would not have died. But this did not make sense because it was her father-in-law's connections that had brought her husband to San Francisco in the first place. She simply could not revisit that situation and would not make the call.

The following year, based on Tres' ravings about New York City, the Northern perspective, and her interest in language studies, especially in Spanish and French, El made the decision to attend Middlebury College. When they accompanied El to college, Harry asked if it wasn't near where she grew up in Lake Placid and whether they should visit her old hometown. She said that it wasn't that interesting in September and that she'd take a pass. Harry didn't let it go. He told her, "It must be of some interest. You fly there before Christmas every year to visit. Why not go now?' She put him off, but he started to think.

Leana knew that she may be in a ticklish situation, and she wondered how much harm there'd be if they did go to Lake Placid. Unfortunately, she knew practically everyone who lived there year round. She would have to tell him about Timothy, and he would think she was cold to have not moved him down to Memphis. Could she avoid all those people who knew that she was adopted? She didn't know, but she did not want to open that box of horrors.

Leana thought, *Perhaps if we stay at a high-end lodge in Lake Placid for just two days, we could take all our meals there. I could have Timothy meet us there too. That could work. Timothy will tell them nothing except about his work, his lady companion, and his investments for retirement someday. Maybe he'll mention Ernestine.* She agreed and made reservations.

When she told him that she had made reservations and talked about Timothy, Harry said, "Honey, why wouldn't you tell me? I'll be as nice as I can be to him. I don't know a lot about that condition, but I'll read up on it." Then he questioned and questioned. How did one explain Timothy to someone who didn't understand? She tried without telling him too much.

The Lake Placid visit went well. Harry and El could see that Timothy and his lady friend, Alice, were nice people. Timothy clearly was not emotionally involved unless the conversation focused on taxes, accounting, and baseball. Alice was sweet and talked about everything else in a quiet but simple manner. Then one of the waitresses, Patty, recognized her and started her questions about Mary Lou's life with the salts of the earth, Ernestine and Lester. She said, "Don't you remember you joined our elementary class in fifth grade? I forget where you came from, but I'll remember."

Harry asked her, "Did you change your name? You don't look like a Mary Lou. Why would you change your name to Leana?"

"Why, because George insisted that the name Mary Lou was not sophisticated enough for the Haylor family. He suggested Leana after some great aunt or his, and I liked it too. It fit me."

Harry then asked Timothy where they lived before they came to Lake Placid. Timothy said, "In a house with Mama and Dad." When questioned further, Timothy was agitated and only said, "In a small town." At that point, Leana stepped on Harry's toes, and he stopped questioning.

Two months later, Harry started calling her Mary Lou. It was exasperating. She asked him to stop, and he would for a while, but then he'd start up again. Finally he said that he would stop with the old name when she would honestly tell him the secret she was hiding. She was so perturbed that she flew to Atlanta for a beauty treatment, which was not something she ever did. *Let him miss me,* she thought.

Her lesson to him was lost. While she was gone, Luanne, Harry's ex-wife, returned to Memphis, dried out and supposedly remorseful over the loss of her children. The children were now in college and could decide for themselves whether they wanted to see her. Luanne retained an attorney—actually, her attorney boyfriend—who went to the courts and filed a reopening of Luanne and Harry's divorce. The filing cited Luanne's mental health problems at the time of the divorce, and the lack of effort expended by the court and her ex-husband's attorney to locate her. Luanne was looking for a division of the property that they'd accumulated when they were married.

Harry was in a state when Leana returned. He barely recognized that she had left for two days. He did not improve at all until the kids returned for Christmas, which seemed to reassure him that his life would eventually return to normal. The holiday was lovely. They entertained as usual, holding their annual New Year's Eve party and enjoying life—until Luanne and her now attorney husband entered the front door with Christmas presents for the kids. All the drama was presented in front of their nearest and dearest. Neither Leana nor Harry lived their private lives in public; for them, the event became a catastrophe.

Not long after New Year's Eve, due to the court action filed by Luanne and her husband, Harry's attorney requested full financial statements from him for the court. Although they assured them that his current assets would not be part of any consideration for judgment, he was hard pressed to understand why they were needed at all. Leana put her foot down. "It's time now to look at everything, Harry. I understand these kinds of people. Your ex-wife and her boyfriend are dirt, and there is no dealing with that kind of dirt," she said.

When they finished the financial review, she understood that his non-liquid holdings were in one holding company, and that he didn't have three million dollars plus interest in liquid funds to pay a court if the decision went against him. He had ten million in non-liquid assets with three million in mortgages. If the holding company was broken up, it would require renegotiation of financing and a sale of some assets. Those assets, once a lien was placed on the holding company's assets, would start a fire sale. She was furious and felt she'd been duped by Harry's lack of planning.

This situation encouraged Harry to attempt an out-of-court settlement with Luanne. It took almost three months before Harry and Luanne could come to an agreement. Shortly thereafter, before Harry could sign the settlement agreement his attorneys had negotiated with Luanne, Luanne and her husband died in a freak car accident. Both Leana and Harry were questioned by the police about the contention between Luanne and Harry. However, Harry and Leana were at a public function during the evening of the crash.

The crash was first explained by a recall problem of the transmission that inadvertently allowed the park gear to go to reverse in 1980 Fords. Ford did not have a full recall and simply sent a warning to the autos' owners. The couple was driving a 1980 Ford Bronco and had parked on top of a hill. When they put the car in reverse, it plummeted down into ongoing traffic and was demolished, killing them both. When police traced their steps, the couple was last seen at a local bar celebrating their potential signing of a deal with Harry for four and a half million dollars, payable over three years in equal installments. Luanne and her husband had been drinking heavily.

The police investigated because it seemed as if Harry was a very lucky man to have gotten rid of his problem on the eve of the payout signing. Added to that potential motivation was the fact that the braking system, what could be reconstructed after the accident, was impaired. In checking with local repair shops, they found that the car had been brought in the week before citing transmission slippage and some braking problems. The brakes were supposedly repaired. They were told they would have to come back for the transmission slippage in order to get Ford to pay for it. It took a lot of paperwork. Luanne said, "Not to worry, we'll have a new car next week."

Four months later, Harry was dead of an aortic aneurism. Leana and the children at the funeral appeared to be in a trance. Although severely affected by Harry's death, Leana was very supportive of Tres and El, and she guided them through the next few months.

Fortunately, Harry had a will and a trust, leaving a large amount to her and the rest to the children. Leana was the designated trustee, and the trust had her monitoring the children's share until they reached the age of twenty-five years.

Leana stayed for five more years, settling the estate. She then told the kids that she must move on because she was too young to grieve any longer. Consistent with her history with her brother Timothy, she promised to visit them every summer, but that was all she could manage. All mail was to be sent to a postbox in New York City. The kids cried, and to everyone's surprise, Leana cried a little too.

# 10

# Dinner at the Club

MONA, BEAUREGARD'S WIFE, WAS pleased to have been invited to dinner at the West Side Country Club by her sister-in-law and JR Randall's wife, Sally. The two ladies had much in common. They each had three children and were noted for their dedication to the West Side community. It didn't much matter to the two whether it was a church, a synagogue in Springfield or Longmeadow, or a mosque that needed help; the ladies were there. If it was the Lion's Club, VFW, or Boys and Girls Club, the ladies lent a hand. They could manage nearly any situation or be worker bees. It didn't matter to them; they believed it was their duty to assist if their calendars permitted it.

Tonight was different, however. Tonight was for them. It was a special luxury for Mona, whose husband was not a member. Belonging to the club wasn't a priority for Mona, and it could never have fit in their family budget. Beauregard loved golf, and so he was a frequent guest of JR when he was not working on a weekend.

The ladies ordered the rack of lamb with spinach risotto, and they moaned over the succulent taste of each morsel. They had also ordered the charcuterie appetizer and wondered whether they would be able to eat their dinner. They were decidedly wrong. They ate and continued to eat. Between their bites, they discussed the merits of breaking their diets occasionally; and then they gossiped.

Mona stopped for a moment and said, "Sally, I'm generally not interested in gossip."

Sally retorted, "Gossip for me is my bread and butter for living. So do what we always do, Mona: I'll talk, and you'll listen.

Mona thought, *In fairness to Sally, I guess listening is also partaking in gossip, as Rudy often tells me. I don't tell him every bit of gossip I hear, but when I do relay a thread to him, well, then, doesn't that make him an active listener too?*

Mona could see that tonight Sally was interested in what she had heard regarding Leana Lonergan, Gar Lonergan's second wife who had died in that terrible accident.

Mona said, "Leana was much too young to die, and I was sorry for her. To be honest with you, Sally, Leana was not my favorite person, and it's not because she was prettier and more sophisticated than most of us. I simply concluded that she was may be a fraud, that she was not the person she presented herself to be."

Sally said, "And what do you think she was presenting herself to be? She ran great parties in that beautiful home of theirs, and she kept it in pristine shape. She did volunteer at the club when they had all kinds of committees—that is, before the new owners took over. She was generally charming to everyone, and I never saw her flirt. But that's why this rumor is so strange."

"What rumor? Sally, Leana's been dead for almost two years, and I never heard anything about her when she was living. I don't remember hearing anything when she died, except nobody could understand why she took a right turn at that time of night when she should have been bearing left to go home."

Sally answered in a slightly hushed tone, "That's why I wanted to talk with you. I think if the rumor is true, maybe Beauregard should look into the accident again. Not that I want to get Gar in trouble, but it's strange that he would disappear shortly after the accident—and not for a month to recover, but twenty or so months."

"God, give me a break!" Mona groaned. "Believe me, Sally, there is no way that I can move Beauregard to do an investigation unless he thinks it's warranted, and I don't think for a minute that he would be moved by gossip."

"I knew you would say that, but listen to me before you close your mind. I was at the Club Ladies Golf Luncheon with Theresa, Sam Chaya's wife, and Tasha, Tom Suri's wife. They told everyone at the table that they thought Leana was having an affair before she died, and you'll never guess with whom."

"Don't keep me waiting, but I have to tell you I find it hard to believe. I've seen all the big-time movers in town try to approach her in an overly friendly way, and she never once flirted. It's very unlike a beautiful woman to not at least shine on some sparkle to other men."

"Well, they said that they saw Leana with Don Turtolo, of all people. You know that brash, very good-looking guy who flirts with every woman between eighteen and forty. And he spends money like water. I think I heard that he's loaded without a lot of debt. JR always says that what looks like money isn't always the case. You have to see how much the person owes. Lots of folks are up today and down tomorrow with cash. So I asked JR, and he said that he thought, but wasn't sure, that Don was financially solid."

"There you go, Sally. Couldn't be true. Leana was well over fifty, closer to sixty, when she died. Somehow I think that she would be able to see through Don. Although I did hear from someone that he was really a good sport, helped at the food kitchen, and was pretty lonely. This friend told me that she thought maybe he had decided that he needed and wanted a wife. I guess his marriage fell apart when he was in Silicon Valley; you know the pressure on those guys working out there. Then he was all involved in his business here. Still, let's face it: which one would you rather have for love, Gar Lonergan or Don Turtolo? No contest in my mind, I'd take Gar Lonergan any day. First of all, he's probably twice as wealthy, and second, he's awfully good looking. Finally, he's just a lovely man, and I do not want to rake up trouble for him. He adored his first wife, as he should have. Madeleine was an exceptional human being. So instead of getting some solace in his life after he's lost Leana in such a terrible way, the town is starting new gossip? I don't think I want to hear it. I've always thanked God that Gar's kids were out of the house by then so that they wouldn't suffer another loss when Leana died."

"Mona, you can bury your head in the sand if you wish, but those kids were not at all comfortable with Leana as a stepmother. Gar's son—I forget his name right now—he adored her for the first year and then completely turned away from her for some reason. The relatives said he moved to California to get away from the situation. and Gar's daughter, Paige, never was comfortable with Leana. Paige used to tell her girlfriend that she had discerned that there was nothing inside Leana; the woman would say whatever she believed would please her current listener. One of my corporate customers for the garden center was Paige's friend, and Paige's version of Leana was not that she had suffered before she'd met Gar, which was her story, but that she was incapable of feeling or feeling the suffering of others. However, she was quite capable of putting on a show of empathy when there was an audience."

"I find that difficult to believe especially knowing Gar. He is intelligent and perceptive, and they had been married a while. Don't you think that he would have noticed this deficit in Leana, especially after having been married to Madeleine, who was so empathetic?"

Sally answered, "Mona, you're married to Beauregard. You don't have to worry about trust; Beauregard takes care of that. He's of a suspicious nature, and as the lead detective in Major Crimes, his experiences make him extraordinarily careful in the judgment of others. But Leana was a different case. She turned heads wherever she went. It wasn't just her looks; she moved as if she owned the world, and on top of that she had the most gorgeous smile, which was invitational when she used it. Gar Lonergan was hurting, and she was the remedy for his pain and loneliness. Besides, I firmly believe that when it comes to a good-looking woman, men are incredibly stupid, and Gar is a man!"

Mona felt trapped in a situation where she really wanted to know more but also felt constrained by her sense of what Beauregard would say if he were here. "So what else have you heard other than that she was seen with some man? Where were they, at some motel? That might make even me suspicious."

"No, they were together at some joint in Palmer or Ware. It was the kind of place that Leana probably would not ever be caught dead—you know, a dive. Also, they were seen shopping at the Natick Mall, I think. Both sightings were out of town, one being over seventy miles away. Now, you explain that to me."

"Maybe Leana was back to work in marketing and was working for Don. Believe me, if you saw my Rudy in New York City with Petra, you would think something was going on, when they were probably on the prowl for info or at a police conference. I will let Rudy know somehow what you've told me, but I can guarantee that he's not going to respond even if he already knows about this rumor. Sometimes it's infuriating to live with him."

Later that evening, after returning home, Mona made some chamomile tea for Beauregard and brought it to his home office. He seemed surprised and said, "Guilt tea because I was forced to make dinner for the kids while you were out gallivanting? Or are you trying to get me to slow down with chamomile? Which is it, dear Bride of Frankenstein?" That was one of his pet names for her.

"Guilt? No, you called for pizza for the kids, which is what you always do when I'm not home for dinner. I suppose it's better than you poisoning them by making that French meat pie your mother used to make. Hers was fattening but good; yours is questionable. But no, I want to share with you what Sally told me today. It's a bit of gossip, but it does ring as if maybe something is not quite right. It's about Gar and Leana Lonergan ..."

Beauregard did not shut her off while she repeated what she could remember from her conversation with Sally. It was surprising that he was so patient and seemed to be waiting for each detail. When she finally finished, she asked what he thought about the potentials of a romance.

He said, "I don't believe it for a minute, but I find it as strange as you and Sally do. Why would Leana be alone with Don in Palmer and Natick? Probably she was with someone else and not Don. I don't think it was an affair; no, not at all do I think that."

That was the end of the conversation.

# 11

# Police Focus on the Non-open Case

Beauregard was holding his typical Monday morning case management meeting at 11:00 a.m. He held the meeting for a few hours to calm any chaos from the previous weekend. The timing also allowed him to organize new work coming in that day. Millie kept notes for the four detectives because as she would often say, "Smart minds are not necessarily organized minds, and for sure my detectives are lousy at record keeping."

In keeping with a practice he developed, Beauregard had Millie take notes for general meetings. She was consistent and reliable, and the detectives accepted her. In some departments, a detective would document meetings, and they did so in his department when the focus was on something of which Millie could not be a part. He knew that Millie complemented his management style: she was the best at nagging the detectives to do what they were supposed to do, and she nagged well. Beauregard thought, *I don't nag well. I don't want to learn either.*

All the nagging in the world would not have been enough to assure proper documentation of cases, and thus Millie was the force in the process. The case management meeting minutes were never left up to the detectives. Beauregard understood that if he let them document the meetings, they would be done days after the meetings, and there would be too much creative thinking going into the minutes. No, Millie would do the minutes, and that way they would reflect some sense of accuracy.

Beauregard addressed current issues and read aloud three notes from Chief Coyne, despite the fact that each detective had previously received the notes. Beauregard wanted assurance that his detectives would never be able to deny they were familiar with the content of the notes, knowing that they might not like much of Chief Coyne's remarks. From the looks on their faces, he got validation: they were not pleased with the extra paperwork suggested by the chief.

Beauregard then left the floor open for news from other investigations. At this point, he told Millie that this would be a session on investigative style, and minutes would not be needed. Millie excused herself without asking a question.

Aylebrook tried to speak but was interrupted by Smith, who spoke over her. "Me first. I have news on the non-investigation. And by the way, does Millie know anything about this?" Not waiting for an answer, he proceeded. "Leana's previously married name on the marriage certificate to Frederick Fraine in New Hampshire is Goldberg, and following that, I found her marriage certificate in New York City stating that she was previously married in 1993 in Chicago. I've made some calls, and that marriage certificate shows that she married Theodore Waleski on December 23, 1993, in the city clerk's office."

Theodore was president of a company called the Greater Chicago Best Mattress Ever. The clerk said that he was a catch—not only wealthy but a good-time player and an altogether good guy. The only problem is he liked his booze and gambling, and he was noted for several DUIs that made the papers. You think with Chicago's murder rate that a DUI wouldn't' be important, but the clerk said that it's always important when someone from money gets caught. Anyway, he died a few years later. He'd had only one previous wife, and Leana listed only one previous husband on the certificate. Her name on the marriage application was Bergerdemaine, and her maiden name was Prior."

Beauregard asked, "How long did this one live, and how did he die? For certain he's dead?"

Smith answered both questions. "He died in a single-car accident, and liquor was involved. He was alone, and it was their third anniversary. According to the papers, he was driving his wife's automobile, which had just been serviced. But get this: the wrecked car did not show the repair that was paid for, and the steering and suspension problem wasn't abated. The estate filed a claim against the dealership and repairer, All Queen City Motors, and there was a settlement. I don't know how much, but the papers say seven figures. I've got a request out for the estate filing, but the problem is that all the assets won't show up in the estate. If Leana was on the bank accounts, she would have simply grabbed the money. Waleski had an adult son who was in business with him, so maybe the business went with him and Leana got the house and cash. I'll try to find out more."

Beauregard said, "Now, slow down. How does this fit in the timeline? Let's fill in the chart. Did the Wolfeboro clerk have her name there in their records when she married?"

Mason pulled up a simple data marriage sheet on the white computerized board.

## Leana Lonergan

- Windsor, Connecticut. Born Mary Lou Court, 1/15/1955, to Cora and Calvin Court.
- Windsor, Connecticut. Death in 1963 of parents Cora, Calvin, and brother Austin Court in house fire. Mary Lou and brother Timothy escaped fire.
- Mary Lou and brother Timothy adopted sometime in 1967 by Ernestine and Lester Prior, in Connecticut. Family later moves to Lake Placid, New York.

- Lake Placid: death of last remaining adoptive parent, Ernestine Prior, 3/23/1975.
- Albany: Graduation with BA in English, 1977.
- San Francisco: married 5/28/1978, to George Smith Haylor III. Maiden name on marriage license was Mary Lou Prior. Mary Lou changes her first name to Leana. Husband dies April 30, 1981, of heart attack at age 29.
- Memphis: married March 18, 1983, to Harry Bergerdemaine. Married name citing one marriage is Haylor on the license. Maiden name listed is Leana Prior. Husband dies of an aortic aneurism. News article that his former wife and her husband, who had sued the Bergerdemaines about past alimony and a fraudulent divorce, died in a fiery accident just days before a financial settlement on the case. Leana stays in Memphis until 1989, tells children they can reach her at a NYC PO box.
- Chicago: married 12/23/1993, to Theodore Waleski. Maiden name on marriage license is Prior. Previous name with one marriage listed is Leana Bergerdemaine. Waleski had one previous marriage listed and one adult son. Waleski died in an auto accident on 2/4/1996. Repair problems on auto not properly done, and alcohol cited as causes of accident.
- New York City: Leana Goldberg?
- Wolfeboro, New Hampshire: married 6/20/2001, to Frederick Fraine. Her name listed on marriage certificate is Leana Goldberg. Her maiden name listed is Leana Prior. Both parties listed that they were widowed. Frederick dies alone on 9/16/2005 on his boat in the middle of Lake Winnipesauke of type one diabetes, age 62.
- Savannah, Georgia: married 11/15/2007, to R. William Chisholm. Her name listed on marriage certificate is Leana Fraine. Her maiden name listed is Leana Prior. He had a couple of previous marriages listed in divorce. She was listed

as having one previous marriage and was a widow. R. William Chisholm died in a boating accident on 10/10/2010 at age 65.
- West Side, Massachusetts: married 5/20/2012, to Edgar Lonergan. Her name listed on marriage certificate is Leana Chisholm. Her maiden name listed is Leana Prior. Both listed one previous marriage ending in death of spouses.

Locke was the first to speak. "She was a busy lady, our Leana. But what about this Goldberg marriage? Can't we get some info on it? She must have really squeezed that one in. She's pretty consistent. She lists the last previous marriage as her only previous marriage and Prior, her adopted name, as her maiden name. Do you guys realize how many husbands she's left dead behind her? Six, with Gar Lonergan left as her widower, meaning at least seven marriages. Two of the husbands die in accidents, and the other four dying early. But she has an ability to walk into a new area of the country and quickly find a husband of means? Well, that just boggles my brain."

Beauregard told Smith to work on the unknown New York marriage to see whether he could find out more about the PO Box in New York.

"And Smith, it looks like this lady had some big assets. She must have left an estate. We never looked at her worth before. Gar could tell us; as the widower, he would be entitled to a share. I think I remember reading that she had no life insurance. But if there was a lot of money going to Lonergan, then this may warrant reopening the investigation into her accident."

Petra and Jim next presented their findings from Lake Placid and Wolfeboro. Petra gave the report. "We had a really lovely time while investigating. We met Leana's brother, Timothy, and found him to be an upstanding member of the community. He has a live-in lady friend, Alice, and a lovely home simply decorated in a rustic style."

Beauregard said, "Cut the interior design part, Petra."

Smiling, Petra continued. "Timothy is apparently successful. He was sad when Leana's name was mentioned. He said that she would always be Mary Lou to him, and she told him that Leana was just her stage name. He had heard a second time about her death from a sympathy letter sent from our lady in Georgia, Myra Kortiac.

"Six months after Leana's death, Gar Lonergan visited Timothy. Timothy really liked him. He said that he knew Mary Lou was dead when she didn't visit him on his birthday in December. We carefully questioned him. He didn't really wish to talk about Leana; it was too painful. His lady friend Alice proved quite helpful. He apparently talks to her in-depth when there is no stress and they are walking in the woods."

Petra retold what Alice had said. "About fourteen months after Leana died, an attorney from New York City sent him a long letter, the gist of which was a request for a bank address to send his portion of her estate along with a copy of the will and estate attached. It took a month before Timothy would read it."

Alice added, "Tim is a genius with finance. He understood the will and estate immediately. Apparently Timothy got 30 percent of her estate; her husband, Gar, got 50 percent; and the remainder went to a nonprofit she had supported for years. Its mission was to help convicted felons with a history of early childhood abuse find quality jobs, housing, and psychological support."

Alice said, "Timothy received over nine million dollars. Leana's death left Timothy bereft. He kept saying that he tried to warn her. I don't know how he could have warned her, or about what. We don't have a phone number for her; just a post office box in New York City. A few months ago, Timothy went on a short trip and would not tell me where or why; he simply disappeared for three days. He was completely distraught after he returned. Autistics often have guilt that is difficult to assuage. Timothy rarely feels guilty because he never does anything wrong. When horrible things happen to Timothy, he is a little different from many autistics. He has such control over his emotions. I credit the training that his mother, Ernestine, gave him and his strong moral code. He lives what his church teaches. Generally rage comes before reason for autistics, and it's what sometimes gets them into trouble.

Not true with Timothy. Well, anyway, I'll stop elaborating on autism. Timothy seems to have finally recovered from Mary Lou's death."

Both Timothy and Alice said that Mary Lou had been married twice, once to Harry Bergerdemaine and then to Gar Lonergan.

Petra said, "As far as how the community viewed Mary Lou, they thought that she was perfect, and they all loved Timothy. There was a general dislike of Jason, the natural child of the Priors. Alice said that they had met Harry Bergerdemaine, and it was nice to be a family with Harry and Mary Lou."

Jim took over the report, summarizing their visit to Wolfeboro, which resulted in lots of conflicting information. "Leana and Fred were the salts of the earth" was one description. Another was that Fred's death had left Leana in charge of Fred's assets, which altered the expected legacies on who got what. Some of his friends who had fished with him regularly said that it was a surprise to them that he didn't have his needle kit with him for his diabetes on the day he died. They never saw him without it.

"One fellow said that it was not unusual for Fred to go out in the middle of the lake and pretend to fish; it was his way of connecting with nature. His friends' view of Fred was that he was a loner. All believed that he had truly lucked out when he was smart enough to marry Leana. Even the ladies in church—and Fred was a regular churchgoer—liked Leana. One gossipy lady asked Fred why, because he was Catholic, would Father Broughton marry him to a Jewish woman in church? After all, her name was Goldberg. Fred told her to mind her own business and sent her away in a huff. The whole town got a laugh out of that because after marrying the two of them, Father Broughton told everyone he was quite impressed with Fred's wife."

Jim continued. "Apparently Fred told a friend that Leana wasn't Jewish or Catholic, but that it would have been easier to marry her in the Catholic Church if she were Jewish than a Protestant. Fred said that marrying Leana, who was raised Protestant, required proof that she was baptized and confirmed, which she did supply. That would not have been required if she were Jewish because of old church rules;

most of the early Christians were Jewish. I don't know if that's true, but Fred believed it was true. Maybe the priest told him."

Beauregard interjected, "This is not a church court, Jim. Stay on track."

Jim continued. "Fred had earlier married a local girl from nearby Alton Bay. He was in his thirties at the time, and she died five years later of a stroke. He was, from their reports, quite broken up. Although wealthy and young, he never married until Leana. One guy said, 'Believe me, it was not from some of our prettiest ladies not trying.'

"Fred had a brother and two cousins who worked the real estate management company for him. The funny thing is he had a will that left everything to them and the Catholic Church. The will was made before he married. Apparently, marriage nullified the will, and when he died, he died intestate, which means Leana got everything that was in his name alone—and that was substantial. The business land was in a trust set up years before, but it had a stipulation that if he died, 25 percent would go to the living spouse, and the rest would be divided between the other three. That is, 25 percent of net profits from the real estate business, because there was a trust stipulation that would not allow the business to be closed if he died until it was no longer viable. Apparently Leana told the brother and cousins that they should split her 25 percent between themselves and Fred's church."

Jim continued. "The estate shows that Leana took seven million from cash and investments and donated four hundred thousand of that to various local charities in the area. This legacy protected her reputation in town, I can tell you that. Smart lady! One of the town residents insisted that Fred had a cache of money that wasn't traceable. He was the kind of guy who wanted ready cash in case he ever needed to buy something quickly. He bought all his cars and equipment for cash; how much of, or where that money went after he died, nobody knows. Most think that Leana would know where it was and took it."

Petra took over reporting to give Jim a break. "I spoke with the fire chief and a guy who was on call that day from the New Hampshire State Police Marine Patrol. They both said that the boat was out of fuel, and Fred was in a diabetic coma clutching his uncharged cell phone in one hand and an empty bottle of orange juice in the other hand. He died five minutes after they found him. They were both upset with the fact that several boats had passed his Boston whaler while he was lying partially propped up, and no one reported it. Probably was a good half hour before a passerby sent a distress signal. I wonder why this guy, who apparently was a bit obsessive, would go boating without his kit—and then also would not check the gas tank, and on top of that not have charged his phone. Besides, Jim got another kernel of information from Fraine's brother."

Jim relayed his interview of Fred's brother Peter, who inferred that his brother's death was disturbing to him. Peter went further, saying, "After all, he's dead. What good would it do to raise questions? He was a good man and a good brother. I don't want to dishonor him." Jim discussed at length with Peter his feelings about Fred, and he led the discussion to Leana.

Peter finally opened up. "You've gotta understand. We all thought Fred was a lucky son of a bitch to get a woman like Leana to marry him. She was awesome, apparently well-heeled, beautiful, and smart. He met her when she rented a major property from him after coming to the Wolfeboro area. She said that she loved Lake Winnipesauke. It was not only a beautiful lake but was also accessible to two ski areas. Turns out she was raised in the Lake Placid area, and this was, as she often said, 'Like coming home but with no negative memories.'

"They were dynamite together, and she got along with just about everyone except my wife, who never liked her. Now, I wondered whether her reservations might be a woman kind of thing. I mean, my wife's good looking, but she's not in the same category as Leana. Also, my wife thinks that I've always been in my brother's shadow. It's not true, but she doesn't understand that Fred was a risk taker; I'm a manager and weigh risk far more carefully than Fred. I really don't think that we would have had such a great business if Fred wasn't at the helm. Also, I have four children and couldn't take financial risks.

Fred could and did, and so he had major ownership of the business. Thanks to Leana, I and my cousins still own the business."

Jim reported that he pushed a bit and said, "So what's bothering you now? Isn't your wife satisfied that Leana didn't keep her portion of the business? Also, Leana has been generous with some of the local charities when she didn't have to be. So help me out here, Peter. What's bothering you?"

With some reluctance, Peter said, "Fred was despondent over the last few months before he died. I asked Leana if there was a problem in the marriage. She denied marriage problems but said something was the matter; she figured maybe his illness was depressing him. She said that he would disappear for half a day or even the whole day, and when questioned he just simply say, 'I'm getting my thoughts together. Can't do it when you're around.'"

Jim reported questioning whether Peter ever asked Fred further questions. Peter did, but he was told the problems were age related. Peter was approached at the funeral by someone in town who relayed information that three or four months before Fred's death, various neighbors and store clerks were questioned about Leana and Fred on one or two separate occasions and by two different men.

Peter said, "One man even asked whether Leana was ever called Mary Lou. This is a small town, and I know that if questions were being asked about Fred and Leana, well, those folks maybe wouldn't tell Leana, but they sure as hell would tell Fred. I don't know whether Leana had a past that was catchin' up to her. I mean, it stands to reason. She had only a short marriage to someone else when she married my brother, and she was no spring chicken. I don't think I ever heard her talk about herself except about some public relations and political experiences. We all deduced that because she seemed to be financially comfortable, she had always been involved in her career. But I can tell you that she was one smart cookie, and I can't believe that she lived alone all those years. She had enough energy to handle a career and a home life. If you want to pursue it, you can talk to Jack Wade, the pharmacist in town. He's the one who told me, and he knows everything that's going on."

Petra continued the report. "I told Jim that I would approach Jack Wade. I have a script at home for my allergies, and so I told my cousin who's a pharmacist here in West Side that I forgot my pills, and if he got a call from the pharmacist from Wolfeboro, whether he could have the next refill done there. Jim and I decided that the wait time for that conversation between pharmacists would take at least fifteen minutes; and if Jack Wade wasn't busy, I could get him to talk. It worked. Jack gave me a detailed description of the first guy who said he was looking at Leana and Fred for a security clearance for some work they were doing for the federal government. He gave Jack Wade a card, but it was bogus. Even the coat of arms on the card for the US government was botched. We guess he was some sort of investigator, and we got a description and a list of the people he questioned. He apparently told Jack that he got info from others and named some of them; one was a lady who owned the Winni-Rest B&B, where the guy stayed. We later went there and found that the guy registered with a different name, but the owner had his license plate. She said that she always checks the plates against registration in her guestbook, in case there are any problems with the bill at a later date. It was a rental car with New York plates. She also claimed she told him nothing about the couple. The second fellow looking for information was described as 'like a dude.' He seemed deliberate and very much focused. Jack told him nothing. Jack described him as older, tall, and good looking, but dressed too cool and expensively for the lake region."

Beauregard was interested in the rental car and said that Mason should follow through. "I hope you got the date of stay at the B&B so that Mason can find out who rented it at that time. What about the rental agency?"

Jim said, "I ran the plates, and it was from an agency in Vermont. You know these agencies do a lot of insurance work, and the cars come back wherever and are sent out where needed. A Vermont agency could have some rentals with three or four different state plates. Normally the plates are from surrounding states, but not always. Anyway, the name on the rental form is a New York City detective named Jerry Silverstein. His agency is called Silverstein Detective Agency, and their motto is, 'We investigate anyone, go anywhere for you.' We'd like to talk to him, Captain, but I wonder whether we'd do better in person. We have his e-mail."

Beauregard chided Jim. "You just came back from a vacation that's supposed to be work, and now you want another one? I can send one of you for a day, but whoever goes had better find out whether Silverstein's there before going, and I don't want him frightened. Also, while you're there, try investigating her marriage to this Goldberg. Maybe Silverstein knows something. Petra, I really need you here because the work is work that will continue after Jim leaves us. Sorry!"

Beauregard noticed that Petra was not disturbed when she replied, "I need to be here for a bit anyway. My dad's having some minor surgery, and I should be in town. You know my mother can't handle anything like that alone."

Mason happily summed up his thoughts on what they had all learned, and with his usual dry sense of humor, he said, "Sounds like some rats were stalking the lady. Maybe they caused Fred to do some searching himself on his lady, and old Fred was figuring out an exit plan from the marriage. Maybe the lady decided on an exit plan for him first. Most interesting lady I've ever heard about. Leana sure beats the ladies in my family for secrets kept. Maybe Gar Lonergan found out about the lady's history and formed his own exit plan for her. Maybe he was compensated well for getting rid of her. I sure as hell would be nervous living with someone with her history. Imagine bringing her home to your kids."

Beauregard then suggested that Mason go to New York City to interview the Silverstein Detective Agency, instead of Jim.

Jim looked disappointed, but Beauregard reminded him, "Do I need to remind you again, Jim, that I need someone who will be available later if there is anything of importance resulting from the interview? You won't be here later. I can't send you. Besides, Mason's going to have to pick up some of the slack until we find a replacement for you. It won't be easy."

# 12

# Gar Lonergan Retains an Attorney

ATTORNEY NORBERTO CULL WAS surprised to get an e-mail from Gar Lonergan requesting him to schedule a golf date at the West Side Country Club on Thursday afternoon. First of all, he'd only ever played golf with Gar in a foursome. Second, Gar had not been around for over twenty months. He checked with his secretary and paralegal, Sheila, about his availability. She said, "Don't worry. Gar already called to see what day you could play a few rounds." Norbie was put out and told Sheila that it wasn't her job to decide whether he was available for golf, and on a week day. She reacted by saying, "God, you men are dumb. He's trying to find a subtle way to retain you, Norbie."

"Sheila, why do you think that?"

Sheila laughed. "Duh! When do any of your friends ask me about your calendar? They know you. You like privacy and don't like anyone knowing anything about you. Given that you do a lot of criminal defense work, I understand; but when a golfing buddy calls and is trying to schedule time for a golf twosome, not a foursome, then the handwriting's on the wall. He simply can't make an appointment to see you. He must have troubles. For a criminal lawyer, I'm amazed how little you see sometimes."

Annoyed, he returned to his office and considered why Gar would possibly need his help. Maybe it related to one of his kids or his employees. Or could he possibly have a problem resulting from Leana's accident? He'd heard some remarks from his wife when she'd come home from her book club about Leana having an affair, but he never saw that in her. However, Norbie knew from experience that one never knew everything about another person.

Norbie greeted Gar on the tee, and it was obvious that Gar was out of sorts. They played a couple of holes before Norbie decided to rely on his paralegal Sheila's wisdom and say, "You have a problem, Gar. Let's cut out this ruse and go somewhere quiet to talk about whatever is on your mind."

So as to not be involved with other members in the club tavern, they chose to hit Luxe Burger Bar in Springfield for a drink; after all, it was happy hour, but it was probably too early to have a full bar.

Gar did not hesitate. "I've got to talk to someone about this before it kills me, and it's getting worse. You see, Norbie, Leana was not the person I judged I had married, not by a long shot. I mean, she was many things, but not what she said she was. She was smart, good looking, classy, and great in bed, and you'd think that would be enough. She tried to be good to my kids. You'd think that it was the whole package. But I had a long marriage to a very loving woman the first time. This marriage was different. It took a couple of years before I figured out what was missing. Leana responded to everything I wanted and rarely gave me the normal tug-of-war that a wife would give. You know, like a 'No, I don't want to go out with that couple,' or 'I hate golf dinners,' or anything. It was strange, almost like being married to a robot, until I learned how to read her better."

Norbie said, "Gar, sounds like every man's dream of the perfect wife. Did you ever ask what her expectations were, what she wanted to do?"

"Of course I did. I constantly asked her. You see, a marriage at this time in my life didn't involve worrying about money. She could have just about anything she wanted, and I gave her open accounts. She never abused them. At first, I hoped that maybe there was no need to discuss wants and needs if you're able to have everything you desire.

But it didn't seem normal to me. Nothing was important to her; she was satisfied with her schedule. I think after a while, I just wanted to get into her head. I'm not proud of it, and maybe I was a little lost because she had so little need for me. I love being needed. I realized very early that she had her own source of funds, but no mail from banks ever came to the house. I rationalized that maybe she got her mail at work because she still insisted on working part-time. I called a friend of mine who works with her, and she said that Leana never got any personal mail. So here I was, spying on my wife when she gave me no reason to be suspicious. I felt no intimacy with her—plenty of sex, but no intimacy."

Norbie said, "I guess you discovered something, or you wouldn't be talking with me. I'm very interested in everything you say. Go on; I've got the afternoon for you, Gar."

Gar's story was filled with little things. Leana would go on a private "health spa" trip for almost two weeks in December, from the tenth to the twentieth. She said that she planned to do this every year. At first he didn't question it, and he discerned that it was just what beautiful and wealthy women did for themselves—except that she wasn't into regular spa treatments the rest of the year. He said that the wives of his friends said that maintenance was required more than once a year. The ladies also tried to get information from Leana about the spa she used. Leana never gave it up.

Gar said, "When I attempted to finagle it out of her, Leana would give me a cold stare and respond with, 'Do I ever question you about your doings? There must me trust in a marriage. I need some time for me.' God, she made me ashamed for asking—but that didn't stop me. No, I found myself obsessed with her spa trips. I would probably have left things alone if I hadn't accidently picked up a parking receipt for Bradley Airport in December 2014. Leana's car expenses were on my business account. I rarely ever look at expenses. It is up to my office manager to make reviews for reasonableness, and if there's a problem, then she brings it to me. In this case, my manager had taken time out for surgery, and I was stuck with the task. Somehow the airport parking receipt was like a neon sign to me, sparkling and changing colors. If Leana were to fly somewhere, then why didn't she ask me to drive her to and from the airport? I would have been pleased to do something for her. Because she always drove her car for her spa trip, I had assumed that she was visiting a spa in the Berkshires or in Connecticut. Now I couldn't leave it alone."

"Didn't you ask her about the receipt, Gar? I mean, if that happened in my home, I'd have asked my wife and have a donnybrook if necessary. I can tell by your face that you didn't. Why didn't you?"

Gar's reasoning was a jumble of rambling that was not at all clear. One was the persistent feeling he'd had all along that there was a worm trying to get out of this perfect apple of a marriage. He also said that his children told him several times that there was something wrong with Leana, that she wasn't normal. His daughter never liked her, often saying that Leana was cold. His son, Paul, liked her at first, but then he took a decided disliking to her, so much so that he moved cross-country with his family because he said he couldn't be around her. Neither of his children had any firm facts or events on which to base their feelings.

"I blamed myself for the problem. I mean, Leana couldn't have been nicer or more generous. I concluded that perhaps the kids never got over their mother's death. I explained to them that I was lonely. Both countered me with the claim that Leana was not genuine, that she was hiding something, and it really bothered them. Paul said that her eyes never showed real emotion."

In remembering his kids' intuition on Leana, Gar said, "I didn't listen to them for a long time. But Paige said something about Leana one day that I was already thinking. She said,' Dad, don't be mad, but have you ever noticed that Leana agrees with just about everything we say to her? I've tried saying some outrageous things, and she just flows with what I'm saying as if what I've said is normal. I've tested her many times, and my friends have too. We all think she's wacked out and hiding some secret, and she doesn't want to cause you to look at her too closely. You know she's smart as a whip, but she never puts a position forward unless it's about business practices, or where to buy clothes, or which hairdresser is best at the cheapest price.'"

Gar said, "Of course, I brushed it all aside. But I knew in my heart that Paige was on to something. I didn't want to believe that this love story of mine was not what I judged it to be. I tell you, Norbie, we can really fool ourselves when we're lonely. I needed someone in my life. I was there for the taking, and all the time I rationalized that I picked Leana, it was more like she'd planned it all out. I see it now."

Norbie tried to be patient, but he was having difficulty. "Gar, what do you see now? What are you really trying to say?" His lawyer's instincts were riled. His fears enabled his brain to think about the possibility that Gar did something wrong, that maybe he should turn this conversation into an attorney-client conversation. He decided to play it safe and added, "Gar, give me ten dollars, and we have a contract. You're my client, making anything you say protected by lawyer-client confidentiality. Okay?" Norbie held him off for a minute while he wrote a simple contract by hand, and Gar signed it. They agreed to meet at his office the next day to draw an agreement of representation. Then Gar started talking, and although he was very distressed during the telling, it was obvious that Gar needed this catharsis and had been longing to share his fears for a long time.

"Norbie, I do blame myself for a lot of what's happened. I married too quickly without thinking through any possible ramifications, but Leana made it so easy. Maybe I never would have had second thoughts if there had been no reason to pick up on things. But the car at the airport thing, I just couldn't let it go. Her computer was locked. At that time, I tried all kinds of possible passwords, but I wasn't successful at access. I traced flights out of Bradley within three hours after she left our home over two years, and Atlanta and Charlotte came up as destinations. I also personally knew the auto parking management company's local manager, and he checked his billing records. Leana charged the car parking to the MLATC Investment Trust with a post office box in New York City."

He shuddered and said, "Norbie, I think I have a big problem, and I just don't know how to deal with it. I've spent the last eighteen months trying to find out just who my wife was, and I'm no closer to the truth. The things I've learned lead me to believe that she may have been murdered and that I will eventually be the lead suspect in her murder. Please believe me, I never hurt Leana. But with what I have found out since her death ... well, nobody will ever believe me."

"Now, at that point I had no idea what the MLATC Investment Trust was. Was it a private employer? Was it a family trust? We never discussed her finances. It was all off the record. She offered to sign a prenuptial agreement with me. I never did, it and she gave me no financial reason to regret that decision."

Norbie said, "Well, what did you do with the information on the car and the trust? I mean, didn't you ever talk about real issues, everyday issues? Things like where were you born, where did you attend college, are there any buddies from the old days, brothers and sisters, other relatives, old boyfriends, friends from your previous marriages—that kind of stuff."

Gar said very slowly, "Norbie, we're all selfish animals, and we men more so. If you think about it in your marriage, and I in my marriages, we men generally won't raise old entanglements for fear the women in our lives might find fault. Women are the ones always questioning what we did before we met them, not us. I was happy not to have entanglements that would interfere in our life together. I was pleased that she had no children. Hell, it was difficult enough for my kids to have me replace their mother in my life. Imagine if she'd had children too, and they got together. They could have really created havoc. At least, that was what I used to think, and I'm ashamed of it. I only considered myself and how to protect my life. I wasn't thinking about Leana then. If I were, I would have been more curious. I would have wanted to know more in order to understand where she was coming from and make adjustments. I didn't want to know, but in the end, my lack of interest has really set me up."

"Gar, exactly what did she tell you about her life? She must have told you something, or you would have seen on the marriage license that she'd been married before. It would tell you her maiden name and place of birth, as well as the location of her previous marriages, the date, and his information. Didn't you follow up at all?"

"No. Originally, I was too immersed in pleasing her, thinking that I was lucky that someone so beautiful, smart, and free was interested in me. Even after I found out about her flying to the South, her previous only marriage was to a guy from Georgia, so that didn't seem so weird, at least at that time. But why not tell me? It would have been reasonable that she wanted to see some family from a previous marriage and that she may be uncomfortable having me there. Madeleine's family didn't exactly welcome my new marriage. I understand that kind of stuff. But why couldn't she trust me?"

"Didn't you question the trust, Gar? What was the trust all about?"

Gar answered, "I didn't know then. I started to notice things. For instance, she had some nice clothes that she bought with my charge cards, but nothing out of line. One night we were at a big political fundraising dinner in Boston, and I overheard two women at the bar night talking about Leana's dress. They said it was a Versace and went for $4,500. One said that she had seen Leana at a fundraiser before, and she had on a scrumptious Chanel afternoon suit. Well, Gar, I didn't pay for that, I can tell you, and I didn't know how Leana could pay that kind of money. When I asked her about her dress, I could tell she was lying. There was a slight change in her eyes that I'd seen before when I questioned her. Her reply was, 'Oh, Gar, it's a knockoff of a Versace. I paid about five hundred for it. Forgive me for not telling you. It is a bit pricey.'"

"But that night, I checked her closet—which by the way, I had built for her, twenty feet by twenty feet with all kinds of built-ins. That dress had a Versace label, and most of her clothes had labels I'd read about in magazines. Only her pants were from Talbots and a few tops were from Chico's, which are local stores. I asked one of the fashionistas in the office about buying knock-offs, and she said that you can buy labels for them separately and sew them in. I accepted that as a possibility, but in truth, I never saw Leana sew anything. I went through my American

Express, Master Card, and Visa accounts and couldn't find a record of a dress purchased for $500. I did find multiple purchases on one slip totaling $489."

Norbie was attentive and said, "I know next to nothing about women's clothes, but I would want to know more about who Leana had been married to and about that trust. Tell me more about that."

"At that point, I asked my daughter about clothing prices for designer clothes. She was no help—had never bought anything that wasn't off the rack—but she had lots to say about Leana, including, 'But, Dad, never does she confront anybody. Something's wrong with her, and I for one can't feel close to her. Maybe it's different for you, but that's how Paul and I feel. Be careful, Dad, I don't feel comfortable with her.'"

Gar continued. "Of course, I ignored it all." He fidgeted for a moment. "Look, Norbie. I have to be at your office tomorrow to sign the engagement agreement. Let's wait on this discussion. You see, I have some papers for you to review, and it's going to be a long conversation. Besides, some people I know are over there, and they'll be interrupting us soon. Okay?"

That was fine with Norbie. He'd already been questioning his choice of setting for a serious talk. The bar was getting busy, and there were more than a few lawyers present—enough to make him antsy about holding a serious conversation with Gar.

# 13

# Brooklyn, New York, 1996

LEANA HAD NOT VISITED New York City since her whirlwind romance with George Haylor. She would have preferred to forget all references to him, and it bothered her a bit to see some places that they had visited or celebrated in together. But there was one thing she valued greatly, and that was a friend she knew who lived in New York when she'd lived there, before she'd met Georgie. His name was Jake Rubin.

Jake had attended SUNY Albany and was a year ahead of her. His only interest in the world was business. They hit it off as friends because they were the only sober students at all the parties at the university. Leana believed that her sobriety was based on Ernestine's rock-solid Protestant training and also her own deliberate departure from the lack of morality of the Courts. Jake's was his background in a close Hasidic family. She smiled, thinking that the two religions could give such common ground. They certainly didn't think they were doing that.

She was here to see Jake. She had contacted him many times professionally for a number of years, but now it was time to talk and put her past and future together in a good financial plan. She had to ensure that Timothy would be taken care of, and she wanted to ensure that Harry's children got a little something, although she knew that they were able to take care of themselves. The rest she could care less about, but there was always a concern that the distant Court cousins knew about her when she received her grandparents' inheritance and could maybe show up in the future if she died, trying to get her money. *That's not going to happen.*

Jake seemed excited that she was coming to Brooklyn. Not surprising to her, he agreed to meet at a Jewish deli near Fulton Street Mall. When she saw him, she was surprised. He used to be a skinny nerdy type, an overbearing business geek. He was now a well-dressed business man of some stature. She mused about how that could have happened. Jake kissed her on both cheeks, feigning the continental habit, but it did not feel artificial to her. She believed that she was an expert on seeing deceptive practices by people. *Hell,* she thought, *I ought to be an expert.*

Jake said, "Leana, you look good, and am I happy to see you. I've had a rough couple of years, and from what you told me when you telephoned, the going's been difficult for you too. Let's have some unhealthy pastrami and coffee, and let's talk." They did so, easily laughing over their past and enjoying kosher pickles, potato latkes, and of course pastrami on rye that was so large Leana left two-thirds of it behind.

"So how are your mother and your dad, Jake? Are they still pulling you in different directions? I mean, it's not every Hasidic boy whose mother is a Quaker."

"You're kidding, aren't you, Leana? How can I be truly Hasidic with a Quaker mother? No, the only Hasidic side of me is in my father and my grandfather's business, which I truly love. We finance anything and everything. As a result, nothing big goes on in Brooklyn or New York City that we aren't a part of. I'm grateful for that. But as to my parent's marriage, well, we could write a book about it.

"I will say that my wife, Rosalind, broke any hold they had on me within a month of our marriage. Rosalind was as good at finance as my dad and me. Maybe that's why they left us alone. Now that

Rosalind's dead, it's been lonely. You know she couldn't have children, and she didn't want to adopt. I would have, but she said no."

They talked some more about Rosalind and about her sudden death in an automobile accident on Gold Street in broad daylight. The driver left the scene. People gave a description of the car, and it turned out to be stolen. "I've been lonely, Leana. Really lonely."

Leana questioned him about her own investment portfolio, which he had held since she'd left San Francisco. She had started investing with a large portion of the fifty thousand dollars the Haylor Family had given her, using the remainder to fund her for her move across the country and other necessities. She had also merged her inheritance, which had been invested with a firm in Lake Placid at a later date.

Leana had contacted Jake when she was leaving San Francisco. He was happy to monitor her funds with a caveat. "Twenty-two grand is too little. I normally don't touch anything under a hundred grand. But for you, Leana, I'll invest and take just 20 percent of any income. Okay? Not to worry—you will never have a negative year with me."

Leana remembered questioning him. "Jake, what if I invest a million with you, and it earns two hundred thousand? Does that mean you'll get a forty-thousand-dollar fee? It seems a bit steep to me."

"Maybe you could look at it that way, but consider this. You'll never have a loss. Our investments never lose. The companies we put money into wouldn't dare lose. Remember, Leana, there's no risk here. Maybe later, when you build up a decent portfolio, we can talk again. Maybe someday you'll want a trust—you know, if you have kids or something. Certainly you'll want a will. I'll set you up with a lawyer."

Leana thought, *That conversation took place a long time ago.*

Now, Leana asked about the total in her portfolio to date. Jake smiled and said, "Impressive, Leana. In fifteen years, you've been able to sock away over twenty million, including interest. It all can't be from a public relations salary. The Memphis and Chicago marriages—well, they paid off for you, didn't they? I heard the mattress king died—conveniently, I hope."

"Don't go there, Jake. My life has been filled with loss. It's as if a dark cloud is above me, always waiting to drop a squall on me. I will not get driven down. I will not be down and out. I've worked my ass off trying to live carefully and in a conservative way, and I've always worked hard. So don't act as if my life is easy. Besides, quite a bit of that money has been earnings, and you got a piece of the action. What do they say in your business? 'Don't ask questions.'"

"Hey, baby, I don't need to know anything. But when you called, you asked about a will and a trust. So I've arranged for us to have dinner with an attorney and a representative of the firm I use for trustee appointments. Look, the one thing that you know is that my family has been in this business for over one hundred years, and we have never had an unhappy client."

Leana's gave her answer too quickly. "Why? Are the unhappy ones dead?"

Jake's face reddened, and in a low voice he replied, "Leana, we go to the wall in collections. You have always known that. That is the reason why we never have a loss. When people die, we pay out every penny they have. Our records are impeccable. You've received, or at least your PO Box has received, our reports for fifteen years. Granted that you've only been a depositor, but I think you know that we are legitimate. So cut with the cutesy accusation."

Knowing she was out of line and surprised at herself, Leana agreed that the remark was not funny, and she apologized. They made plans to have dinner at nine in a private dining room at the Hotel Pierre on East Sixty-first Street. He offered to send a car to her hotel, but she said she would be in the neighborhood. He didn't argue.

Leana carefully dressed for the private dinner in slightly subdued but sophisticated New York attire. She dressed in black, of course, showing her curves with great style; but it was not such a knockout outfit that it would immediately focus attention on her. She was not here to do that; she was here for business, and part of her business was to demonstrate that she was not to be screwed around with. They would figure that out instantly.

Jake was waiting for her in the lobby and gave a soft whistle.

"Well, let's hope my guys can keep their minds on finance tonight. We're meeting with Aaron Goldberg and Alfie Stein. Both are real professionals and are in charge of my dad's and my estates. You're smart doing this now, Leana. Listen carefully about irrevocable trusts, trustees, New York law, et cetera, and think about the ramifications from any choices if you were to marry again. I know you've had a couple of marriages so far. Think it through. No decisions have to be made tonight, but don't waste their time. It'll cost you."

The private dining room at the Pierre was lovely, and service hovered around the single table set for four. Two men were standing with drinks in their hands, waiting for them. The taller one was Attorney Aaron Goldberg, and the other man was a gnome of a man named Alfie Stein. They were, from her perspective, quite successful looking, and she was not put off.

Dinner was a long but nice affair with non-inquisitive small talk—what New York professionals were best at—not like small-city conversations where everyone wanted to know one's history. Here in the city, many people had histories that they did not want to be known, and good manners seemed to allow them their privacy. After dessert was served, a special New York version of Grand Marnier soufflé, the raison d'être was discussed.

Leana was impressed with Aaron and Alfie. They were concise in explaining the law relative to what she reasoned she wanted. However, both questioned why she wanted so much secrecy about her affairs. Aaron asked her why she believed it was important that she would always file a tax return as unmarried and single. Perhaps she would marry again or have children. She said that it wasn't important to them, perhaps, but to her it was very important. "My financial interests are and should be of no importance to anyone but me. I have learned that only I am able to be trusted to take care of myself, and that's the way it will always be. If I marry, he will have to understand that we are each separate economic beings, almost like two friendly corporations working side by side."

Alfie had no problem with the arrangement and said, "A lot of wealthy men would be happy to not have a wife question him about money. The only thing is, some men want control over a wife, and that would mean her money, even if he had a whole lot more. I'm all for women's lib, especially about supporting their efforts to plan their own financial future. I put my wife in a business that she loves, and she has made it very profitable. A happy wife is a happy life, as they say."

Leana questioned him about what business she was in. He laughed and said, "Well, women in a strict Hasidic community must cover their heads when they're out of the home. The modern Hasidic woman often wears a wig, which is after all a head covering. Some of the most beautiful wigs in the world are made by wigmakers in this community, and they are costly. Sarah, my wife, has expanded the business and sells to cancer patients. They are individually fitted and feel natural. Sarah feels good about her product and what it's doing for her clients. She gets to travel every year to Russia to buy hair, and that's a big plus for her. She's independent financially if I should die, which is important to her—despite the fact that I will leave her and the kids more money than she'll ever need."

Leana then explained that her future was unknown at this time, but she knew how much of her wealth she would leave to specific beneficiaries. She believed that a trust would be the way to go but wondered whether a beneficiary could be someone unknown now. For instance, if she were to leave a spouse after her demise, then she would want that spouse to be a beneficiary, if for no other reason than to insure that she wasn't completely leaving out the spouse. She would not want a spouse attempting to contest her decisions. She understood from their previous conversation that appointing a professional trustee was an important step. She looked at Alfie and said, "Jake says to trust you. I will, but you need to know that I don't take kindly to games. I could seriously upset anyone's life if he does not treat me well. As a trustee, you need to understand that I am not your everyday client. It's imperative that you be honest, reliable, and discreet."

Everyone present assured her that she would be treated well. Leana said that she would use the same post office box address as in the past, and she would call in once a month for a conference. If she did not call within three months, they could assume she was dead. In that case, she gave them the address of Carly Calderon, a woman who opened her mail, organized it, and responded if necessary to business problems and sent her weekly reports. That woman would have her e-mail address and a current cell number different from the one on which she would call them. "If I'm dead, someone else will answer it, and you may get the death certificate from a spouse if there is one at that time, or through normal legal process. If I were to have children, then I would make changes to the trust for them. Therefore whether the trust is revocable or irrevocable, you decide what's best based on my needs. I expect, Alfie, that you will do the trust tax return."

They agreed that Leana would meet Aaron at his office on the Avenue of the Americas the following day at noon.

The next day, when she arrived at Goldberg's office, Leana was not impressed with the extravagant legal offices she had just entered. First of all, she knew that she must pay the overhead as part of her fee, and she begrudged paying Aaron so he could look grand. She could hear her mother Ernestine saying in her ear, "If a person is too flashy, then beware. It probably means insecurity, or worse." But Aaron was very good looking and did not appear at all insecure. She had researched his practice. He and the twelve other lawyers in his firm, a small firm called Goldberg and Associates, PC, had offices in New York, Paris, and Israel and served a select clientele. That's all she could discover. She was now part of that select clientele.

Aaron came out to meet her as she walked into the extraordinary and too-large reception area. He kissed her on both cheeks in the continental style, and she liked it. It was New York City, after all, and anything went. They retreated to his office, which was large but sparsely furnished. She decided that he liked lots of space, maybe because he was a good six feet four inches tall. She felt dwarfed by his presence. They spent the better part of three hours together, which included lunch brought in by his secretary and papers to sign brought in by a male paralegal, Kevin, whose legal knowledge was impressive; he immediately responded to every question posed to him. When he left, she asked Aaron about him. His response was that he was a brilliant attorney who was disbarred. He got snookered by a street-smart lawyer who laid all the blame on him for the swindle of an important client. Aaron represented him for gratis because he personally had such dislike for the smart-ass attorney. Kevin did not go to jail but was disbarred for two years. Aaron now had an employee who was not only smart but who was totally loyal.

At two thirty, Aaron said that the rest of the work was his, and he would have papers ready to sign in a few days. He then gave her a deadly attractive smile and an invite. "Have dinner with me, Leana. Make no mistake about it: it's not for business. Business stays here. I'm interested in you. I'll have a car pick you up. There is a new, upscale Italian place with the best food in town I'd like to show you. Please join me."

She did. And she joined him for the next week every night, and sometimes for lunch. She wondered how he got any work done. They went to the Met for opera, and to the Museum of Modern Art. They had lunch after a walk in Central Park. He window-shopped with her. She wondered, *Is this too good? No, I am in control.*

Finally she asked when her papers would be signed. She decided that it was time to move on. One reason she was pushing herself to move on was based on an accidental meeting. She ran into her first husband Georgie's sister, Martha, at Bergdorf's. Martha cautioned Leana, telling her to avoid seeing Martha's mother in the city. Mrs. Haylor had decided over time that Leana was responsible for George's drug addiction and death. Martha said that one of George's friends insisted that George was too knowledgeable about drugs to ever overdose. Martha didn't believe that for a minute but said that her mother would make trouble for Leana.

That evening, Leana told Aaron that she was anxious to move on and settle in a new life. He appeared upset and asked her where she meant to go. Leana said that she believed she would like some area in New England around a large lake; she'd always liked Lake Placid but didn't wish to return there. Aaron discussed the pros and cons of living in the city versus living in a lakeside community. He said, "Why not do both? Why not stay here with me, and we'll find some lakeside community for a vacation home? I'm lonely, Leana, and you are exactly what I want in my life. I'll treat you very well. You can work in any field, just not in my legal and financial area. You come up with what you want out of marriage, and I'm certain I can go along with your wishes."

Leana couldn't share her fears about Mrs. Haylor making problems for her, and she did have fears, but despite those fears she was intrigued at the offer. She and Aaron had not even kissed yet, but she felt a strong attraction to him and realized that a marriage to this powerful, wealthy man could work—and his importance would keep Mrs. Haylor at bay. She believed that Aaron and Mrs. Haylor didn't travel in the same circles.

*Well, Aaron,* she said to herself, *I do like your company, but I definitely have some rules for marriage.* It took four hours of discussion and explaining her vague reasons for her concerns before her preliminary requirements were accepted, and they pounded out the marriage and prenuptial agreement. Aaron had some rules of his own.

Leana's rules centered on her privacy, her desire to have an annual large income from him in addition to any work income she would make on her own, her desire to file a separate tax return, and her insistence that he never ask questions about her background. Aaron required her agreement to never discuss specifics of his business, her acceptance of his requirement that she entertain with him, and finally her agreement to attend all required religious activities that she as a spouse was allowed to attend. He explained that it would require some knowledge of his culture. She had no problems. He insisted that she must be faithful. She said that wouldn't be a problem for her, specifically stating, "I believe in fidelity in marriage."

They married quickly at the home of a justice of the peace in Brooklyn, who was a close friend of Aaron's—and who appeared surprised that Aaron was marrying. There was no celebration, just dinner for the two of them and some great sex.

Leana called her friend Jake the next day and told him about her new marital status. He was not excited and said, "Leana, I understood you might sleep with him, but marry him? Not a good idea. There's a lot you don't know about Aaron. Be careful. If you see a problem—and I know you don't hide from problems—then you must walk away." Although she was upset, all the urging she could muster and direct at him did not make Jake say anything more.

Leana did not meet any of Aaron's family until two months later, when they were invited to Shabbat at his sister Ruth's home in Crown Heights. She realized that their visit was special and that Aaron had not shared the Friday night dinner with his family in almost two years. This made her introduction to his family a double occasion: long lost prodigal son and new sister-in-law. The conversation was stilted at first, although Aaron was hugged as if he were the most precious member of the family. He was loved by them, but he appeared to be uncomfortable at their display of affection.

Leana was carefully examined by his two brothers and their wives, as well as Ruth and her husband. Fortunately, again Ernestine's training in good manners supported her early acceptance by this ultra-Orthodox Jewish family. Leana immensely enjoyed herself. Ruth was a wonderful hostess who gave insight into the meaning of the traditional and religious aspects of the dinner, and she further discussed all the important Jewish holidays and their history. The food was excellent. Ruth was a wonderful cook and housekeeper, and the whole family, including five adult nieces and nephews, were friendly and interesting. Aaron was constantly ribbed about his childhood escapades; the essence of which surprised Leana. Her new, and to her very conservative, husband was apparently always into something as a kid and was known for his risk taking. *Perhaps there is a great deal more I don't know about Aaron*, she thought.

She learned quickly that Aaron did not like the spotlight on him or his work. All entertainment was not held at his lavish, 3,600-square-foot apartment on the Upper East Side; instead, they entertained at venues outside the home, at clubs and restaurants. Even the building where his apartment was situated had a conservative look from the outside. It was only upon entering the lobby that the full beauty of the building was in view. Best of all, nobody who was not expected could get past the doorman; security was in full view.

Leana loved the privacy of it all at first. Later, after she viewed maybe a dozen people hustled out of there, albeit quietly, she began to wonder. But life was good, and there were no surprises in her daily life. She found marketing work with an upscale agency focused on art, which engaged her as its public relations agent, and she enjoyed her life.

There was one disruption in her life, and that was in her meeting of a lover from her first job. She did not like old ghosts, who may know too much about her, rising. The meeting resolved an old insecurity. She felt again that a dark cloud was following her. She talked to Alfie, and the potential problem went away.

A couple of years into the marriage, she received a call from Aaron at work, which was unusual. He started not with a hello but with, "Leana, don't talk with Alfie or his wife. Do not under any circumstances e-mail or write to them. Trust me. They are being monitored, and you don't want your name noted."

"Why are they being monitored? By whom, Aaron? And for what are they being monitored? He's my damn trustee. I need to know if I can't trust him. Tell me, or at the very least remove him as trustee now. Do you understand me, Aaron? Now! I can't have any problems. What have you gotten me into?"

His answer scalded. "You're a big girl, Leana, and no innocent. You knew you were playing high-risk poker here. You don't get big earnings like this without risk. This is the last phone call where we discuss anything related to business. Who knows who is next? I'll be at home at eight tonight. I have to put some controls in place, one of which is a change in trustee for your trust. Remember: do not contact either one of them. I know you're supposed to get a wig from Sarah. Don't pick it up." Then Aaron hung up.

Leana was enraged. She made some excuses and left work. She sat on a bench in Central Park with a pretzel and mustard and a coffee, thinking that she may as well eat like a tourist because she felt like one at this moment. She felt taken. *You fool! You think you're so smart. Good-looking and successful husband! All on your own terms! You should know better by now. Men disappoint women and will say anything to involve you, but you're on your own when there's trouble.* She remembered back to her husbands, her father, and her birth father.

There were only two men in her life whom she trusted, and they'd died of disease at an inopportune time. Aaron was not worried about her—he was worried about himself. She could bet she knew who was monitoring Alfie: it had to be the FBI investigating money laundering. She could not afford a close look at her past life. If Alfie was being watched, then Jake would be next, and then Aaron. Would Alfie talk about her? How could she get out of this mess? Why would Aaron be worried? Then she realized that Aaron would be the linchpin on the FBI's case—and she saw today that Aaron was frightened. Frightened individuals do not behave smartly.

*Time to take Jake's advice!* She would move on, but not before removing a liability. She made a call to Chicago.

Six weeks later, after burying Aaron within twenty-four hours of his death from a serious heart attack that had killed him instantly, Leana scheduled a sale of their condominium, which he had put in both names. She took her smaller share of the trust he'd left, with his siblings getting the rest, and left for a safer location. She was well considered by the family she left behind. Only Alfie and Sarah, who were in a kind of exile, bore her any ill will, and that was only in disappointment at her excluding them from her life. Some of their other friends also felt some rancor at her quick departure, although they wished her well.

# 14

# Gar Lonergan Reveals

Norbie set aside a few hours for his conference with Gar, and he took copious notes. It was unfortunate that he would have to do this manually, but he needed to be able to write down hard facts while keeping unintended confessional statements off the written intake statement. *Some of this stuff is for my ears only,* he thought.

Norbie heard Gar's slow start. It was the same approach as when his kids decided to tell him the truth about one of their escapades: slow, and then the rhythm would come. The faucet of truth eventually splashed loudly. Norbie knew that everything Gar told him was the truth, or at least what Gar perceived as the truth. Norbie knew from past clients that the lens of the teller was not always clear of cultural stigmas.

Very early in the marriage, Gar had started noticing Leana's ability to change the tone, mood, and subject of conversation in a manner that at first seemed charming and later felt controlling. In the beginning of the marriage, he could not see a connection in the conversations that triggered her altering a conversation. Later, he realized that there were many connections. Any question about her history before her previous marriage was one that made her laugh about some joke she had heard recently, or she'd interrupt with a football stat that no one else had ever heard. She refused to go to California, New York City,

New Jersey, Memphis, and New Hampshire with him on business or vacation trips. He considered her refusals strange. Each of those areas had been locations that he was required to visit. She loved business trips, which allowed her time alone with him—or so he believed at first.

A long time later, after he realized that his wife was a walking designer showcase model for West Side, and after investigating her trips south, he started snooping into her paperwork. She had a checking account at a local bank. He watched and saw in the mirror what looked like a password as she was typing into her computer. The word she typed, as he guessed from the position of her hands, looked like "nstuloy," and so he tried it. It wasn't the first time he'd tried to crack her computer, and it didn't work. It took him a day of thinking to realize that he couldn't see the exact keys she was typing. The next day, he put his hands on the key board and tried different keys near to the letters he thought he saw in the mirror. After about twelve tries, the password "Marylou" surfaced. This was the only normal word. He had tried all small letters and then capitalized the first letter, and voila, it worked.

He was disappointed in what he found. Leana only kept three months of bank statements. A twenty-five-thousand-dollar deposit was made to her account from a trust named MLATC on the first of each month. She spent twenty thousand dollars on clothes, shoes, jewelry, and presents. That amount was greatly extravagant for western Massachusetts living and their lifestyle. Her account showed his deposits of eight thousand dollars per month. He had believed that for a wife who had no expenses for the house, her car, presents, or anything, eight thousand dollars per month was pretty generous. Apparently she never needed any money from him. And what was this MLATC trust?

"I asked my broker, who was once on the big board in New York and retired here, about the trust. He has always advised me well. He said that information on private trusts was dicey to discover, but he would try. Later, he found a connection to some private banks in the

Hasidic community about which he was not willing to follow. It was at that point that I was about to ask Leana about the trust when I got a note in the mail, and this is it. I kept it."

The note read, "You are a fool. Your wife is cheating on you with Don Turtolo. She is not nice. Nobody likes her. I feel her evilness."

Norbie read the note and said, "Sounds like a woman who's jealous. Is this all you have?"

Gar then said that he had more notes, but they came later and were not from this person—at least, he didn't think they were. He said, "But this note got me thinking. First of all, not for a minute did I think that Leana would cheat, and if she did, it wouldn't be with Don Turtolo. She despised the man and complained vociferously many times about his approaching her.

"The trouble is that I got reports that they were seen together. It didn't compute, so I started thinking about Don. Now, I have a lot of connections with local banks, and I asked about his, you know, his fiscal health. Don was paying everything on time, but at the last minute, and I was told that additional credit was cut off. In fact, he has two lines of credit that must be paid down next month or else they'll not be renewed. He's a big spender for show. One banker told me that he paid one line of credit about six months before Leana died, and it came from a trust account out of New York City. That info hit a raw nerve with me. Leana would give money to a good cause, especially if it involved helping children, but she was the type who felt that you don't give money to bad causes, and Don would be a bad cause. I therefore concluded that she was being blackmailed by Don."

Norbie asked him what he did about it. Did he ask Leana? Gar said that he wouldn't do that because he'd have to tell her that he knew she had money, and that would mean telling her how he knew that, and how he knew about the NYC trust. Also, although his information said that it was a trust, he couldn't be sure what kind of trust it was.

"Norbie, I decided to find out more about Leana. I hired a local detective agency called Hunt and Find, and I asked them to do computer record searches on Leana. The computer nerd behind the search is Jeffrey Hunt. It took him several months. They found a history of six marriages before me. All her husbands died. She had no children. She has one brother, and she changed her name to Leana from Mary Lou, which explains her password on her computer.

"I've seen enough movies and read lots of books, and I know that this great marriage was just another slot for Leana in her life's plan, which was in my mind about money. I have a lot of resources, and so my first concern was that I was going to die like the others. Now, I know that you think I have an active imagination, but there were questions about one of her husband's deaths.

"Then I concluded that there were a couple of things I could control: my will and trusts for my family. You know that I use that attorney you once referred me to who specializes in wills and trusts for my personal affairs. You do everything else. In fact, you must remember sending me to him. Well, I changed my will. He had a fit that I was excluding Leana completely and worried that she would attack the will if she outlived me. I told him that she couldn't afford the publicity, and that he was to make any attacks on the will after I died a public event."

Norbie responded, "How were you able to keep your relationship going during this period of discovery of Leana's history? Was she on to your change in attitude toward her?"

"I reasoned I was doing well until she asked me if there was something wrong, if she had done something wrong. She wanted to go to the Caribbean to relax and renew our relationship. She said that I was exhibiting great stress, and of course she was right. I put her off and said that we could go after Christmas. She told some people that we would be vacationing after Christmas to help me deal with stress.

"I theorized for a while that Don was being paid to kill me, and so I maneuvered to have lunch with him at the club. Probably I wanted to see if he exhibited any guilt; you know he's not that smart of a guy. He told me my wife was a special woman. I agreed, thinking at the time it depended on how you define special. He did not appear guilty.

Norbie, this is why I'm concerned. I believed that nobody knew about this stuff about Leana.

"So at first when she died, it was a relief. I felt sorry that she died that way; it was horrific. But for me it ended well. Then I got two other letters—very different letters—and they made me run. The information I gleaned from tracing Leana's past convinced me that she may have been a serial murderer. I ran away and tried to forget, but you can't run forever, can you?"

Gar pulled out the two letters he had mentioned. The first stated, "Good work. You got rid of the bitch. Now I don't have to do it." The second said, "I'm watching you. You have not gotten away with this. You'll be hearing from me in the future."

Gar sighed. "You can see why I ran, Norbie. But now I need to face the music. I can't live like this. Please believe me, I did not and could not kill Leana. I want to go to the police. I've talked to my kids, and they agree. They think the stress is making me ill. I've explained that if I do go to the police, there will be publicity, and they will probably implicate me. My only alibi is that I was with my son. So that's what I want to do, Norbie."

Gar explained that he had talked with a woman who knew Leana in Georgia named Myra Kortiac. Myra had visited the police and talked with Beauregard. According to Myra, her conversation with the police was short, at least by Southern standards. She estimated that she was there for over two hours. She told me that Leana had been married to a Fred Fraine from New Hampshire before she'd married a guy named Chisholm in Savannah. "I pulled our marriage application certificate, and it shows only one previous marriage, which is the story she told me. Myra's history on Leana supported the report that Jeffrey Hunt gave me."

Norbie thought, *I'm not in favor of Gar's choice of this path. Going to the police at this time is foolish. Maybe later.* In a concerned voice, he said, "Gar, you've sat on this information for a long time before talking to me. Give me some time to find out a few things. I have a good relationship with the West Side police. Let me talk to them about the accident first. Do you think the writer of these letters sent them to the police as well as to you?"

Gar did not think so. He had not been questioned by the police since Leana's death, and he acknowledged the fact that the spouse was the first suspect; at least, that was what he'd heard from television. He finished his thoughts with some explosive news. "Norbie, I received a very large sum of money from Leana's trust—over fifteen million dollars. It gives me additional motive. I know that I am wealthy, but to the police, fifteen million dollars is big money, and they will see it as a motive to kill, or at the very least, an additional motive to kill. I didn't kill her. I don't want to die in prison for something I didn't do."

Norbie answered, "Hold on here, Gar. Just give me some time to investigate. You have two serious motives for killing your wife, and maybe an alibi that is not the best, but I believe you. Give me time. I'll call you in a few days."

# 15

# Detective Jim Locke

BEAUREGARD KNEW THAT MILLIE was quite proud of her decorating skills, and with good reason. The detective conference room was a blast of balloons, hanging crepe paper, good-luck signs, and a table filled with the likes of Panera sandwiches, ricotta cheesecake from the Italian bakery, chips, chili from Millie, a tray of hors d'oeuvres from Mona Beauregard, mushroom soup from the Crepe House, sweet potato pie from Mason's auntie, and a tray of fruit brought in by Petra. Petra felt that there should be at least one healthy dessert, but she truly believed that the fruit would be there tomorrow after the party as part of a diet recovery plan.

Jim Locke was finally leaving the department, and there was a real sense of loss. However, there was also gain. First, Petra was wearing a two-carat diamond solitaire, and a wedding was scheduled in three weeks. Second, Jim wasn't going far. He was joining Hunt and Find, Private Investigators, as a partner. The unit wasn't losing Jim; instead, it would have a trusted outside vendor for the department. In the past, when they'd wanted to distance themselves from a case but still needed info, it was difficult to know whom to trust, mainly because many of the private investigators in town didn't have the legal and police knowledge to know what not to say or do.

Beauregard was pretty certain that they all agreed Jim was a pro.

Jim was also an awfully good guy, and although the detectives were happy for Jim and Petra's love for each other, they clearly also counted his leaving as a loss for their work. Who would replace his solid interpersonal skills with victims, witnesses, perps, and the public?

Millie had also put up wedding bells over Jim's chair, and the ribbing started. "Finally you've become a man. No ordinary man takes so long for a first marriage. Maybe Jim is a slow learner and just now took a how-to sex course. Naw, he simply couldn't stop interviewing—just didn't have time to jump into bed before. Petra is a born special ed teacher." On and on went the ribbing of their colleague. Jim and Petra, although laughing, wore a permanent shade of scarlet on their cheeks for the rest of the afternoon.

Beauregard judged that this party was interesting. Parties were not allowed in the department; normally it was just a small cake. Yet even the chief and half the department walked in and out of the conference room, grabbing goodies and making low-level remarks at Jim. *Sometimes work needs a bit of happy,* he concluded.

He was really pleased for this couple, and further, he believed that this marriage would work. Jim took the edge off Petra, who had a previous short-term, bad marriage right out of high school and for years wore a circle of distance around her. Jim had found a way inside that distance. As for Jim, Beauregard believed that Petra was the only woman he ever saw Jim show passion for. He knew it would work, and he rarely said these things about a couple. *Love is such a strange passion,* he mused. He was better at seeing the truth behind other passions than any truth behind a love match. Now, his wife was a pro at love. She'd told him a long time before he knew anything that there was something there between Jim and Petra, and that it would work if they ever got around to finding each other. Per usual, Mona was on the mark.

Beauregard now had the job of replacing Jim in the department. *How does one go looking for a balance in a psychology guy who is also police?* He'd already received four possibilities out of ten applications. They were not the same as Jim. He didn't personally like two of them despite their skills. He deduced that their egos would never fit with his people. The other two options included a fifty-year-old woman who had been a social worker before joining the force. She had four grown children, looked like a model for silver vitamin pills, and had a sharp tongue directed to all wise asses. Beauregard kind of liked her. He believed that with her history in the department, no one could push her around. She also could keep secrets. The only drawback was that her husband was a criminal lawyer practicing in Holyoke. Often West Side perps were connected to Holyoke perps. That was especially true in the drug trade. *I'd have to really watch out for leaking if she comes on the unit. She may be closemouthed, but pillow talk is always a potential danger.*

The other possible pick was a tall, kind of goofy, thirty-five-year-old guy who played violin in a quintet or a jazz quintet. He was equally at home as part of classical concerts at Smith or Mount Holyoke as he was at any jazz workshop or bar. The resulting bonus of this sideline included his knowledge of many kinds of people and an ability to relate to all kinds of folks easily despite his almost gawkish appearance. He also knew all the drug deals happening in the area and had been in the town's drug task force partnership with the district attorney's office. He could keep his mouth shut. What to do? Well to start with, tomorrow he would interview the two of them, and maybe one of them could be ruled out. He would also have a talk with his other detectives to see how they viewed them both.

The party did not stop at the conference room. Like all good parties, it continued, and this time at Jim's request. They had dinner at the West Side Country Club. He was a member and would now use his membership for business. They met his new partner, Jeffrey Hunt, and a rollicking time was had. The club was a lot noisier than usual. Police parties were generally noted for an abundance of raucous comments and general glad-handing, but they were not usually in a country club setting. Petra and Jim's wedding reception was scheduled there, and Petra took this opportunity to do some extra scoping. Perhaps she could learn more about the viability of her wedding plans. The staff made some suggestions that the event planner had never mentioned. Petra believed it was always good to talk to the doers and not just the planners. They knew what could go wrong.

Beauregard saw Norbie at the club, and they talked. Beauregard felt a bond with Norbie, which was not normal between a defense attorney and a police captain. The bond was based on an earned history of trust between the two resulting from experience during the famous, or infamous, child serial murderer case, where a child was the murderer. However, the child murderer was difficult to charge because her mother claimed to be the killer. Beauregard trusted Norbie for his good instincts, his discretion, his ballsy moving forward because it was the right thing to do, and his lack of ego. Norbie never took the prestige of the arrest; he had a tight lip. His clients—all of them—trusted him. Beauregard trusted him too.

There was one thing that bothered Beauregard about Norbie: his skills were honed to get information through conversation. One never knew whether Norbie was trying to con one into talking, or whether it was just small talk. Sometimes Beauregard's sixth sense said that Norbie was on an informational gathering path, but not always. Tonight he was confused. Was it pure gossip, or was there a reason behind his interest in Gar Lonergan's wife's death?

Norbie seemed interested in whether or not the gossip he'd heard about there being someone in a truck at the accident scene was bogus.

Clearly, Norbie had heard about the neighbor's interview, and so Beauregard said, "There was some conversation around that question, but nothing came out of our investigation."

Norbie then asked if Beauregard knew Leana, which was questionable in and of itself. After all, Beauregard was a cop who didn't travel in Leana's or Gar's circles other than as an occasional golf partner. He answered in exactly that way. Norbie stated the obvious: that Leana was one good-looking and smart lady, and it was a shame that she had to die that way. Beauregard was now suspicious. Norbie never said the superfluous or the unnecessary. Therefore he must have an interest in the death. What that interest was, Beauregard didn't know.

Beauregard made the decision to play with Norbie, which was always dangerous. He was not in Norbie's league when it came to word games, but he was now curious and decided to hang out a worm and see if Norbie would bite.

"You know, Norbie, a funny thing happened around Leana's death. The department got some funny notes about the death inferring that maybe it wasn't all that it seemed. We couldn't find anything to go after, but those notes are still there. I think that Leana may not have been all that she appeared to be, but other than that, I have no information."

Norbie was interested and questioned the wording on the notes. The fish had bitten. Beauregard said, "I really can't remember the exact wording, and I probably shouldn't say unless you have a client whose interests require disclosure."

As expected, this closed the conversation, but it tickled Beauregard's interest in the case. *Is Norbie representing Gar? If so, why did Gar think he needed representation?*

Beauregard went to the bar to say goodbye to Petra and Jim. Jim was talking to Jeffrey Hunt, and Beauregard heard Jim say, "Wasn't that an accident? Why would Gar want to know about his wife's history?"

Beauregard backed away and found Petra at the other end of the bar, discussing her wedding plans. He was forced to listen to the specifics of her wedding plans, which were of no interest to him at all but would be valuable if he could remember to tell his wife, Mona. The conversation would go a long way to assuage her feelings that he was only involved in crime solving and not in everyday living.

# 16

# Hunt and Find, Private Investigators

Jim Locke's first day at his firm started out just fine. The location of his new work was in a building near central Springfield and had great parking. Although much of the work was computer based, there were also the security and physical investigation sections that made ample parking an absolute necessity. Jim spent the morning with Jeffrey going over open investigations and reviewing security clients. They broke for a nice lunch at Mom & Rico's, eating from the buffet of Italian homemade specialties. Jim opted for macaroni pie and roasted peppers and onions; Jeffrey, with his long and skinny frame, ate from an assortment of pastas.

Continuing their review of clients, Gar Lonergan's file was presented and discussed. Jim groaned when he saw its contents. Gar had used the firm in the past for investigations of vendors' financials and other records checks. However, this time he was investigating his wife, Leana. Bells rang for Jim. *What are the ethical requirements for me now? Clearly from the file, the firm knows almost as much about Leana as the police. What is new to me is that Gar Lonergan knew most of this before Leana died—a fact that Beauregard and the detectives do not know. The knowledge speaks to motive. What responsibility to relay this potential motive to the department do I have?*

*I could speak with the district attorney and have him subpoena*

*Hunt and Find's records for a grand jury. I won't do that without informing Jeffrey first, and if I do go forward that way, it is pouring gasoline on a tiny fire that may be just a flame. On the other hand, I feel that ex-cop tug-of-war going on in my psyche, between keeping quiet for personal reasons and the strong draw toward law and order. Haven't I preached many times to witnesses about citizen responsibility to uphold the justice system with their input? Now I'm a citizen. Just what is my responsibility? Further, Gar Lonergan is invited to my wedding. I believed when I left the department that all these ethical teasers would disappear.*

Jim left work alone at two thirty with the excuses of required banking and getting coffee. He needed to think. Over a perfectly constructed and overpriced cappuccino, Jim decided to solve this problem in the old-fashioned police way. On his wedding day, he would drop a hint to Beauregard, not Mason. Mason would never take a hint; he would dog someone for the whole story and not leave it alone. But Beauregard would follow a clue on his own, with that well-developed nose for detecting. Now that he knew what he would do, Jim had another problem, and this one was even bigger.

Petra would be after him to tell her about his new work, his first day there, and how he would be conducting cases. He could anticipate her questions on interviewing techniques, types of computer systems, and types of cases. He did not want to shut Petra out; it had taken a lot of work to overcome her reticence about entanglements and get her to engage in love. She came first, and therefore he would be very careful to say nothing about this case. He didn't have to worry about Jeffrey saying anything. Jeffrey never talked about business to outsiders. In fact, as a computer nerd, he was more comfortable talking to machines than people.

That night at dinner, Petra relieved some of the stress he was feeling when she said, "Jim, I've been thinking about our separate careers. I hadn't really before, until today. We probably won't be able to talk about our cases in detail every day, which is what we have been doing. I have a duty to keep information in house unless it's already public. And I guess that you can't talk about your clients. They probably often come to you because they have some quasi-legal problem that may border on police interests, at least in some cases. I hate to say that, because you know I have a police nose and want to discover everything. But Jim, you and I are most important. I don't want us to get into some ethical bind. You do understand, don't you?"

He said he did, and he meant it. He was grateful because lying to Petra was not something he wanted—and it was not something he believed he was good at.

The rest of the evening was spent writing table place cards for the impending wedding, and it was a job that he never wished to do again. He stated often that big weddings should not be allowed. Petra's wacky Aunt Jean was seated with a group of his dull relatives. Petra groaned, knowing that Auntie would be the life of the table with her stories about her life in the Federal Foreign Service as a secretary. At age eighty-nine, much was forgiven her. His relatives were relatively sedate next to Petra's. Their friends were all ages and careers, although the police would be heavily represented.

Jim knew that Petra's mother did not want this beautiful wedding to turn into a drunken police ball. Her friend had once been to a police wedding, and it was too wild and unrefined, she'd explained. Petra knew the wedding referenced and pointed out to her mom that in that case, the couple was in their early twenties. Maybe that was the cause of the excitement, not the fact that the groom was on the force. Petra's father told her not to worry because most of the chaos at a wedding was like childbirth and was mostly forgotten a week later. How could he know that, considering he'd never experienced childbirth?

The next morning, Jim pulled the Lonergan file and brought it to his office. He compared it to the computer file and saw that, like in police work, there were notes in the margins that were not transferred to the computer file. Some of those notes held extra details showing Gar's understanding of his wife's actions at the time of each interview. There were also half a dozen interviews, some in person and some over the phone. That alone showed Gar's interest in and stress over the subject matter, which could speak to motive.

In the first interview, Gar was in a state of disbelief, which was abated over time when he realized he'd been played. To his credit, he never said anything about violence to Jeffrey and appeared to think that there must have been some early childhood abuse in Leana's history. Gar simply could not imagine living Leana's life and keeping quiet about it. The last interview was particularly problematic. In it, Gar said that he should have listened to his children, but he did not. Now it was time to solve this situation. He said he would see his lawyer about a will and trust, and whether an annulment or divorce would be better. That was in late September, shortly before her death.

Jim considered Leana's history again—about what kind of experience created this masterpiece of deceit or maybe a psychotic murderer. Reading the file reminded him that Leana crossed the country from New York State to California to Tennessee to New York City to Chicago to New Hampshire to Georgia to Massachusetts. She was like a salamander, easily adaptable to her environment. She fooled astute men, not novices.

How come the state registries didn't pick up her multiple marriages? He'd have to check into that. Probably there wasn't interstate computer tracking then. There should be now. Gar and Leana had married only a few years before. Maybe one had to ask questions and develop an interest for the state in order to have the state investigate the truthfulness in a marriage application. Jim knew that in Massachusetts, he and Petra had filed a marriage application in West Springfield, and it took three days to get the license. What did the registry do in those three days? Maybe just check in-state, or maybe the registry just served as legal verification for taxation? He'd better find out. He wouldn't ask Jeffrey now, even though he may know. He didn't want Jeffrey honing in on this case and his reservations. It was too early in his business relationship to create a problem.

# 17

# The Wedding

IT WAS A BEAUTIFUL, cold, but sunny day at Saint Agatha's Catholic Church in West Side. The bride was dressed in white. Her great aunt had reservations about a previously married bride wearing white for a second marriage. Petra's mother and dad said the opposite: that the first marriage was a like a gimme in golf, not one to be counted. Jim agreed with them. Petra wondered why it had taken her so long to close the door on her early marital mistake.

Petra felt like a first-time bride. She felt beautiful in her dress designed by Pollardi. Her matron of honor, Camille, lived in Lexington, and when she'd heard that Petra was finally committing to a life of wedded bliss, she was so excited that she dragged her to a great bridal shop in Lexington. Petra, Camille, and her mom had enjoyed two hours playing Cinderella going to the ball. It gave Petra back the sense of being special, being with her mom choosing for the big day, and giggling over the possibility that there may someday be grandchildren. She cried a little over this birth of reassurance about the future. She was sure that Jim would help make everything work, at least as well as any planning can assure what is to come. She loved him and trusted him.

Petra's dad cried when, at the altar, he handed his daughter over to Jim. He later explained that he cried with relief. He had believed that she would never marry again, and he was certain that Jim Locke was going to be the best son-in-law—better than what he and his wife would have chosen. One of the West Side officers sang the "Our Father" with such beauty and fervor that the crowd almost forgot he was nicknamed Traffic Ticket Tommy. Father Brewer, known for his brevity, engaged in a three-and-a-half-minute homily about marriage and his personal feeling that this couple belonged together. The couple walked out to the hymn "How Great Thou Art." Jim had chosen the hymn. Probably it was because they both liked Elvis Presley's award-winning version of the hymn, or because they both believe that there was divine direction in their getting together in the first place.

Then the guests drove the two miles to the country club. The photographer, Hamilton, a young man and an immigrant from Poland, offered his services to the couple. He could airbrush away just about any problem in a photo. His fees would normally not have fit in Petra's budget but were offered today for gratis—his wedding gift. He'd known Petra's first husband, known he was a bad dude, and helped coax Petra out of the marriage. He was thrilled with Petra's decision to put that marriage behind her.

Petra insisted on candid shots only. She wanted no posed shots, leaving Hamilton the tough job of getting the couple together and looking cool before there was too much going on. Once the bar was in action, he was sure that someone would spill a drink on the bride when trying to wish her well, or her hair would get mussed. Hamilton was a pro, and he quickly got an action three-quarters shot, with the beautiful landscaping of the club as a backdrop, of the couple giving each other a loving smile. The result was a timeless photo of a beautiful woman and her handsome husband. He hoped that the rest of the day would be a piece of cake.

Rocky Belisle and his band played a combination of standard wedding, jazz, and traditional rock and roll. Jim and Petra were adamant in choosing the music. Rocky also added selections from the traditional love and wedding genre. They danced their first dance to a sung version of "When a Man Loves a Woman." The guests appeared to appreciate that this was one happy wedding and so let down their hair.

Norbie sat at table number six with Gar, Beauregard, Mason, and Millie and their spouses. There was easy talking in this group, with the spouses being responsible for setting the stage away from police work and the law. Millie's husband was with the fire department, and he jostled the cops over the fact that the fire department was now the first responder to many emergency call events. A debate ensued over the relative merits of police over fire as first responders. Naturally, fire was outflanked at this wedding.

Gar whispered to Norbie, "Big difference between this wedding and mine to Leana. I think I'd forgotten what real relationships look like. In real relationships, I suspect that they giggle together, have silly fun together, and are not worried about being sophisticated or saying the right thing. Leana and I, to outsiders, looked like one of the hoi poloi getting married. We were dressed perfectly, photographed magnificently. I hoped that this, my second marriage, would be as good as my marriage to Madeleine. I considered myself lucky at my age to get such an accomplished woman, like a Spartan conquering an Athenian woman in battle. I forgot about the interpersonal daily fun of learning about each other. I was in such a hurry then! I didn't think enough of myself and my family to work things through. And to be honest with you, I now wonder every day whether Leana would have put me down like a dog if she knew that I was changing my will and trust and was thinking of filing for divorce before she died."

Norbie abruptly turned to Gar and said, "Please, no discussion here. But is there anyone you talked to about making those changes in addition to your attorney?"

"Yeah, didn't I tell you about Hunt and Find, the detective agency? When I got the last report, Jeffrey told me I had better smell the roses. We had a discussion, and he pushed me to meet with my probate lawyer, which is what I was going to do anyway."

Norbie responded with a nod but was not happy. *Another leak in the information boat.*

To further complicate matters, his wife whispered to him, "Did you know that Jim has left the force? He's now working as a PI with Jeffrey Hunt. Mona just told me. You'd think that Petra's mother would have told me; I play golf with her on a daily basis. I've heard every detail about the wedding but not much about the groom. He's certainly a nice man—you'd think that she'd have said more about him before today. Norbie, are you listening to me?"

He was, but he was not a happy camper. Knowing that his wife needed more confirmation from him, especially as she continued to point Jeffrey Hunt out over at table seven, he said in a kind and husbandly way, "Honey, you know just about everything happening in this town. What would I do without you?" And to be certain that his wife moved away from this subject, Norbie did the unthinkable and asked his wife whether her friend's dress was a designer dress.

With a disgusted note, she said, "Norbie, haven't I taught you anything in our marriage? That dress is definitely off the rack, and not even a high-level rack." Then she turned her attention to Mona, whose conversation would be much more satisfying to her than her husband's.

Norbie got up to go to the bar, and Gar followed him. Gar quickly caught up and said, "I heard that. A cop is going in business with the investigator to whom I spilled my guts. We'd better get in and talk to Beauregard before Jim does."

Norbie asked how Gar came to be invited to the wedding, and the story was similar to his own story, except that in Gar's case, Jim's mother was a good friend of Madeleine's and had been wonderful to him after Madeleine had died, although Leana had cooled the relationship. He never saw much of the groom's parents after his marriage, except at the club. The invitation to this wedding was probably partly an apology for staying away.

Norbie told Gar to simply enjoy the wedding; there may be no ramifications. Jeffrey was not much of a talker, and maybe the file would not be open for Jim. Jim would be going on a honeymoon, and besides, it was a closed file. Gar appeared to be consoled but said, "We can't wait too long. I've got a bad feeling about this, Norbie."

Norbie was certain that he also had a bad feeling about this. *Once a cop, always a cop.* Nosiness was a trained trait and became engrained, and the one thing he had heard about Jim Locke was that he was interested in everything about everyone. He was notorious for his long interviews with witnesses, let alone perps. He remembered Jim on the stand against one of his more infamous clients. Jim's attention to detail had almost tripped up his case. No, Jim would eventually read Gar's file, and he would do something then. Just what he would do, Norbie didn't know.

Beauregard was suddenly behind Norbie and said, "Your wife and Mona are plotting to get us out on a foursome. Help me, please. Mona does everything well except play golf. Get me out of this, and I owe you one." Norbie immediately agreed. He didn't think that owing one to Beauregard had anything to do with work, but good vibes were also worth something. They discussed a current case when Beauregard said, "What kind of a guy do you think Gar Lonergan is? Why do you think he disappeared after his wife's death? Seemed a little strange to me at the time. Maybe a different way to handle sorrow, huh?"

Norbie looked at Beauregard with his best blank eyes, but he felt the bony finger of inquisitiveness pointing at him. He knew that Beauregard was testing him, trying to figure out whether he was representing Gar. He decided to play it safe and tell a partial truth. The world and its citizens know that a partial truth and a partial omission are often far more effective that an outright lie.

"Beauregard, I have known Gar for many years. I've represented him in a couple of business cases where a large corporation in his industry was famous for threatening criminal action in order to get a quick settlement on a civil case—frowned upon under the law, but happens often. Civil lawyers get antsy when they are threatened with a criminal case. I know both sides of the law and had handled a case for an employee of Gar's who had some trouble. Gar's a really good man, a really stand-up guy, if you know what I mean."

Beauregard nodded his head and said, "Seems that way to me. I never did understand why he would choose the second wife he chose, given that we knew Madeleine. They were as different as two women could be, don't you think?"

Norbie gave an answer that he later worried he may regret. "Beauregard, you and I know that you can't always trust what looks good. Gar is no different from you or me in that way. But there are not more than twenty people here that I would stake my life on their honesty. Gar's one of those twenty."

The bridegroom intercepted Beauregard at the bar just after Norbie left him to return to Mona. Beauregard shook his hand and gave him a guy hug, telling him what a lucky son-of-a-gun he was in capturing Petra. Jim said in a low tone, "Look, I've received some information, and I think you have to look at Leana Lonergan's history and her finances. I can't say any more, but I'm telling you it could be worth your while." Beauregard instinctively knew that Jim had a lot more to tell him but couldn't. He would miss Jim's ability to ferret information, and he thanked him as Jim was pulled away by his new mother-in-law.

The bride threw her bouquet. The groom, to the hoots and hollers of a herd of police, took the garter off Petra's shapely leg and threw it to the beer-soaked squadron; the winner was Traffic Ticket Tommy, who to this date had carefully avoided marching to the altar.

The party went on until early morning, long after the bridal couple left in their car overly decorated with "Questionable" signs. It was an affair to be remembered for many reasons.

# 18

# Silverstein Detectives

The office was a twenty-foot by twenty-four-foot rectangular front for a busy digital warehouse positioned in a separate large lot adjacent to a small suburban mall. The receptionist had a nametag on her ample but seductive breast that said, "Lettie, Receptionist." Lettie was engaging. Mason figured that Lettie was well paid because her presence made one forget one's problems, and because her charming manners were a cover for her real role as warden of the premises. He reasoned that her nametag should say, "Lettie: You can't get beyond me, don't try." He, with what his friends called his overblown self-esteem, was going to try anyway.

Before entering Silverstein's offices, Mason had done some reconnoitering. There was a 2017 white Land Rover on the left of the building blocked by two trucks; the plate said SILV100. He decided that Mr. Silverstein perhaps was not shy or afraid of confrontation; he was certainly not trying to be invisible. Mason also noticed that the parking lot for the agency had over twenty-five cars parked, with only a couple of vehicles having magnetic agency signs attached. He suspected that this was a busy enterprise, probably a lot bigger than the PI agencies located in his home area of western Massachusetts.

Mason gave his best smile and said, "Lettie, I'm here to see the boss, and I hope you will tell him because I know he's on the premises.

Tell him, please, that I'm from western Massachusetts and need his help, if he is able to help. Also tell him I'm a cop, if you haven't guessed that already. I'm willing to wait for his availability. Tell him I'm not here to compromise his work or his clients."

Lettie took two seconds to eye him and said, "Your name, Mr. No Compromise?"

Mason took out his badge and showed her, remarking, "No kidding, Lettie. I am Mr. Smith, or Detective Smith in this case." He received her winning smile and a slight jab.

"Where's Angelina, Brad?"

Enjoying the fun, Mason responded, "In case you haven't noticed, Lettie, I'm a little darker in skin color than those folks."

Lettie apparently enjoyed the repartee because she told him it would be a few minutes; Sid was with a client.

While Mason waited twenty minutes, he saw a lot of work action. This was a going concern for sure. At least half the people coming from the back warehouse scanned him as they walked out the door—cops for sure, he intuited. Sid had quite a few cops, ex-cops, and cop retirees working.

Sid Silverstein, a man who was all of five feet six inches tall and solid, with some extra girth, walked out of the back office and greeted him. *A Napoleon for sure,* was Mason's first conclusion—but a Napoleon with a brilliant smile.

"How do you do, Detective Smith? You've passed the first test: you've entertained Lettie, which is not an easy thing to do. Come along to my office, and we'll discuss how I can help you without any compromise on my part. I'm not sure of my geography, so please tell me where in hell in western Massachusetts is West Side?"

Mason gave a verbal tour guide of the area and its statistics.

Sid smiled and said, "I remember. You had that kid who murdered all her friends. How'd you solve that when the feds were a bust? Nice job. You were on that case?"

Mason knew that he had Sid now. He'd give him the scoop on the six serial murders and how the feds and staties didn't solve them with their expertise and how the West Side detectives did. Sid would pay him back with info on Leana. *Nice exchange*, he rationalized. *Just the way the world ought to work—tit for tat.* The conversation began.

Mason told Sid that his department was investigating a two-year-old suspicious accident death based on new information. The woman who died was Leana Lonergan, whom Sid may know under other names. He explained how many times Leana had married, gave Sid a few of the married names and her previous locations, and asked if he had information he could share.

Sid said, "Maybe I have some information, but I can't put my client in any jeopardy, so I won't name the client. By the way, in our investigations of Leana Goldberg, we ran across two other trails of investigators, and they were not pros investigating. Why don't you ask me questions about her, and I'll try to answer them? Might bring us to the same place. It will certainly show me that you have info already and therefore reduce for me any compromise I might have to make."

Mason determined that Sid could not really use any information he would give against the department unless his client was involved in Leana's death. Still, he would have to be careful. Cops always knew that any of their ill-advised words could hurt them in court at a later date.

Mason asked about Leana and Aaron, whether the marriage was good from friends' standpoint, whether Aaron was a stand-up guy, how Aaron died, and whether anyone questioned where Leana went when she'd left the city. Sid had not anted up right away.

Sid started a discussion with, "Detective Mason, have you ever met anyone from the Hasidic community in West Side? I mean, do you know anything about ultra-conservative Jews and their way of life?" Mason had to admit that he did not. He believed that there was a small Hasidic community he had heard about in the Springfield and Longmeadow areas, but he had no experience with them as individuals or as a group.

Sid told Mason that he wasn't sure he could explain, even in general, what it meant to be brought up as an ultra-conservative Jew in America, as well as the implications when a person withdrew from that community but did business on its fringes or deeply within that community. In other words, a person lived a quasi-Hasidic life whose social, religious, moral, and business interactions were only partially maintained. He explained that Leana was Aaron's third marriage, and not one of his wives was Jewish. Aaron loved business, finance, and making money by taking shortcuts; that was his religion.

Mason wasn't sure how to interpret the ramifications of Aaron's behavior. What could it have meant? Mason had grown up in a tight-knit African American, female-dominated family that was churched fifteen hours a week to keep him from gangs and drugs and steer him on the right path. He understood how powerful the family tug could be. Mason knew that he'd pulled away from some of his culture's emotional attitudes, but he tried his best to be a good son, brother, husband, and father.

Mason knew that he could never do business with his family, however—that would have killed him. He liked the structure of the department and his computer work. If he worked with the men in his family, one thing was for certain: he'd be in lifelong psychotherapy.

"Sid, how does someone do business, and in this case as a lawyer, and represent this group of religious folks if he knows he no longer believes what they believe?"

"Well, Mason, there's the rub. Aaron was a top-notch international private corporate attorney with financial connections everywhere, but his main source of clients and funds were from the community from which he was trying to distance himself. What's more amazing is that the community trusted him in business. They wouldn't trust their daughters with him, but in business he was golden."

Mason pushed further and asked what this had to do with Aaron's death. He was surprised by the flat but direct answer.

Sid said, "Unequivocally, the Jewish community had nothing to do with his death."

Mason had one of the answers he was searching for: Aaron's death was suspicious, and Sid believed Mason knew that. The fact that Sid didn't even try to feign, "Was there a problem with his death?" was the hint.

He remembered that Aaron was a wealthy and healthy athletic type who'd died suddenly of a heart attack. How to question Sid to get his reasons for being suspicious about Aaron's early demise was his concern.

Mason questioned Sid on who was there when Aaron had died. Had he been brought to the hospital, and had there been an autopsy? Or instead, did the community intercede for a timely ritual burial—and if so, why was it allowed?

Sid smiled but did not respond directly to the question. Instead, he said that he was surprised that Mason would ask that question. He wondered how much Mason understood how any segment of the population could isolate itself enough from the general population to enable it to maneuver or avoid some legal requirements.

Mason answered just as cryptically. "I think if there are enough really good friends in high places, then social cultural norms practiced by an entrenched or vocal minority, such as religious or politically active group, especially in these times, may be more powerful than legal requirements, as you put it."

The two men laughed at each other and themselves, but the foundation was laid for a more open conversation. After a conversation that went back and forth for about twenty minutes, Sid told a story in a hypothetical example.

The story imagined an investigation into high finance by the FBI. The implications were very serious, and even some small publicity could topple a multibillion-dollar, maybe even trillion-dollar, industry that was spread over four continents. The industry was carefully controlled with the right people in high places and serious containment of process, so few knew all the connections and nobody talked out of turn. Sid said, "Remember, this culture is a carefully structured and controlled culture that has worked for two thousand years for the good of the goals of the community, not for individual and personal goals."

One piece of information was stated firmly by Sid. "This is not organized like the Italian mafia. First of all, the mafia was careless; Italians generally have a difficult time separating family from business. They talk in their homes about business. The Jews typically do not. Business is business; family is family."

Sid explained that there was no small talk. However, one weakness in the system was that the wives were now highly educated. Take for example a wife who independently owned her own business, was ultra-conservative, but was required to travel outside the country without her spouse on business. She may learn more than what was healthy for her or the group. She may become more American and have loose lips. And what if a wife was brought into the financing part of the business that may be 99 percent legitimate, and she was smarter than all the men? She could be a threat. If that threat should disappear, maybe by accident, then it may attract attention from the government, resulting in its attempt to know more about the workings of this industry. So there could not be any hint that the community would be involved.

"Now, imagine how financial investment could over time perform at a high but level rate despite recessions and booms," Sid said. "This group of financial investments—and I say group because I don't think anyone knows its size—did perform at a steady, over 25 percent annual return for thirty to forty years. That simply cannot happen. You and I know that over time, companies, people, or nonprofits can't pay what they've borrowed, and they often go bankrupt. In this case, everyone pays back their loans. There are incentives in place for proper loan repayment. One incentive is that someone takes over the assets or the business to relieve the debtor. Now, you and I know that the relief may be more like a robbery, but it's better than the alternative. Another incentive is the time-honored practice of 'unhealthy enforcement,' which I won't explain but which I know you will understand."

Sid continued. "This group had a most active division for unhealthy enforcement, and in this case it would have been used, except it wasn't required. Somebody else did the job for them. Naturally, enforcement was pleased to help clean up. Using their connections, a well-regarded and religious doctor was contacted and seemed willing and able to discuss the technical aspects of a sudden coronary for this important man who died under his care with a long but recently made-up medical history. No need for an autopsy. The doctor was supposedly there at the death. A quick burial was required by the culture, and a sad, sad formal service with great moaning was held. Moaning was particularly great by the FBI. The important man being buried was the linchpin for their case. He was a renegade from the community who may have been extraordinarily talented, but he knew too much and liked his comforts. He would not stand up under stressful FBI interviews despite the fact that he was a tough adversary in contracts and civil court."

Mason was dumbfounded and said so. "You mean the FBI couldn't figure out what happened—like, raise the body, do blood testing and analysis, interrogate those close to the attorney? This is nuts. In West Side, they'd be all over us. This community is supposed to be isolated or closed. It doesn't sound that way to me. It sounds to me as if they have tentacles of influence everywhere! That would mean the enforcement side is absolutely not legal."

Sid smiled and laughingly said, "Of course this is only a hypothetical case, Mason. But don't kid yourself: this happens everywhere."

Mason regretted his emotional response. He was certain that Sid would think he was a novice, and he wasn't. He asked, "Who else would be interested in the demise of this upstanding lawyer? Perhaps it wasn't a sanctioned hit, but could any of the other players who were at risk take it upon themselves to act? I mean, if there is an enforcement arm, then in my experience, those guys are not easy to control. Or perhaps there was also a personal motive, and maybe his spouse or a shamed family member did the dirty deed."

Sid said that maybe in this hypothetical case, the spouse had some enemies, and an investigation could blow her life apart. The question remained how she would have done it. How did she know enough to contact the right people in a timely manner? Probably the whole truth would never be known. "This wife could keep her mouth shut, in this hypothetical case. Also, she blew town really fast. Her nearest and dearest, including some old enemies, never even knew she left. It was that fast—in this hypothetical case."

Mason suggested that the wife must have known where to go next and must have planned a setup for herself. Would she have pulled some money out of this quick exit? With great seriousness, Sid inferred that the wife was an investor and understood the game. She came away with some good money, but she had more already invested in her own name. She simply took her fair share. In fact, the professionals talking said that she was someone who just wanted her fair share, no more. They respected her—and probably respected her more if she did arrange her husband's death.

Mason said, "Sid, enough about this hypothetical. Would it be infringing if we talked about anything you know about any investigation into Leana Goldberg before and after her New York City life? For instance, did you go to Chicago or Wolfeboro, New Hampshire or Memphis, Savannah or San Francisco to investigate? If you did get some info, it wouldn't affect the affairs of your client or clients, would it? I mean, maybe you can help."

Sid was serious when he responded. "Well, I didn't bother with Memphis because the husband died of natural causes, and the police were not even investigating his death. However, maybe she and the husband were involved with the husband's ex-wife and her new husband's deaths. The police were investigating that death but came up with shit.

"The Hayley death was promising, and I was directed to that one. Her former sister-in-law, Martha Haylor Jenkins, pushed me to investigate that death. She gave me a retainer, and I did some work on it. Flew out to San Francisco and met with some of his druggie friends—at least those who were not dead. That was a sad time for druggies then. The stuff was everywhere. His business friends theorized he was all right; a bit overprivileged was the only negative comment. That, and his many absences from work. One of his ex-girlfriends was vehement in saying that Georgie could never overdose; he was too knowledgeable about drugs to do so. Funny thing—her name was Leana too. This gal said that Georgie would never commit suicide and that he was too much in love with himself; he was the kind of guy who could always think up a new angle. She didn't like his wife and believed that the wife was sick of Georgie. Knowing what we know about her husbands' demises, maybe she was right. I know that my client, Martha, said that she always understood that Georgie wasn't fair to Leana, but her mother who I believe was paying my fee and is about ninety-five years old now, could never let it go. Leana ran into Martha when she first came to New York, and unfortunately Martha said when she told her mother that Leana was in the city, Mama definitely appeared unhappy.

"Martha's mother never said anything while her father was alive, but now she wanted to prove what she knew was the truth: that Leana killed Georgie. Martha later learned that there was a payout from her father of about fifty grand to Leana to never talk about Georgie's death again, and she didn't think Leana ever did. Martha discerned that her father was not unhappy to see Georgie go—not that he wasn't upset, no! But he told her that Georgie was a manipulator who would never be normal, and that God maybe did the right thing in taking him so that his mother would not see his total disintegration to nothingness. They're wealthy people, and in my experience the rich are sometimes really strange and cold."

Mason prodded Sid with questions about smoking guns in any of Leana's husbands' deaths.

Sid said, "If someone wants to go to the trouble, all the cases together could support investigating Leana. But now that she's dead, what agency would care? A dead serial killer is no danger to the community. I suppose you could make a case that Leana probably had some help with the killings, if she did them—and personally I think she did. I think that if a party had the interest and the funds for a long-term investigation, something could be proven. But think, Mason. You'd never prove it in the Haylor case, and the Memphis husband

and Leana are both dead, so you might have serious problems finding evidence that they killed the husband's ex-wife and boyfriend. I don't think either one of them knew enough about cars to pull off that one. I think that Leana had help. I think she had one or two doers who were willing to assist her in murder. Who they might be is probably not easily discoverable. Maybe she had enough drug knowledge to stop Aaron's heart, but I don't think she was the driver in Chicago, or that she bumped the pontoon boat in Savannah. Maybe she staged the Wolfeboro's husband's death herself. She was smart. Now, who killed her, Mason? And don't tell me you don't think someone did. Maybe one of the doers was blackmailing her. Maybe one of the folks on her trail was searching for her. Difficult case!"

Although Mason spent another hour with Sid, he garnered no additional info. Mason realized that Leana had made a lot of enemies in New York, and perhaps she was killed to ensure her continual silence. If that was the case, they waited a long time, allowing her two new husbands before moving to kill her. He loved the concept that big money was cleaning up the trail, but he intuitively felt that Leana was removed for personal reasons.

# 19

# Opening the Leana Lonergan Case

BEAUREGARD CALLED CHIEF JIM Coyne and told him that they were opening an old accident case. The chief was not happy but accepted Beauregard's decision when he explained that there were too many things connected to the case that could not be ignored. Beauregard then said the one thing that the chief didn't want to hear. "I have this feeling, Chief, that if we don't get on top of this, it's going to bite us in the ass in the future, and the mayor will direct all negative publicity at us." Beauregard knew that the chief was worried about taking a fall if Beauregard was wrong. Beauregard was mostly always right, but he also knew that any decision he made today to not investigate would be on his shoulders. He sometimes hated management.

"Well, Beauregard, give me written reasons why we are reopening this case. I know damn well you must have already done some investigation, so include that in your report. I'll say I sanctioned it, but you'd better keep me in the loop. I don't like that you went off on your own and investigated something that was not on the agenda. Don't tell me it didn't happen, and don't let it happen again."

Beauregard was surprised at the limited reaction he got from the chief; it could have been a lot worse. He sat at his desk ruminating about his work. *Most cases are never completely resolved. Even when I catch the felon red-handed, I can never be sure I have the motive straight. Everyone lies. People spin the truth even when they're trying to tell the truth. My strength is my truth radar, which is pretty good, but it's not perfect when interviewing a serial killer.* His mind went straight to Anya, the twelve-year-old serial killer who had recently pleaded to six murders of her friends and one attack. He couldn't get out of his mind one of the last things she'd said. "I couldn't do it all alone." Was that a lie? His radar told him it wasn't, and that bothered him. Did one of her friends assist her? Did he overlook something? It was possible. He was deeply concerned that someone would be murdered in the future. Would it be because he hadn't paid proper attention. *Shit, there wasn't a lot of satisfaction in this work. They talk about closure, but often closure is elusive.*

The other detectives joined him in the conference room, including the newly transferred detective to Major Crimes, Ashton Lent. Ashton was skinny and rather goofy looking, and of all things, the detectives heard that he played violin. Beauregard pointed out to the other detectives that Ashton could have some insights into drug use in the area and all the bars. They were informed that Ashton played violin both in classical concerts and in jazz bars and was supposed to be musically talented. However that musical reputation was wasted on the folks in Major Crimes. This was his first group interaction with his new peers. Beauregard thought, *It's rather funny. Ash seems totally at ease. He should be worried. Getting along in the department is a priority; every cop knows that.*

Beauregard also knew that he'd originally wanted the female applicant, but a turn in her family responsibilities resulted in her withdrawing her name, so Ash it was. He should be happy. Everyone in the squad knew that Ash was the only viable remaining applicant—and better yet, there was no political pressure to appoint him, so there was no resentment or feelings of distrust around the selection of the new guy.

Beauregard announced that they were opening the Leana Lonergan case, and everyone but Ash raised a cheer. Beauregard handed out a summary sheet of known facts and then asked Petra to give a presentation of how the squad had come to reopening what was supposedly an auto accident case. Mason then updated them on his interview with Sid Silverstein. The information transfer took almost two hours, requiring a short coffee break.

On their review renewal, Ash shared that he knew a little about Leana. He met her and her husband Gar at a Mount Holyoke chamber musical night. He had been playing violin, and Leana had come up to him and complimented him. He'd asked if she played violin, and she'd said no but that her brother played and was quite good. Ash stated that he thought Leana was charming. She'd requested his playing schedule and had showed up at four of his venues, two in bars. Gar had accompanied her twice.

Ash had seen a creepy guy approach her one evening when he'd played at the Iron Horse in Northampton. As she'd left the ladies room, she'd pulled him away from where her husband had been sitting and had vehemently argued with the man for a few minutes. She'd then written a note and handed it to him, and he'd left. "I noticed all this because she and her husband were distinctly different from the likes of this guy."

Mason wanted a description of the guy, which caused Ash to blush. "Well, you know, jeans, muddy-colored T-shirt, and a worn leather bomber's jacket. He wore sneakers and had three days' growth of beard with lots of silver in it. His hair was long, and he walked like an inner-city kid with his pants showing a plumbers' crack. His face wasn't distinctive, but his walk was. That's all I remember. But it was not a normal interaction, that I know."

Beauregard asked him if he could place the guy as Southern versus Northern, or city versus country. Ash could not. They continued with a discussion as to what direction they would move. Mason had a report on Leana's early childhood that triggered a serious conversation on whether an eight-year-old child could have knowingly started the fire that killed most of her family, and why the one brother would be saved. There was a complete report on the investigation, and the original detectives could not find a smoking gun but were deeply suspicious that the cause may have been deliberate.

Beauregard was just about to sum up their findings more completely and again open the meeting to directions for further investigation when Ash said that he noticed something in the accident file. "You know, Captain, I'm surprised that the chief let you open this case just because the victim looked troublesome or maybe is a serial murderer. After all, she's dead now. Despite that fact, I do think that the accident smells. You know, sometimes I have a problem not with what's in an investigative file, but with what's *not* in it."

Beauregard was aware that Ash did not know that the concept of "what's been ignored or overlooked" was a favorite of his. *Well, I'll be. Ash, you go right ahead and explain.* He nodded to prompt Ash to continue.

Ash explained, "I looked at that accident investigation to see if folks in charge had looked for large equipment available in the area. They searched for town equipment and said that they looked to local construction companies in West Side. They even called the big equipment rental companies in Springfield, Holyoke, and Chicopee. You know there are some single-owner construction companies in Agawam, East Longmeadow, and even Enfield, Connecticut, who are known to loan their equipment off the books for some big money. The investigators never contacted any of them. One of my friends in a rock band drives big equipment and gets some big money for small work by connecting companies in need to sources of equipment—kind of an underground connection economy. These connections are always in the off hours and on Sunday and mostly off the books. The biggest problem for them is they don't want to be noticed. I think we should investigate some of them as a possibility, because that woman witness sounded really stable and sure of herself, and the lights she talked about were seen by other witnesses. On top of that, Leana was supposed to be a crackerjack driver. It does seem possible and even likely—in fact, more than likely—that some big truck was there with construction lights. If so, it could have caused that accident by its actions. It would have taken really heavy lighting to throw this Leana off course, and big equipment to push that oversized jersey barrier off a bit. And why wasn't she going home at that time of night? Where to the right would she be going? West Side is a small city, and there isn't much going on in that direction; in fact, it's kind of rural."

Beauregard thanked Ash and immediately pointed out that a list of Leana's and Gar's friends had never been made. Perhaps some of them lived over in that direction, and she was going for a late-night drink, although she was not known as a heavy drinker. He agreed that Ash should follow through on the construction equipment concept. As to the Lonergans' friends, that was a more delicate matter. He asked Petra if she could quietly investigate the Lonergans' associations using a list of addresses from the country club, and perhaps she could question both Leana's and Jim's parents as to who the Lonergans associated with on a regular basis without raising awareness that the accident case had been reopened.

Beauregard informed Mason that he wanted a real murder board created with all that was known about each of Leana's marriages and her early childhood. "Make a list of the type of enemies she could have made in each place. Some of them we know about, but there must be some who would want her dead long after their experience with her. Remember, seething revenge is a motive. Somebody else may have loved one of these husbands, or perhaps we should follow the money. Mason, you know what to do. We'll meet in forty-eight hours. Meanwhile, I'll follow the gossip mongers."

Beauregard called his brother-in-law and asked for a golf date, which was a surprise to both of them. JR Randall was pleased to drop everything for golf. He wasn't too interested in knowing the reason why Beauregard would want to golf in the middle of a workday. He knew that Beauregard, a man of few words and vices, must need something, and because his wants were minimal, JR figured Beauregard was looking for something—and the only something Beauregard was ever interested in was information.

The two played nine holes, and at about five in the afternoon,

Beauregard suggested they not play on but instead have a beer in the clubhouse downstairs bar. JR smirked at him and said, "Just who do you want to talk to, and may I at least ask what this is about?"

He received no answer, which was an answer for JR. It meant that this was about police business, and it was to be on the QT. They sat over a couple of beers until Beauregard saw his victim. Part of the usual crew from the church, with the addition of that idiot Don Turtolo, had entered the club house after playing eighteen holes, which was why they had not crossed paths with Beauregard and JR on the course.

JR thought that Beauregard must be really hard up for info, because to him it was obvious that Don was Beauregard's mark. It was very unlike him to be so obvious, and he couldn't imagine what would spark Beauregard's interest in Don Turtolo. That obviousness must be a ruse to pull in somebody else. Anyway, JR was here for a good ride. His work gave him only superficial info involving outside life. Here was a police investigation right in front of him. He was sure of that because Beauregard had only two interests: his family and police work. Everything else was nonessential.

Beauregard noticed that Don Turtolo was not in a good mood at first. He'd played lousy golf against what could be considered by the guys as a golf inferior. To make matters worse, they were also older and, as heard previously from Don, on their way out. Actually, they were in their sixties. Beauregard's brother-in-law had said that all the old guys on the course dressed so traditionally that they aged themselves—and maybe did that not unconsciously. Beauregard sometimes thought, *If you believe that you make enough money, then you can afford to let yourself go to pot and look old. To be truthful, I always dress old myself, at least according to Mona. Then again, I don't have to look prosperous; I'm not in that position. Don has to look prosperous. Although he looks stressed. Maybe life has caught up with him.*

JR told Beauregard that he had heard some rumors that money was tight for Don, who needed just a small cash-flow infusion to tide him over until his current project was finished and he got his payout. Beauregard thought, *Those rumors abound against half the members here. Sometimes I can get some evidence of financial trouble when I see the list of members in suspension. Although the club used member numbers, JR always knows who is who. I notice that the new owners don't have a list posted anymore. I like that change. I like privacy—except when I'm inquiring.*

Beauregard noticed that Don drank his beer and then ordered a vodka and tonic. Beauregard and JR sat next to him.

Beauregard was the first to speak about how JR was only one stroke ahead of him today. JR reacted with, "You were going downhill. That's why you decided nine holes were enough. You're afraid I'd cream you."

Beauregard shook his head and said, "Some days your heart's not in it. Work just tires you out. Today's one of those days, JR. I can't control my work world like you're able to." Don was in total agreement that there were days, and there were days.

Beauregard asked him about his work, questioning intelligently as if he knew a lot, which was a surprise to Don. Beauregard said that his wife had told him about the photo albums his firm had sold, and that there was a lot more to his business than that. Beauregard expressed interest in his experience in Silicon Valley and found that Don, once he was talking about himself, was just as verbose as Leana's friend from Georgia.

Beauregard decided it must be the sales side of both Don and Myra; it was probably what made them successful. Beauregard asked Don about West Coast living's effect on his marriage. Did he think the lifestyle interfered with everyday living?

It took about forty-five minutes of listening before Beauregard went in for the kill. "Don, I know that you were a good friend of Leana Lonergan. Folks tell me that they saw you with her for lunches outside of town, and that there may be something between you two. I mean, did you have a business or personal relationship with her? It's not the norm for married ladies to meet with single guys, especially good-looking guys like you. Is it true that you met with her frequently? I'm not just being nosy. I have to put some things at rest related to her accident."

Beauregard had decided in advance that Don was not a killer for a couple of reasons. First, he was depressed after she'd died, and second, Don was not that kind of bad actor. If Beauregard had not been certain, he never would have approached him. He thought, *I don't normally do my interviewing in an intimate bar setting at a country club.* However his question raised an immediate reaction from Don.

"Don't look at me. I heard that there were some questions as to whether Leana died accidently, but you can't blame me. You'd better understand that I was out of town that night. I of all people wanted Leana to live. Her death caused me a severe cash-flow shortage; and I do think things between her and her husband were off a little, if you know what I mean. It looked to me as if the marriage was winding down. I liked her a lot and was perhaps waiting in the wings for her. It was not easy to tell with Leana how she felt from day to day."

Beauregard stated, "Don, you haven't answered my question. What was going on with these luncheons with you and her, and how many were there? I know about a few. Doesn't sound like there was romance going on given the dives you two lunched at, and the Natick Mall. Give me a break—what guy goes to the Natick Mall without being forced to by a girlfriend?"

Beauregard thought Don looked cornered, and so he was not surprised when Don quickly attacked. "Look, I wasn't blackmailing her. Don't go there, Beauregard. I asked her to invest in one of my businesses that had a working capital problem, and she did. The problem resolved, and she decided to leave the dollars in there for future growth. Point of fact, she had promised me another cash infusion to be given two days after her death. Her death was damn inconvenient for me."

Beauregard now had a deep interest in Don's businesses and insisted he tell him more, specifically about how much money Leana had invested. He was bowled over by the amount: $1.4 million invested and not repaid. He wondered whether he should read Don his rights and decided that maybe he should.

Beauregard insisted that they move over to an empty table despite the fact that nobody could hear their conversation because of a deep discussion about football and the Patriots' star Tom Brady. Two at the table were not Patriots fans, which always encouraged a verbal war. Their excuse in moving was that nobody could hear themselves think due to the football saga being repeated over and over, with caustic criticism slammed at both teams.

Don was visibly disturbed when Beauregard read him his rights. Beauregard feared that he was about to ask for an attorney when Beauregard said that perhaps they should continue their conversation at the station. Don clearly didn't want that; their leaving together would be awfully hard to explain. Beauregard was quite certain that Don believed because he was innocent—well, maybe not innocent of some smaller issues—that this situation was, in his mind and using his favorite business term, containable.

His story was a revelation to Beauregard. Don said that he had business relations with the Haylor family in New York City, and through his former brother-in-law with the son of the mattress king in Chicago. Each had spoken about Leana, and not in the most positive way.

Over drinks, Martha Haylor Jenkins talked about her deceased brother and his untimely death. She said that her mother hated her brother's widow and was investigating her; the widow's name was Leana, formerly Mary Lou. Martha asked Don what kind of woman would change her first name. Because Don already was caught up in Leana Lonergan's beauty and personality, and because Leana was not the most common woman's name he had ever heard, he asked Martha what this Leana was like. Maybe because he wanted to, he believed that the two ladies were the same, and he showed Martha a news photo of Leana with Gar that he kept in his wallet. Beauregard thought the guy was really smitten to go that far.

Martha couldn't believe it but excitedly assured Don that despite the years, the woman in the picture was Georgie's wife. Martha had seen Leana, though briefly, in New York City a few years before. She was uncertain whether to tell her mother about this new marriage; her mother had taken following Leana too far. Martha believed the investigation was unhealthy and an obsession, which was very unlike her mother. However, didn't her mother have the right to know? At the very least, she would tell her mother's investigator, who would not be emotionally involved and had so far displayed some common sense in the investigation.

As to the mattress king, Don's former brother-in-law recognized Leana from the photo Don kept in his wallet. He told Don that she was something but was maybe too smart for Don to fool around with. The mattress king's son, Ted Waleski Jr., had business with Don. He'd bought multiple photo albums through purchased software as a perk given to each of his buyers of a king-sized imperial mattress set (which were blatantly overpriced). Over drinks after his contract was signed, Don questioned Ted Jr. about his dad and his mom. With no emotion, Ted said that both his parents were out-of-control drinkers. His mom and dad would have killed each other in a drunken brawl if they hadn't divorced. Their divorce was a relief to all the relatives, and especially to Ted.

Ted Jr. had not seen his former stepmother since she'd left Chicago as quickly as she could after his dad's death. He said that Leana had reaped a lot of his father's loot despite his having a will that supposedly protected his assets from the marriage. Ted Sr. apparently had lots of money on the side that wasn't in trusts, and he had Leana's name on each of the accounts—not surprising because his dad couldn't balance a checkbook. Ted Jr. also implied that there was a lot of buried money from some transactions his dad had with some of his buddies with whom he grew up. They were "connected guys," and he himself wanted to know nothing about them. They often would come by and talk with Leana at the house; they really liked her.

Ted Jr. thought that maybe all that cash around, and the big-time and good-looking hoods hanging at the house, were the lures his father hung out there to get Leana to marry him. He also said that his mother often talked about a stash of big cash that her ex kept at the house. She could never find it when she was married to him, or else it would have been included in the divorce. She insisted that it was over ten million and that her husband kept it for escape money. He was deadly afraid of the IRS getting a complaint about him and putting a lien on his business and accounts; he wanted something he could fall back on if he had to quickly leave the country.

Ted Jr. said, "After all, my dad was bigger than life, an advertising genius. But he was a heavy drinker, and up close he was not particularly charming. Why that beauty Leana would marry him had to be about money. She lasted three years until he died.

"Funny thing about the law suit on his accident is that it was my father who brought Leana's car in for repairs, not Leana. They couldn't blame Leana for not repairing her car—Dad brought it in. The repair guy was relatively new, but he said that Dad came in to reclaim it at closing time, and the regular clerk had gone home. The substitute guy, a salesman, told my dad they hadn't gotten to it yet. He even paid for the repairs with his credit card. Just a glitch in the system and my father's drunkenness, I guess."

Ted, Jr. didn't hate Leana. In fact, he believed that his father's marrying Leana was the one intelligent thing he'd ever done. "He was mostly sober during those three years, although he was going downhill toward the end."

Beauregard was interested in Leana's history, but he was more interested in Don's relationship with Leana. He said, "Don, maybe you didn't want to pay back the million dollars. That's a big enough motive to do away with her. I notice that you spend a lot of time with Oakie, the gravel and asphalt guy here at the club."

Don said, "You mean Ray O'Conner?" Beauregard replied in the affirmative. Don was genuinely confused. "So what? Oakie and I go way back. We went to grade school together. Why would you be interested in him and me?"

Beauregard ignored this question and instead asked, "You know you owe over a million bucks, plus implied interest, to Leana's estate. Were you ever going to tell Gar about it? And furthermore, why in hell would you have the balls to ask Leana for that kind of money without asking Gar? Just when did you find out her past history—before or after she loaned you money? It plays pretty weirdly for me. Just imagine: I go to a club member's wife asking for a loan, and not to the husband who has plenty of money. What did you have on Leana? You're gonna have to fess up, Don. I can't leave this conversation this way. You know that."

Don's answer was bizarre. He said that he'd made a play for Leana, and at first she'd simply ignored him. But when he'd insisted, she'd become very angry. Basically, she'd told him to learn to play like a good little boy in the sandbox and leave married women alone. This had been his sole motive to retaliate. At that time, he hadn't been thinking about money at all, although he'd had some financial distress. He'd entered into a new investment that had required a lot more capital than originally expected. He had two partners with deep pockets who'd had no problem keeping up with the new funds required; in fact, they'd been willing to buy him out. This problem had been concurrent with his increasing the size and diversity of his IT products, which had also required increased funding. He couldn't get additional financing and had been nervous about accessing available "entrepreneurial special funding," which carried interest rates that were much too high.

In anger and in ignorance, Don had told Leana, "Don't pull your morality lecture on me Leana. Husbands in New York City and Chicago—who are you kidding? You're no babe in the woods."

Don said that she was as off-centered as he had ever seen her, but she recovered quickly. He'd been himself totally surprised when she'd said, "How did you know Aaron Goldberg?" He hadn't known him but was astute enough to know that this would be an issue for her, and so he'd decided to punt, as he called it.

Taking a chance he'd said, "Finance. I've needed funds at various times, and he always helped me find non-bank financing." Don had thought that this was a good overall story because all kinds of people in the professions and business would perhaps be knowledgeable about financing alternatives, especially if they were from New York City.

Her reply showed him just how wrong he was. "How much are you looking for, Don? And don't give me any shit about a personal relationship."

From there, they'd met four or five times outside of West Side in little out of the way spots. He didn't remember seeing anyone he knew in any of the spots, but he said that Leana was squirrely about it. She'd loaned him as much as a $1.4 million, but he had paid back $600,000. Paying back the rest right now was not possible. In six months he could probably do it, but never was interest ever mentioned.

"Leana told me, 'Don't ever mention my past to anyone. Do you understand? You will be one very unhappy camper if you do.' She also said that if there was a good investment I had, she may be willing to cough up some more capital if I could follow through. She had no problem with the size of the loan."

Beauregard told Don that in order to avoid an interview at the station, he was to write up everything he had told him, including being advised of his rights. He inferred that any loans to Leana were not what he was looking for, but if for any reason Beauregard did not have a signed interview statement on his desk in the morning, then he would make the loans his business, and Gar would be the first to be informed.

The two rejoined the other table, and the guy talk continued. The subject changed to ISIS.

# 20

# Mary Lou's First Love, 1976

It was the summer before her senior year at SUNY Albany. Mary Lou was excited. She had an interview in New York City for an internship at a boutique marketing and advertising firm. Mary Lou knew that any public relations experience would serve her well when she looked for her first professional job, and her faculty advisor told her that if she did a decent job this summer, there may be a possible job offer in it for her. *If I get the internship, you can bet that I will give it everything I have.*

A week later, her faculty advisor informed Mary Lou that she was getting the internship and that he had given her a glowing reference. She was pleased and waited to hear; it took five days. She had almost given up when she got the very professional call.

Mary Lou shared an apartment owned by the firm with three other interns and one employee. Apparently, the marketing firm found that putting interns up for a few months twice a year was a cheaper way to test worthiness for employment than direct hire or hiring through headhunters or employment agencies. It worked for her. She met Jack Leahy, assistant advertising director at the firm. She worked in the marketing research section of the firm but gave several research reports at the weekly advertising board meetings. After the second meeting she presented, Jack held her back and complimented her work. He then asked if she would like to have a drink with him after work. She agreed.

Mary Lou met with Jack in a bar in the Village, which had a college hippy feel to it. It was kind of what she was used to, and she felt comfortable. She and Jack hit it off immediately, and they met very often over the next three weeks. He was good looking in an all-American athletic kind of way, and he was immensely entertaining. Mary Lou generally was a more serious young woman, and she found herself taken up with the jovial back-and-forth banter. She quickly developed an ability to keep up with him. He was informed about everything. She asked him how he knew so much about so many issues, and his reply created a basis for her goals for the rest of her life. He said, "Look around you, listen, and absorb. People aren't interested in you—they're interested in themselves and information about things they don't know. You can use relationships for sales and for personal connections, but only if you are able to forge a relationship that makes you unforgettable."

Jack practiced what he preached. He was unforgettable, as was that summer in New York City. They walked Central Park in the rain and in the sunshine. They saw a couple of Broadway shows. They shopped in offbeat shops. He showed her how to shop for value. Then they finally slept together. Mary Lou was in love. She shared her background with him, or at least most of it. He was kind and considerate, and he told her that she must forget the worst of it, but she should always remember the lessons she had learned. She somehow felt cleansed and forgiven.

About two weeks before the end of her internship, he told her at lunch that he was taking a new job, a partnership interest in a firm in Los Angeles. In fact, he was leaving the next day. She was upset, maybe even bereft. He was not the first man she had slept with, but he was the first one who'd left his mark on her psyche. "Jack, what does this mean for us? I have one year left at SUNY, but I could just as well do that year in Los Angeles. I have only my brother to think about, but I simply send money for him and see him once a year. I have no ties."

His answer devastated her. He explained that he wasn't the kind of guy who was interested in long-term relationships; his background, which he had not shared with her previously, prevented positive relationships. In fact, he was fearful of long-term relationships, let alone marriage. He was crazy about her, but that was because he had no responsibility for her and didn't have to report to her.

He said, "Mary Lou, you are absolutely the best of any of the women I've ever been with, but I am not for you. You will see that in time. I'm about business, about my financial future. I cannot now, and probably never will, include a personal partner in my plans. It is a fact. I will miss you, and you will miss me, but this is not personal. I will not, I cannot take you with me. I will not tell you the firm I'm joining, and furthermore, I do not want to keep in contact with you. I believe that a hard break is kinder to both of us. Do not think for a minute that you don't mean a great deal to me. You do, Mary Lou. But this is what has to happen for the good of both of us."

Something from her past prevented Mary Lou from crying in front of Jack. He walked away, but not before paying the luncheon bill. She went back to work and acted as if nothing was wrong. One of her colleagues told her that she had heard through the grapevine that Jack Leahy was taking a great position in advertising and marketing as a full partner in a firm in LA. Mary Lou nodded as if it meant nothing. When she left work, she took in a movie, and in the dark Mary Lou silently cried for two hours.

On the next day, Mary Lou started her new life—a life with no romantic notions. Jack Leahy was gone, but what was not gone was office gossip that had been previously controlled by his presence. The gossip informed Mary Lou that Jack had been at the firm for five years, and his work was highly regarded; in fact, the firm had been scheduling a promotion to partnership for him in the autumn. His departure left the firm scrambling for a replacement. She also heard that Jack had a favorite intern twice a year, every year. In point of fact, one favorite was the daughter of a very important client, who'd raised hell with management over his relationship with her. Management overlooked his peccadillos because of his fabulous ability to satisfy most clients.

Mary Lou was now faced with wondering whether she had been truly had. She considered carefully every word he ever said, reviewed the most intimate sex acts they had experienced, and ruminated over his wonderfully thoughtful advice. She reviewed the restaurants, shows, parks, retailers, and events they had shared in their short time together. He had exposed her to a sophisticated lifestyle—one she wanted to live. Every past moment she remembered included not one debate, or argument, or sense that she wasn't the most important person in the world to him.

That perfection in all those moments now enraged her. She reflected, *My soul soaring above the universe was the one fantasy I had daily when I was with him.* Leana felt like Mary Lou who could not believe that she, with the affronts she and Timothy had faced in their early childhood and her difficulty dealing with her obnoxious stepbrother, could be taken in by a con artist. Jack was a con artist, of that she was sure. He had inflicted on her such enormous emotional pain. It was inconceivable that she had let her guard down, but she had. What was worse was that she was in a long line of naïve women over whom Jack had cast a spell. She, who considered herself wise in the ways of the world, was one of the stupid ones. She said loudly when she was alone in her room, "No, no! I won't allow this to happen to me again. And why should Jack get away scot-free?"

Mary Lou finally concluded that the time spent with him, despite her ultimate disappointment, was well worth her investment. Mary Lou decided that if she had known it was a limited engagement, it wouldn't have hurt quite so much. She felt it was so damaging because she'd expected it to be so much more—she'd thought it was real! She could not believe that she had been so silly as to think that life could work out this easily. No, she was a Saturday's child and would have to work for a living. She was not Cinderella.

Her managing partner in the firm asked to see her in his office the second to last day of her internship. This was highly unusual, and she hoped that it had nothing to do with Jack. It didn't. His approach to her was mainly on her work, which he said was exceptional. "Mary Lou, you are exactly the kind of employee we are looking for to start a management training program. You have set standards in your presentations that have been beyond what our senior employees have given us. It is surprising in one so young to see this attention to detail, to directions, and to embracing creative solutions to typical problems. We are impressed with your performance. On our evaluation sheets, we have seen nothing but praise, even from your peer internship colleagues. Your living style has also been evaluated, and the management of the firm condo you occupy with others has also praised you as responsible and reliable. We have noticed, however, that you seem to have entered a relationship with Jack Leahy, and we wondered about that. I'm sure it was a mentoring relationship, but if there was anything I should know about, please tell me now."

Mary Lou thanked the universe that she had had the opportunity of a few days to recover from Jack to enable her to view his impact on her in a more positive way. It allowed her to answer with apparent frankness. "Thank you for asking. Jack Leahy is a powerful mentor and has taught me a great deal about marketing and public relations, which will be invaluable for me in the future. I want to stay in this field and believe that his input has helped direct me toward success. I am entering my senior year at SUNY, and I needed work experience and a focus for my career. From the beginning, Jack appeared to me to be a free soul who is all about work, and I can't thank him enough for his assistance. Unfortunately, he didn't tell me he was leaving, or I would have tried to arrange an office party for him with our internship group. I know he helped several others even more than he assisted me. I'm sorry to see him leave us."

Mary Lou was offered a job after her graduation in June. She was also asked if she knew the names of any of the young women interns to whom Jack had given additional mentoring. She quickly named three, picking a few that she had seen in Jack's office and who had given her the most difficulty while she was there. She knew how to return a "favor."

She returned to college with a more realistic picture of life and romance. More than once she said to herself, "Thank you, Jack Leahy. The class was great, but the final exam was deadly."

# 21

# Collaborating at the Station

THERE WAS AN EXTREME aura of business in the conference room. The detectives were reviewing the white boards and the emergence of what appeared to all of them as another honest-to-god, real serial murderer who was maybe murdered herself. Although the two-year-old protracted investigation was daunting, it also excited the detectives. Mary Lou, alias Leana, had operated and possibly murdered in six different states. None of the localities she lived in had open cases related to her; in fact, those authorities probably had no idea that there were murders in their area. This was the stuff television shows were made from.

Ash, who the detectives now believed had the most cynical world view of them all, asked, "Nobody knows that there were murders unless we tell them, and we can't prove any of it. What district force wants an old case opened, especially when the suspect is now dead? On the other hand, we have enough information to know that Mary Lou or Leana was a mark for someone. Who was in the area? How can we find out? Looks interesting to me, but this won't be easy, Captain."

Beauregard was fascinated with Ash's easy way of looking at the big picture. He deduced that Ash had saved him a lot of time trying to bring focus to the work for his crew. He assigned Petra the task to report on the Lonergans' friends. He gave Ash the task to bring them up to date on the squirrely guy he saw at the Iron Horse concert in Northampton, and also to pursue the truck equipment alternatives.

Next, Beauregard started the reporting by distributing a copy of the written and signed interview with Don Tortola. After the report, the detectives were to make recommendations for the murder board and where they should move next.

Beauregard began. "Let's start with the debris Leana left behind her. There has to be a bunch of disappointed people; people left with money problems or with personal loss problems." He then told the detectives that there was always a motive for crime. Often investigations did not discover motive if it was not a concern—for example, if there was enough evidence and a confession to convict, then motive was not so important.

"However, in this case, motive may be the only direction we have unless we get some info on construction equipment used that night, if that's what happened. So let's start with people who were hurt at each juncture of her life. Have we missed any period of her life where there was change?"

Ash said, "Although I agree that generally other police district personnel may not want to reopen a case on their books, I think that if we phrase it right, if we let them know that we have a couple of serious possibilities for her murderer, and as a result of our investigations her history will all come out, then they'll want to be part of the solution. Take it from me, we must hustle them into believing that we know more than we know. I'm telling you we need all the info they may have about people questioned, if any, around any of the so-called accidents related to Leana's husbands."

Beauregard thought that Ash expressed it all in a nutshell. "I'll give you all a few days to bring your ideas to me."

Mason and Petra decided to start calling police departments for lists of those most potentially impacted directly by Leana's life and the loss of her husbands. Ash asked how much interviewing was done on the Lonergans' associations. Petra had a list but had not yet followed through, and she had not yet questioned her parents or her in-laws.

She was told to put that off until the next day. Ash then left to visit owners of construction companies who had big equipment from the list he had already compiled.

The phones at the station became very busy, and mostly with outgoing calls. The call center found that the detectives were using three lines all the time for outgoing calling.

Beauregard had left a message for a guy who grew up in a nearby city but who was now a detective in San Francisco. Beauregard had wrestled against him in high school and was certain that he would be interested in the case simply because of their history. The detective's mom and dad now lived in West Side. He would have a vested interest. Beauregard recognized that there was nothing like a personal connection to bring folks to the table to assist.

As he hung up, he had what he called a brain burp; others would call it an epiphany. He yelled to Mason, "What the hell? We never got Leana's post office box. There may be mail in it. It was probably paid for until the estate was settled. Maybe it was paid in advance, and there's something in it of interest. And we need to go through her computer. I know that her husband looked at it and said that he didn't find anything, but we haven't looked at it. What do we need for a warrant, Mason? And which judge at District Court would be most favorable? Damn, most of them are members of the West Side Country Club. You'll have to see who's on the schedule and hit him with as little notice as possible. I guess that we'll have to get a reliable informant to tell us that the post office box still has mail in it that could be pertinent to the investigation. It's been two years. Maybe we can talk to Turtolo again, and he can state he had knowledge of the post office box."

Mason said, "Captain, I think we get Sid, the New York detective, to leak the post office box address. Maybe we can get info from Ted Jr. from Chicago about her getting mail from Ted Sr.'s estate attorneys. The attorneys in New Hampshire were probably directed to send all mail there too. Hell, the post office box may be the nexus for us. We don't want the husband to know we're successful until we've gone through what's there. If we find anything, then maybe we can take the next step and go after her computer, if he still has it."

Beauregard nodded in agreement. He had second thoughts about his conversation with Norbie, Gar Lonergan's attorney. He regretted raising the specter of an investigation into the accident. If Norbie smelled his client as a potential suspect, he would move to protect him. Maybe he'd even close the post office box if he knew about it, and certainly he'd dump the computer. Beauregard was deep in legal mumbo-jumbo when Mason approached him.

"Captain, I was just talking to the marketing firm where Leana worked right after college. It was during the time period that she met her first husband, right after she graduated from SUNY. Funny thing is that her then supervisor is now the senior partner in charge. He said that before her full employment engagement, she served an internship there during the summer before her senior year in college, and she was the best intern ever to work for them. Her name was Mary Lou then. He had been informed—although she denied it—that she had had a serious affair with one of the junior partners at that time, a Jack Leahy. He said that Jack was a really cool womanizer who left a trail of crying ladies behind him. Jack relocated to Los Angeles and later back to New York, where he was a big time player in commercial real estate after selling his ownership interest in one of the most successful advertising firms in the city. This was right about the time she was involved with Aaron Goldberg. This Leahy guy was killed coming out of a little restaurant across from the Metropolitan Opera by a mugger who didn't take anything. It's still an open case in New York, but maybe Leana was involved. Maybe she was cleaning up on old memories, if she had been dissed by this guy. Seems he's never changed his ways. He finally married and had some kids, although the marriage into a wealthy and important family seemed to not have been a love match. He continued to have short, romantic interludes after his marriage. At least, that's what this guy said. Here's my report. Maybe our Leana is good for this murder too. Not a husband, but a disappointment to her—and think how this must have killed her self-esteem. She was just a kid."

Beauregard asked if Mason had reviewed her college years, and he had. "She never got in trouble there. Her professors regarded her as very talented. There were pictures of her with a financial investment group that included a guy who Sid told me was a master investment counselor for the New York Hasidic community. I'll follow that lead next."

Beauregard instructed him to add all this info to the murder board and said, "Make sure we have every bit of her time accounted for. She seemed to be doing okay from the age of eight to when her adoptive parents died, but check again on that. Make sure there were no surprise bodies or unexpected deaths up there. I recall that she didn't like her stepbrother. See if he's still alive."

Beauregard was not himself; his radar for missing the obvious was buzzing. What the hell was bothering him? He shook his head and, as was his pattern, reviewed all the new information, trying to make it gel with what was previously known. He grabbed the original accident report compiled by the fire department and the police and kept repeating to himself, "What don't I see? What should be there and isn't?" He then looked at all the fire investigator and police notes and did the same thing. "That's it—I'm going to the scene," he said loud enough for Petra and Mason to hear, but he did not stop to explain what scene or why.

Twenty minutes later, Beauregard stood at the apex, the point where Leana would make a decision the night of her accident: the decision to go right or left. Even now, with big barrier guard rails, some cars would sometimes seem to stop before deciding to go one way or another. He figured that these were autos driven by people unfamiliar with the road. But Leana was familiar with the road. Still, under the right circumstances, if bright lights were in her eyes, he wondered if it looked safer to go to the right even if she wanted to go to the left.

He then looked down the hill on the right to the neighbor's house, the one who had seen the bright lights that night. She lived down in the dingle. He wondered why the lights bothered her more than usual. Her house was down below, and the lights should have shined above her roof, where they would not be such a bother. They would have to be extraordinarily bright, and if they were turned to the road, they shouldn't have been a problem for the neighbor. However, it could be a problem if they were turned one way, angled toward the neighbor's house and then reversed when the right person came by, if the operator of the lights was waiting for Leana or someone else. He'd need to talk to Ash to see just how lights like these worked.

# 22

# Attorney and Client

Norbie met with Gar, his client. He set the meeting using the guise that he needed a fuller understanding of the letters sent to Gar. Because Norbie had reviewed the letters, Gar was perplexed as to why it was necessary to have a meeting with him, and particularly on a Saturday.

Over coffee, Norbie laid out on the conference table what looked like a visual diagram on Leana and her life. Norbie said, "Captain Beauregard"—Gar noticed that Norbie did not use his familiar name—"has intimated that Leana was not all that she appeared to be. He then confirmed that there is some suspicion around her death. My instincts kicked in, and I've had Sheila, my paralegal, do some digging. This is what she found, and I don't believe for a moment that this is everything of importance." With that, he directed Gar's attention to all Leana's marriages, her change of name from Mary Lou to Leana, and the location of the first eight years of her life.

Norbie pointed out that not one of her previous husbands outlived her marriage to them. "Now, Gar, if I have this info, then the police have this info. You don't have to be brilliant to infer what they may be thinking. They will know from your marriage license, which is public record, that she lied on the form. They will wonder whether you discovered all her past marriages and were moved to kill her. Maybe in the last few weeks before Leana died, you figured out that she was trying to kill you. After all, killing her husbands may be Leana's substitution for divorce. Death is a lot less messy than divorce. And finally, not only are you the husband of the purported victim, but she also left you so much damn money, maybe more than what you had yourself. All are possible motives for murder, and I am deeply concerned. Added to that is your request to have Jeffrey Find, the PI, investigate her background. He even tells you to divorce her. It's a matter of time before Jim, his new partner and formerly one of Beauregard's detectives, gets wind of all of this. We need to approach this as if you have been charged, because I suspect that you may be charged in the near future. Most important, you must not talk to anyone about Leana and the accident unless I direct you. As you know, clients often get themselves in hot water by denying stuff and then trying to explain in-depth their denial. Later, they regret their explanations."

Gar's characteristic ruddy complexion bleached out to a grayish white, and he almost whispered, "This can't be true. On all levels, Norbie! I would have just divorced her. If I knew all this stuff about her, I could have had the marriage annulled. I could never hurt anyone. Besides, I was with my son all that evening. I couldn't be two places at once. You don't believe I did this, do you? What the hell? I've had a lifetime of clean living, and you think that they could arrest me for murder? Norbie, maybe you're overreacting. What real evidence do they have that it's a murder, and what specific evidence do they have that I murdered my wife?"

Norbie listened and waited patiently while Gar gained more control over himself. After all, Norbie had lived a lifetime telling clients and relatives what they did not want to hear. He knew that the process could not be rushed. Gar then asked the question that demonstrated that he was in the right place in the process of setting up his defense. "How do we do this Norbie? How do we find out what the police think? And how does any of this help us in preventing arrest?"

Norbie said that until Gar was arrested, there was no requirement that the police share info with them. He decided that they had a couple of avenues to pursue in planning a potential defense that would give them a heads-up on the case before they were hit with an arrest—not an absolute occurrence, but one that he believed was not only possible but imminent.

The first avenue was to use Gar's relationship as her husband to get some records on her everyday dealings, specifically her financial dealings. Norbie had many questions about these dealings for Gar to answer. Second, they would need their own private investigation. Norbie suggested a guy from Worcester who was an attorney and a former cop, as well as an investigator. "I would like to make him co-counsel; he would then come under protection, preventing anything he found from being discoverable. I want him because he is unknown in this area. He will be able to ask questions without it being linked to you or me. He would not maintain records. In all our work, we will be doing the police a favor. We'll be looking for alternate theories of the crime, if there truly is a crime. That really means that we'll be looking for an unknown subject out there who may have wanted Leana dead. Take my word: we're going to find at least a few of them. So I need you to okay the expenses.

"For your mental attitude toward this, I don't believe for a minute that you murdered Leana, but it doesn't matter what I believe. What matters is that I find an alternate theory before the police go after you. I may not be able to, but it's what we should be doing now."

Gar had recovered a little upon hearing that Norbie believed in him. In a thoughtful voice, he slowly said, "Go ahead. Hire this guy, but I want to meet him. I have some good gut instincts when it comes to people working with me. I want to make sure that he believes in me too. And don't say what you're thinking—that if my instincts were so good, why were they inactive when I married Leana?"

Norbie tried to reassure Gar about Leana. He explained that from his perspective, Leana was a very high-operating sociopath who wiped away problems only when she felt at risk. He told Gar,

"Probably anyone would be sucked in by her beauty, brains, and class. You know, the only way to outsmart a sociopath is to watch her for a couple of years or longer. Then you may—and I say may—catch on. Normally the sociopath can't keep the act up for really long periods of time. Gar, in your case, you felt you needed a wife. Leana filled the bill beautifully. Don't blame yourself. If she was murdered, then someone from her past caught up with her and saved you a lot of divorce litigation, and potentially your life."

Norbie went on to say that Estefan Buenaros, the attorney from Worcester, would be there in ten minutes. "I want you to meet him and to feel comfortable with him. You may call him anytime you remember something that you are unable to remember today. But call only me about strategy, and never talk to anyone else about this case."

Estefan was a few minutes late and apologetically explained to the other two men that the traffic on the Pike West was loaded. "Sorry to be late, but can I ask you what the hell's going on? Getting here was a bear, like everyone was going to Springfield. But once I hit the city, there were few cars whose destination was Springfield."

He told Gar to call him Steve. From that point on, Gar considered that the conversation resembled an interrogation, so much so that he directly asked Steve if he believed that he was guilty.

Steve laughed and said, "Norbie would never have brought me into this case this way if he judged you were guilty. As to what I think, it probably is not important. But if Norbie thinks you're not guilty, then you are not guilty in my mind. Now, let's cut the 'poor me' routine and get down to business."

Steve grilled Gar about his marriage. He asked questions about Leana's daily routine, her friends, their common friends, any written materials she left behind, publications she received as well as her mail, her relationship with the children, trips she took during their marriage, her medical history, what he knew of her childhood, and her likes and dislikes. Finally Steve asked if they could search her room and her computer, and whether he knew about any post office box.

"Be my guest. No one's in the house right now. Let's go. But the computer will be a disappointment. I told you, Norbie, that I'd been through it, and there wasn't much in there."

Steve responded immediately, "Gar, I can do things with computers you haven't dreamed of. Perhaps she's erased some history. I'll recover anything that's recoverable. There was a reason her computer was password protected and she used a word she didn't think you'd ever know for her password. By the way, it was a very weak password, so I'm assuming she wasn't a techie. She was in the public relations field, which means she was probably facile in words and pictures. Is it a Mac computer? We need to discover her post office box number before the police. Do you have her key ring? Perhaps it's there. In any case, we'll go through all her clothes, her pocketbooks, and everything connected to her. Have you thrown away any of her personal things?"

Gar said that the computer was a Mac and that he had not thrown away any of Leana's things. He explained that at first he went out of town to recover, and when he returned, he realized that he was in jeopardy and reasoned that he should leave everything alone until after he consulted with Norbie. Both lawyers sighed in relief, and they left for Gar's home.

# 23

# Detective Ashton Lent

Ash had already visited several construction sites in Massachusetts and now was at ALL Construction, Inc. (ACI), in Enfield, Connecticut. The company had a load of heavy-duty equipment and several large hangars for storing equipment. There was no security, and so he started to walk around.

A big, husky guy who could have been an ad for ANSI Class 2 and 3 work wear wandered over. "Who are you looking for? Most of the trucks are gone, so if you're looking to use one today, you're probably out of luck."

Ash couldn't believe that an entry had been given to him without his having to work for it. Reading the man's nametag, he said, "Chet, I don't need a truck for today, but for a couple of weekends from now. Soon I'm going to need a construction lighting package and a heavy-duty truck with maybe a plow in front. It's for some road work, and it will be in a precarious place. I have company insurance that will pay for any damage to the vehicle, but I really don't expect problems. The job is for the nighttime and for maybe an hour in duration. Have you ever rented out such equipment before, and would you be willing to do that for me? I need to know how much. This job is really important, and I need help." Ash pulled out a card he'd gotten from a friend with a construction logo on it but no name.

Chet looked at the card and eyed Ash. "Good company, but I thought I knew all their people. I don't know you."

Ash dropped his friend's name, Dempsey, and said that he was doing the work for him.

Chet's response tickled Ash. "Look, we don't rent out equipment for that kind of job anymore. A couple of years ago, we got a big payday for a truck and lighting for the same kind of job—more than three times the normal fee. The lights came back smashed, and the front of the truck looked like it had been in an accident. The guy who rented the truck eventually paid for the damages. Actually, he paid for the whole job in cash, but that didn't help. The truck was out of commission for two weeks, and we had to order new lights. I manage the equipment here, but if I were you, I'd talk with the owner. For big money, he might change his mind given the work is for Dempsey, who's a stand-up guy."

Ash thought, *Could this have been any easier?* He may have found the weapon in the supposed accidental death, but he was uncertain how to proceed. He suggested they go up to the office, where he could give his particulars for Chet's boss.

In the office, Ash asked when the negative occurrence had happened. Chet had the date embedded in his mind: early October 2015. Ash asked who this jerk was, and what was his story when he brought the equipment back.

"That's one of the problems. I got reamed out by my boss because the guy, when he finished with the equipment, dropped the equipment off in the middle of the night. We used his large deposit to pay for everything. It totaled nine grand. We had his license. The guy's name was Nick Latorska, and he was not from this area; that was the reason he needed the truck. He was from New York or New Jersey, I can't remember which. Talk to my boss. He may give in to you; especially because you're local."

Ash thanked Chet and said that someone from his company would be back. He didn't lie. Beauregard would be looking for the records that same day. He called Beauregard and told him he had found the vehicle. Beauregard said, "Well, now we probably have a murder. We still will need a connection—not just that date, but connection to evidence at the scene to that equipment. We have pictures of the marks that equipment made. Let's hope that they're distinctive and can be matched to that particular vehicle. I'll get Petra on this now."

Ash was a happy camper. He thought that this small success would perhaps cement his position on the Major Crimes Squad. He knew that they had originally been looking at someone else for his position, and Ash did not want the captain to ever regret appointing him. He liked this job. Other than when he was playing his violin, this was the only situation that felt like home to him. Now he would direct his efforts to his second task.

Ash was getting together with his group for a jazz gig at an engagement party at the Wykoff Country Club in Hoyoke. The group he was playing with was with him at the club in Northampton, where he saw Leana meet with the squirrely guy. Jock, who played bass with the group, never missed anything. Also, Jock played with many different groups around the area. He hoped that maybe Jock had seen the squirrely guy before (and maybe with Leana) at another event. At the very least, maybe Jock saw some detail that Ash had missed, or he saw him with other people who could be identified. Two years was a long time, and Ash's only hope was in the fact that nobody missed looking at Leana without remembering her.

It was a loud and celebratory crowd at the party. The couple, both in their thirties, had been living together for eight years and had finally decided to tie the knot. This was not a sedate crowd, and Ash and his group played their hearts out, granting every request made by the couple. Finally, they had almost an hour break. After hitting the buffet table, Ash made sure he sat next to Jock.

Jock immediately recalled seeing the beautiful blonde that evening. Further, he had seen her at some other classical music venues. He also remembered the squirrely guy. He said that he was a hanger-on with all kinds of fundraising organizations—kind of a runner or gofer for their needs. Jock thought that he worked the political circle and had heard that currently, he may be working for one of the state representatives or senators in the area.

"I don't remember which one, but I'd check all their offices. He's the type who would hang around the office all day in case he heard something. He's a sleazebag."

The next day, Ash hit many political offices with no luck. Then upon leaving the last one, he entered a coffee shop nearby, and there sat his target. Ash sat at the table next to the squirrel and ordered coffee and a pastry. He turned to the man at the next table and said, "Don't I know you? I think I see you at a lot of political events, and maybe even musical events. Hi, my name's Ash."

He was rewarded for his directness. "Nice to meet you, Ash. I'm Chip Nielson, and you probably have seen me. I work with all the nonprofits and get around. You look familiar to me too."

Ash explained that he was a jazz and classical violinist, and perhaps Chip had seen him play. He said that he played the Iron Horse and many other venues. "I think I might have seen you at the Iron Horse one night quite a long time ago, maybe two years or so. I frankly wouldn't remember you, man, but you were with one good-looking and classy head. You were arguing, if I recall. I decided at the time that I wouldn't waste time arguing with her. She was worth the soft touch, if you know what I mean."

Chip's response was memorable. "Oh, Mrs. Uppity Bitch, the lady who didn't want to talk to me! I knew her from Chicago when she was married to the big mattress guy—you know, one of those guys who is on television all day and night talking about his four kinds of mattresses priced at the lowest prices in town. I did some work for him. He was a good guy but had alcohol and gambling problems. I used to place bets for him. It was a great job. She was always trying to stop his gambling. You know there was talk around his death. He normally didn't drive when he was drinking. I would have driven him on that night, the night he died, but I got a call that someone had broken into my apartment. I told him to stay at the club, and I would pick him up later. Instead, he drove himself. That was unusual, so I got this chance to ask her about it, and she blew me off. She said I was never to approach her again, or she would say that I had tried to touch her. Man, I don't need that kind of trouble. You know I'd never be able to work here again, if she created that kind of trouble."

"What would make her threaten you with trouble, Chip? So she was previously married to an alcoholic gambler. No big deal. Why would you think for a minute that she would create trouble for you? I heard that you were at other venues with her, and you approached her." This wasn't true, but he said it anyway. "Give it to me straight."

Chip told Ash, "You know she's dead. She's that broad who was killed in a one-car accident in West Side a couple of years ago. Hard for me to believe; she was pretty careful about taking care of herself. I just asked her what really happened to Big Ted, her husband, and she got all wild and angry. Well, that made me wonder. Did she have anything to do with his demise? I approached her several more times, hoping to throw her off her game. I told her that it was pretty convenient that for the first time in fifteen years, Big Ted drove himself that night after a few drinks. Then she threatened me. I don't like people thinking they're better than me. I used to cover up for her husband to protect him from the press. He was well-known, and the press would have loved to get seedy stuff on him. So then she thinks she's too good to talk to me? Pisses me off, I tell you. And I still think there's something there. Her car! When did Big Ted ever do errands for Leana? I couldn't imagine him taking any car in for service. There was something there, I tell you. Did you know the clerk who told him the car repairs were done only worked there two days and then left a week after the accident, with the excuse that he thought he was going to be fired? The insurance company investigators couldn't find him later for his deposition. Turned out when he was hired, he used stolen papers. At least, that's what I heard."

"Are you trying to say that Leana hired someone to do away with her husband?"

"All I'm saying is something smells there. I've never understood why the car dealership didn't push an investigation. Instead, their insurance company made a big payout. Although I do know the dealership was owned by one of Big Ted's friends. Maybe a settlement was better for the owner than an investigation."

Ash got Chip to talk more about political campaigns, and he made a date to see him again for a drink at a local bar the following week after requesting his address, so that they could meet at a place nearer to him. Ash would not be there.

# 24

# Attorneys Search the Lonergan Home

NORBIE AND STEVE STARTED their search in Leana's walk-in closet, which Steve remarked was the size of a two-car garage. Even Norbie thought that his wife, who had quite a collection of clothes at home, would be envious of the stash of stuff in this closet. Norbie went through all the pockets of all dresses, slacks, jackets, and coats, looking for stuff. He then dumped the contents of all fifty-five handbags and evening bags, all loaded with junk—the same habit used by every woman he ever knew. Leana never completely emptied a purse after using it. He disposed of all the tissues left in the purses except for one with writing on it; just like his wife, if there was no paper, she would write on tissue, and even on her wrist, if it was important.

While Norbie went through all Leana's clothes, Steve worked on her computer. He also noticed that she had a locked desk. The desk was truly beautiful and had two deep drawers on each side and one slimmer one in the middle. The middle drawer's lock controlled locking the other two drawers. The top was clear of any item except for the computer and a decorative statute of two lovers; he realized it may be a copy of one he'd seen in a museum. This extension to the couple's bedroom had all the dressers and cabinets belonging to Leana. He would attack those drawers next.

The other side of the bedroom had an office for Gar. The desk was loaded with papers and had a small laptop sitting on it. He wondered whether Leana's desk always looked so clean compared to Gar's, and so he went out to the great room and asked Gar. Gar said that Leana was generally very neat and very private. When asked about her locked desk, Gar said that her desk was an antique French desk that had cost him over twenty thousand dollars, and he didn't want to break the lock; he had not yet gotten around to having a locksmith rekey it. "I haven't gone near her stuff. I want it all to be over; but we don't always get what we want, do we?"

Steve said that the lock was a simple one, and he could easily open it with a paper clip and a binder clip. Gar said to go ahead and joined Steve in her office, because Steve wanted him in there when he opened it to inspect the contents.

It took about forty seconds for Steve to open the lock and access all the drawers. Inside were piles of papers, a cell phone, and a key ring. Gar had not yet given the two men Leana's key ring. He went into his bedroom and retrieved it. Most of the keys on this ring were very different from the newly discovered ring. Steve said that one of the keys on the new ring was certainly a post office box key, and one was a bank safety deposit box key. He and Gar started looking at the papers from the desk drawer.

Norbie joined them at that moment with a stash of junk from Leana's clothes from the closet. He laid the stash out on the top of one of her dressers, which was clear of decoration other than a tall, beautiful lamp. He saw that the other two men had what looked like a scoop of info, and so he left his stash to join in any discovery made. There were her local bank statements, and Norbie had seen many of them before, but not all of them. There were statements from a MATLR trust whose balances were staggering. There were also bills for the post office box and a list of contents in the safety deposit box. They also found her and Timothy's birth certificates, her baptismal certificate, her Bachelor's degree, all her marriage certificates, several prenuptial agreements with former husbands, her former husbands' death certificates, copies of all her former husbands' trusts, a copy of an agreement and a check for fifty thousand dollars from an attorney in San Francisco, attorneys' letters with copies of legacies awarded to her from a couple of her previous husbands, a list of donations made to various charities (with one for abused children that showed more than ordinary amounts), several threatening letters dated some months before she died, and two threatening letters dated even earlier. They found a poem written by her when she was twelve years old. Gar read it aloud and teared up, saying, "Too bad this little girl had to go the other way." The poem was just two stanzas long.

You all died, and Timothy and I have our chance
To live like normal folks, to sing and to dance.
We were happy to be together, but not alone.
Yet we found that even with an ice cream cone,
The cream may have a nut with a sharp lance.

The lance then tries to stab you when you're down.
You have to watch out for you both—no smiling, just frown.
If you look happy, he will take your dream apart.
He's your new brother, but watch him with a start
To protect yourselves from his squeezing your crown
Of thorns!

Norbie wanted to know if they all agreed that Leana was talking about her stepbrother Jason, and they did.

Steve said, "I wonder if she was being paranoid? Maybe she was on the money with this guy. Let's look at the paperwork in here and see if there's any connection to him. Gar, did she ever talk about him to you?"

Gar said no. In fact, he knew nothing about Jason at all, but that was not surprising because he knew almost nothing about her life in general. Norbie told Gar to return to the great room; it was best that he didn't have more information about Leana at this time.

Norbie then suggested that he and Steve each take a pile and inventory them as to importance; each would verbally explain what was important and decide what to do with them. "Remember, we are looking for credible evidence that someone had it in for Leana. Look for that kind of stuff."

Norbie then went through all the dresser drawers. He left the room to ask Gar if Leana kept any stuff anywhere else in the house, and he was told she had a locked hope chest in the basement—one of the few pieces she'd brought with her when she'd moved in. Norbie requested that Steve break it open while Gar was in the basement. Norbie and Steve would inspect the contents after they went through the desk drawer contents.

The basement was beautifully finished, and Leana's New England hope chest did not go with the contemporary furniture. Therefore a unique modern tapestry had been thrown over it. When opened, the chest revealed files, neatly organized and going back to Leana's and Timothy's childhoods. Norbie had to decide what to do. After he went through everything, he would have to decide where to store it all. If Gar were charged, the police would get a warrant to search the home. He had absolutely no reason expressed by the police that they were looking at Gar, but Norbie's instincts were sending him signals to protect as if they were.

Norbie told his client that he was going to remove all the files and personal stuff, examine them, and then dump anything that was not relevant to his defense unless he had use for some of it. He would see whether the safety deposit box and the post office box were still paid for. If there was anything of value in the safety deposit box, he would give it to Gar. He reminded Gar that he would have a witness with him when he opened both items. Gar said that he trusted Norbie and didn't think that it was necessary.

Norbie said, "It *is* necessary. I need a witness for what I do, for my own protection."

He again advised Gar about discussing anything related to the case with anyone; he specifically said *anyone* over and over. "Anyone includes family and friends." With that said, the two attorneys began the process of removing records.

Two hours later, Norbie, Steve, and Sheila, Norbie's secretary, opened the post office box to find about thirty letters. The latest stamped mail date was about fifteen months after Leana's death. Leana had paid for the box five years out. The trio then met with Gar at Leana's bank, and after proving that all the proper authorizations from Leana's heir, Gar, were there, they were given access to the box.

A first look at the contents took away their breath. There was a mass of beautiful jewelry, including three enormous diamond solitaires. Under the jewelry was a manila envelope. They removed the manila envelope but decided to leave the jewels and left the bank for the office.

# 25

# Surprises, New York City, 1996

LEANA WAS ENJOYING A beautiful sunny day walking in Central Park. She was quite pleased with her new situation. Aaron would do for a husband, and she truly hoped that she had reached the designated point of contentment in her life designed by Ernestine's God. She was very comfortable in their extravagant condo and had found work that she valued but that didn't require her total efforts; it would not drain her spirit and zest for life. Perhaps she may have found some balance. After all, she was at the hair salon at 7:30 in the morning, enabling her to be at work at nine. All was going well, and she saw no rocky road ahead.

Leana headed for Bryant Park. One of her associates had said a jewelry craft show had about five tents set up, and there were silversmiths there who were selling their own work; although priced quite high, they were beautifully designed. Leana grew up in the Lake Placid community, and she remembered Ernestine telling her that handcrafted work was always the best because it had spirit in it.

As she approached the first vendor who was actively trying to engage passersby, she heard someone call her. "Mary Lou? Mary Lou, I can't believe I'm seeing you after all these years!" She shivered, feeling a sliver of fear slicing through her heart. She turned to face Jack Leahy in the flesh, looking quite well after twenty years.

Leana felt a sheath of absolute and distressingly overwhelming anger. It took over her body, and she blushed—not from embarrassment but from almost uncontrollable rage. She felt his sexual interpretation, or what he thought was his insight into her, and she thought, *You completely misunderstand.* The fool thought that she was thrilled to see him. He moved over to hug her. She put her hands directly in front of him, which kept him from moving forward.

With a big smile, Jack said, "Don't tell me you're not as happy to see me as I am to see you. You look wonderful—actually, incredibly beautiful and very well coiffured. Not the college girl I remember, Mary Lou."

Without thinking, she said, "Jack, my name is not Mary Lou, so please don't say that again."

He stepped back to take a broader overview of the situation. "So you're not happy to see me again. I thought that you understood the situation when I left. Look, you were a kid. You weren't ready for my lifestyle then."

Leana noticed the wedding ring on his left hand, and as her eyes stared at his hand, she said, "Well, you finally settled down, Jack. That was not supposed to be part of your game plan."

With one of his infectious laughs, he said, "No, it wasn't, but it was one of her game plans, without which I couldn't get what I wanted."

"So you married. Do you have kids?"

He answered that he had twin boys who were twelve, and he asked her if she had children.

Her answer surprised her. "Well, almost, but I lost the baby." She realized that she had never acknowledged to anyone that she had ever been pregnant, and that by saying it aloud, she was letting go of a secret. She believed in keeping secrets. She thought letting others know her secrets was risky, almost dangerous.

Jack gave all the silly condolences that people give when hearing of another's loss without having the least bit of knowledge of the circumstances. She almost laughed at his pretense of kindness. Now she really could see herself in his eyes: pretty little college girl who was in love with him—and now maybe he could have another fling. No, she would be in control, and she would cause him some pain. Let him feel something other than success at manipulating others.

Jack sensed that Leana was angry still, and he said in his most charming way that he would enjoy catching up on her life. He asked her to join him for lunch. She agreed and gave a beatific smile. Her smile reassured him that she was capable of being recaptured by his charisma.

They ate at a small Italian restaurant that was quieter than most. She did not let him order for her, as she had been in the habit of doing years before. She noticed his serious evaluation of her outfit and her manners. *Well, Jack, I'm my own girl now. Don't you think for a minute I'm not!*

He did tell her that she was quite the lady. Leana elicited his history and discovered that he currently was out of the public relations and advertising industry. He told Leana that he had sold his two agencies. Right now he had ownership in several businesses in New Jersey that were managed by their original owners. He had ended up in investing in businesses once he had made enough capital; she learned that he decided he'd rather do that than work too much. It was now time to enjoy life and take care of his health.

He asked her why he could not call her Mary Lou, and if not that name, then what name. She said that she had changed her name to Leana because it more correctly fit her lifestyle.

He said, "Leana? What is your last name?" She answered it was Goldberg, and a strange scowl crossed his features before he recovered. "Leana. I have to get used to that name, although it is a pretty name and more fitting to your persona. Is your husband Aaron Goldberg?"

Leana realized that despite the city's size, coincidence had reared its ugly head. Without showing her disturbance and without even the slightest hesitation, she told him yes and said, "Why? Is he your attorney, or perhaps he handles trusts for you? He does for most of the Hasidic community and for those who are particularly savvy in international finance. I must say, I wouldn't have thought that he would be your choice for an attorney. Together, you two would exude too much mutual testosterone! Don't be insulted; we women also have testosterone, and surely someone who's as sexual as you are got a good dose of it from the gods."

"Do you live in Brooklyn, Leana? I somehow can't imagine you in Brooklyn. You're an East Side town girl. How well do you know Jake Rubin and Alfie Stein?"

The question was startling because she had not mentioned either man. Her brain raced about what she knew and what maybe Jack knew. It was a time to be careful. "I went to university with Jake. He was such a nerd. I know a Stein woman who makes wigs for the Hasidic women and cancer patients. Is she related to Alfie Stein, Jack? If he's her husband, then I may have met him in her shop."

She met his eyes while noting that Jack was inspecting her face, probably looking for evidence of deceit. She thought, *He's not the only one who can deceive.*

He lowered his head and said in a whisper, "If you meet them with your husband, do not talk business. Have nothing to do with their business. Do you understand me?"

Leana almost screamed out loud at his arrogance. *Imagine his thinking that I will still listen to every suggestion he makes. He's no longer my mentor.*

Instead of expressing her real thoughts, Leana replied earnestly, "Jack, Aaron is a trust lawyer and a Hasidic Jew. I have no reservations about his business. And as to Jake Rubin, he is an awesome investment counselor to very important clients. I really don't know Alfie, but his wife is the best. Have you had business dealings with them? Please share your concerns, and maybe I will be able to understand your reservations."

Leana realized that he had ordered another glass of wine for them without her permission. It annoyed her to no end, but she was after other game, and so she let it go.

"Well, I am unable to share concerns with you, now. But I'm telling you that I will be contacting you in the near months, and you will want to talk to me then about their business dealings. I had some dealings with Alfie and Jake, but never with your husband. Those dealings put me in a spotlight that I didn't want. Thank God my wife's family is so powerful. They were powerful enough to prevent my being brought in, except for information. Until today, I didn't know you were married to Aaron, and nobody else knows. But that information will be out there for all to see shortly after today, and it will cement the two's connection to Aaron. It's probably best that we don't see each other again, for your own sake."

She looked at him and with the haughtiest tone she could muster said, "Don't worry, Jack. We'll never see each other again!" Then she walked out of the restaurant.

Leana had difficulty deciding between calling Aaron, Alfie, or Jake—or all three. She walked for a half hour thinking about what must be going on. No decision might be the worst decision for her. Also, she knew that whoever was trying to make connections among the three had to be a governmental agency, and she would eventually be brought in as a wife. She knew she could not afford a careful look at her history.

*Think like a manager,* she told herself. In the end, there really was no choice. Aaron would want to know personal details about Jack and would eventually hold it against her, and he would talk to the other two. Jake knew finances; that was his gift. He could threaten, she thought, but he was not the bad-ass guy. Alfie was the one, but she could not get to Alfie without leaving a record. Leana called Sarah, Alfie's wife, and asked if she could come for a fitting for a wig.

Sarah greeted her, and they had some girl talk while Leana got fitted for a wig priced at $5,700, for which she would get a 15 percent discount. It was to be in a light brown and blonde color. While she was being fitted and making decisions, she shared with Sarah her conversation with her old colleague, Jack Leahy. Sarah could not hide her awareness of Jack Leahy, although she tried. Leana pretended not to notice and instead said, "Jack must have been in trouble financially or something, because he seemed to be inferring that my marriage to Aaron was important information, and I could be hurt by it. He didn't want anything to do with me. What a jerk. Can you imagine that I once worked with him? Have you ever heard his name before?"

Sarah said that she had heard of Jack Leahy; he had invested in some major real estate in Manhattan that later burned down and was under investigation. Two people had died in the fire. There was a large mortgage on the property, which Leahy had been having trouble paying. "I mean a *big* mortgage, Leana. A mortgage of over 25 million. The building was insured for over 150 million. Leahy's probably a thief."

They talked for another hour, and Leana left the shop knowing that the info was in good hands and would be passed on.

Two weeks later, Jack Leahy died, the victim of a mugging. She did not cry. She did not wonder. Some things simply happened in life at a convenient time.

# 26

# Inventory Control

After returning to Norbie's office, Norbie, Steve, and Sheila took about two hours to sort the items from Gar's house. Sheila carefully documented every item on a spreadsheet developed according to Norbie's strict standards. He ruled paperwork with an iron hand and would say before anyone could argue, "Document as if we're going to court tomorrow and you need to be able to quickly access all data."

Unusual for attorneys, Norbie loved the ability to sort by different headings: date, description, rule of law, evidence level, et cetera. Once he learned it could be done easily on Excel, Sheila became the expert at the software and at teaching Norbie what he needed to know to improve a document and more easily access info.

Next, they opened the letters from the post office box and documented dates, content, sender, and more. Finally, they opened the manila envelope taken from the safety deposit box. It contained a long letter from Leana to whoever found the envelope. Its contents were a revelation and as close as Leana could come in sharing her secrets. It was typed on a high grade of paper; dated February 20, 2015; and signed.

To whoever may read this letter,

I must have passed. I assume that it is you, Gar, reading this because I left the key to my safety deposit box locked in my desk. I imagine that you would not discover it immediately, knowing your genuine good manners and desire not to invade my space. I hope it is you reading this letter because I want you to understand that my bequest to you has hopefully demonstrated, in the only fashion I know, how greatly I respect you. If I could allow myself to feel extraordinary emotions such as love and devotion, then you would be the direction for such feelings. I know that I am different from most people. I am afraid that you may know that now. I do not apologize for my actions, dramatic as they may seem to be to you. I have acted as well as I could have given the life circumstance I have been forced to face. I never harmed anyone who did not set out to harm me or mine first, or who was not an immediate danger to me or mine.

Perhaps if you have by now received some knowledge of my life, you may think me evil. Let me tell you that there are levels of evil, and I acted with malice when I was faced with malice, deceit, and lack of loyalty. I never acted without reason. You are an honorable and kind man who will probably go to your grave lacking insight into my actions.

Remember that you and your children were never at risk. Neither were the children of my second husband. Neither were my brother Timothy and his girlfriend. I discriminate when I act out.

This letter is not a confession. I will not acknowledge any past sins—first because I don't believe in sin, and second because you would bring that knowledge forward and jeopardize your family. I do not countenance foolishness in the name of doing the right thing. There is only situational appropriateness.

I hope that the financial settlement you will have already received will be used by you and your family. Remember to support those like myself who, though jaded, were treated so badly that it is amazing we are able to wake up each day and bring positive feelings to many people.

I myself do not fully understand the ups and downs of most people's minds—not even yours, Gar. I woke every day of my life with one thought, and that was how I would survive the day. If during that day I could do more than survive, then it was an extraordinary day.

For every new situation I entered, my motive was to find safety, security, some comfort, and maybe contentment. For all my experiences in dealing with negative people, I still was not always able to foresee disloyalty and deception in others. I advise you to look deeper into the actions of others before you lay your trust again.

My final request to you is to please contact the police if my demise is other than from normal medical ills. I am currently quite healthy; I have no chronic diseases. Therefore if I die suddenly in an accident while crossing the street, or in a mugging, or in a car accident, or from a tree branch falling on my head, do not for a minute believe that it is accidental.

I have recently settled satisfactorily with one person who knew of my past. However, I have received several threatening letters stemming from my past, and I believe the threats are serious. I think the police should look at my background in Memphis, Savannah,

New York City, Chicago, California, Lake Placid, and New Hampshire when searching for my killer. Some letters came through my post office box. Two came to our home. The phone calls came to our landline. Those are my leads.

Now I say goodbye, and thank you for your love, which I have been incapable of returning.

Leana

Sheila said, "I think that this is one of the saddest letters I've ever read. I know that my take stems from my Catholic foundations, but Leana was a tortured soul. I don't believe she could have stopped herself, so maybe there is less responsibility. I know she was a killer and surely was some sort of sociopath or psychopath. I don't know the difference myself; she appears to have been somewhat self-aware of her problems. However, she really wasn't sorry for anything she did, and she always blamed it on her situation. Although, Norbie, you notice she says that she wasn't always able to recognize negativity in others. Maybe the sociopath can't recognize another sociopath. If that's true, the rest of us are really in jeopardy. I'm telling you, guys, this job brings me to some really low levels in people's lives."

Now that everything was documented, Sheila left the conference room. Steve was the first to state that the letter could be turned over to the police because it clearly demonstrated that Leana had no fear from Gar and was pointing to others if she died suddenly.

Norbie agreed but pointed out, "Leana believed that Gar had no information about her past domestic lives. Her letter was dated February 2015; Gar had already received some info from Jeffrey Find's investigation into Leana's life by then. It doesn't leave Gar off the hook. Helpful, Steve, but it may be a double-edged sword."

They looked at the correspondence from the post office box. There were several letters from a woman in New York City named Carly Calderon. It appeared that Carly served as an administrator for Leana's business dealings and would send only relevant summaries of her work to Leana's post office box. Most of the letters had to do with changes in investments and signature requirements for various documents. She referenced the MATLC trust, but she also referenced other trusts from which she listed her transferring checks to the MATLC trust. She listed them under the list for checks that she endorsed for deposit with Leana's name on it. She included three threatening letters that were sent to her to forward, and she was concerned about how anyone could have found out about her and her location. A later letter said that she had changed her office address and phone number, hoping that that would stop the threatening letters; there were a very limited number of people who now knew how to contact her.

There was a letter dated Christmas 2015 from Timothy Prior, Leana's brother, and it was heartbreaking in its simplicity and sadness. It read, "You have not visited me as you promised. It is the first time you have missed, but I know what it means. I know you must be dead. I miss you. I'm okay. Maybe you'll read this from heaven. I'll be all right. You did a good job protecting me. Thank you, Mary Lou. Love from your brother, Timothy. P.S., I hope you didn't suffer."

The final piece of correspondence was from a company in California requesting confirmation on information that a Mary Lou Prior, aka Leana Goldberg, was now Leana Lonergan. Carly had attached a note saying that the logo of the company was bogus. This letter was dated early September 2015, before Leana's death.

Finally, Carly sent a letter saying, "Per your instructions, this is notice that I have closed all businesses after I discovered notice of your death, and I have notified your trust attorney. I attached and sent to him the newspaper article on your death, along with other documents necessary for him to proceed."

Steve said, "What the fuck? She's sending a letter to a dead woman. What's the purpose of that, do you think, Norbie?"

Norbie's only response was that Leana probably thought that Gar would know all about Carly from some of the documents in the desk, and when he saw this letter, he would know that everything was as Leana had instructed. "She was nothing but thorough."

The two attorneys then started to review Leana's history of marriages. It took three more hours. They wondered how any one woman could move to a new area and so easily establish herself as a professional. She apparently had no difficulty obtaining well-paying jobs using references from previous employment, all showing a stunning work history. Each of her marriages left her in better financial health, and she socked most of it away in banks, later moving all her money to the MATR trust. This move didn't happen until shortly before her marriage to Aaron Goldberg.

There was an employment contract with Carly Calderon, made before Leana went to Chicago. The focus of all her records was to give a trail of her life, but not to give insights into it. She did write a note describing how she truly distrusted the following: everyone in the Haylor family outside of George's sister Martha; everyone in Savanna outside of her friend Myra, and in particular Myra's husband; everyone in Chicago; her stepbrother Jason, who had recently gotten in touch with her; her sister-in-law in New Hampshire and her goonish friends; and any of her relationships in New York City excepting Aaron's family, who she said were good people. She said that her stepchildren from her Memphis marriage were special, as were Gar and his children.

Norbie couldn't believe this treasure trove of detail so devoid of emotion. Her remaining effects supported her having lived a high-end lifestyle. She had one hundred pairs of shoes with labels that were unknown to him other, than Jimmy Choo. She had five fur coats of different lengths and different animals. He knew about that, having shopped with his wife when she'd bought both a mink coat and a lynx coat.

Finally, there were a number of pieces of paper with telephone numbers with various area codes. Leana had a habit of jotting down numbers on ripped pieces of paper and never including the name connected to the number. Steve said that he would follow up. Norbie had some thinking to do about all this new information and in what directions he would move.

# 27

# The Detectives at Work

BEAUREGARD HAD NEVER BEEN busier. Ash's leads required the dogged work for which the police were most famous. Beauregard grilled Chip, the small-time hood or political gofer, for about two hours. It took almost an hour to impress upon him that this was serious business. He repeated the story he gave Ash with only a few little changes, mostly to increase his importance to Ted Sr. in Chicago. His story was consistent in his insistence that Ted Sr. was not about to run errands for his wife.

Beauregard asked, "So why this time?"

Chip said that Ted Sr. didn't want Leana to divorce him. He had said that she was too smart and would go after everything, and she knew where everything was. He inferred that the business was one thing, but there was a lot he had that no one knew about. Chip decided that maybe Ted Sr. was trying to be nice to her and offered to have her car serviced.

When asked why Ted Sr. wouldn't have had Chip take the car to be serviced, Chip replied, "Well, he didn't think I could be trusted with the car. I'd totaled his son's car a year before, and I could only drive when I was escorting one of them."

Beauregard ended the interview with his last question. "Chip, just whom did you tell back in Chicago about Leana being here in a new marriage?"

Chip tried to evade the question with the memory loss routine, but of course Beauregard persisted with veiled insinuations that Chip could be held for obstruction.

With a great deal of bluster, Chip admitted that he had been ticked off about Leana's treatment of him at the Iron Horse, and so he'd told Ted Jr. and some of the hangers-on in Chicago who believed that Leana had interfered with their activities, especially their gambling activities, with Ted Sr. He finished with, "I don't think at this time any of them even think about her at all. Although there was talk about his hidden money cache, and they concluded Leana grabbed it all. Some of it was owed to his gambling partners, which could have been a problem for Leana."

Beauregard suggested that Chip remain in the area. If he had to be located, he would be held and charged. Beauregard didn't say for what Chip would be charged, but he said just enough to put a little fear in the lying bastard.

Beauregard then attempted to put the facts together on the accident. They had gone to ACI in Enfield, the construction company that had leased equipment to someone, and tested the vehicle in question. The company had fortunately had their insurer pay for all the damage and then picked up the money from the guy named Nick Latorska, so the company was more than reimbursed for the damage. The insurance company inspector had really good pictures of the damage, and so they had no trouble matching the damage to the on-site pictures they had at the scene. Even the tracks matched. There was an irregularity in the tires that showed in all the photos. They could prove that this vehicle was at the scene on that night and that there was no work authorized for any vehicle to be there. The source of the broken glass was now connected to the high-powered construction lights that required replacement. The lab had sent a piece of the glass to the source vendor and received a match.

Beauregard announced that the question now was, "Who is this

Nick Latorska, and how do we find him?" Chet and the owner of ACI agreed that the photo on the license looked exactly like the guy who'd presented himself, but the license was a forgery. They started looking in New York and New Jersey for a match to the photo. The detectives were grateful that this accident and murder occurred after 9/11. Before 9/11, the FBI couldn't use e-mail, let alone have an interactive base between states for license registrations. There was a national move from the federal government to establish fusion centers for information access among federal agencies and with state and local agencies. Massachusetts had the Commonwealth Fusion Center, and the detectives were excited about the possibility that there may be technology allowing a search for the questionable Nick Latorski, who was a person of interest.

Beauregard put Mason in charge of the contact and ferreting out whether what they wanted was available, and if so, what they had to do to get the info. Meanwhile, he said they could not sit around when there was still much to do. "We now know a great deal about Leana's past, but what is really known about her friends and colleagues here in West Side? Petra, have you done any research on her friends yet, and have you talked to your family? Leave Jim's family out of the conversation for now, and make sure that your family doesn't get suspicious about your questions."

Petra replied that she had held up on interviewing based on the other work they were doing and on Beauregard's request. "Don't you remember, Captain, you didn't want anyone to get suspicious until there was evidence of a crime? I'll start now."

Beauregard was slightly abashed when he realized he was the one who'd slowed her down. Normally no one could slow down Petra.

Ash immediately agreed to split the list of Leana's friends with Petra to speed the process, and she was grateful. She thought, *If only I could let him interview my parents ... But that would blow everything apart. Their loyalty would be to Gar, if they got wind that he was in any way a suspect. Mason always says that family and friends are family and friends, and you can never be sure that what they say is the truth about family and friends. Or at the very least, you can be certain that family and friends will immediately be informed that there are police out there questioning.*

Ash started calling, and the message was identical: "This is a follow-up on Leana Lonergan's accident. We are ready to close the case and need information for a final report. We are interested in whether you were in attendance at the West Side Country Club on the night of October 12, 2015, and have knowledge of what time she left the club."

That message would be their entrée to a visit with the contact if the conversation left them with any inkling that there was more information to be gathered. On their list, they had Leana's closest supposed friends, but based on their new knowledge of Leana's past, both detectives were certain that she maybe didn't let anyone get too close to her. They were particularly interested in whether she was talking to a particular individual before she left. The notes from the accident investigation were not telling. Finally, they wanted to know why she'd turned right, away from her home, instead of going left toward her home.

Ash and Petra made fifteen successful calls out of eighteen attempts. Of the fifteen calls, only four contacts recalled that night. One call to a Marjorie Evans resulted in what could be a new bit of information. Marjorie recalled that Leana had spent a great deal of time early in the evening talking to a new waiter, which was unusual for her. When questioned about the waiter, Marjorie said that he was older and had only been working for a couple of weeks, and then he'd left after Leana had died. He seemed to be nondescript but competent. Marjorie thought that the club normally had better luck with their employees; most wanted to stay in their jobs. She couldn't remember whether he had left after the dinner (which was a fundraiser) but before the late bar, when there were only a couple of wait staff needed. Usually, practically everyone stayed for the late bar at the club because generally it was the most fun.

Marjorie also didn't think that Leana was the type to visit her friends late at night. In fact, she said, "Leana took good care of herself, and that did not include visiting at one in the morning for a social hour. She'd more likely go home and go to bed."

Petra left Ash to finish up a report for the morning on the calls and to try the other three calls again while she visited her parents. She stopped for some gluten-free cookies at the kitchen restaurant in town, which she knew would make her parents ready to talk over coffee. *God forbid. How did they survive all their lives eating regular flour?*

In her mother's kitchen—and it was definitely her mother's kitchen, with herbs crawling up two walls in vertical planters where there was an abundance of light—Petra sat gossiping with her parents. They were more than pleased to have a few minutes with their daughter sans her new husband. She casually told them about work and then mentioned that they were closing the Leana Lonergan accident case. The statement made her mom and dad pause and say, almost in unison, "That's almost two years ago. How come it's just being closed now?"

Not completely lying, Petra said that the case had always been between two units, accident and major crimes, and so it was never closed because each unit was under the understanding that the other unit was doing it. "I don't think that it's uncommon in any business, Mom. After all, it was a strange accident, and there was a report by neighbors of strange lighting and trucks, so it had to be investigated for causes other than accident. You know Leana was never seen drunk and was a great driver. It was suspicious, but now the case is getting closed. We're just doing a last-minute review. Mom, what have you ever heard about Leana and Gar? Gar seemed pretty broken up when she died. Was he that broken up when his first wife died?"

Petra's mom replied, "Gar's first marriage was extraordinary by anyone's standards, and I think any woman who walked into a second marriage with him would have some difficulties. First of all, Petra, Gar brought home a woman who looked to everyone in West Side like a runway model with a high IQ and a regal profile. Leana did not look like a wife and mother, and she never pretended as such. Her manner was cool unless she was working to invite you into her presence. Don't think that she couldn't be charming; you'd be wrong. She had charisma, and I understand from people who worked with her that she could close a deal with a client in a heartbeat. So we understood why Gar fell for her. Why he married her so quickly without looking at the big picture, and without seeing that his daughter had such reservations, none of us could understand—except maybe your father."

She and Petra looked to Petra's dad, whose only response was, "Hell, honey, she was hot, and every guy in town considered Gar lucky. If the marriage had lasted, you'd all be wrong, and it worked out for a while. It was only toward the end that there seemed to be trouble."

Petra was not very interested in her father's hyper-masculine take on the world. "Tell me, Dad, what was the problem in the marriage?"

Without thinking carefully before responding, her father said that one of Leana's colleagues said she was getting phone calls from a caller who always left the same name, John Albert. Leana had decided it was a phony name, and to his knowledge, she never called back. That raised a red flag because Leana was great at returning calls, even difficult ones. Also, the firm's offices were on the first floor of a commercial building and faced a large driveway next to the parking garage. Leana's office was one of the large ones facing the driveway, and she'd insisted that the same car was constantly driving by. Leana had asked this woman to watch for it when she was out of the office, and the woman did so. She got the plates for Leana; it was a rental car. "Maybe Leana was being stalked, maybe she had someone on the side that she couldn't get rid of, or maybe her past was catching up. A woman like that must have had a few loves in the past, don't you think?"

Her mother retorted, "And they think women are the only ones to gossip!"

Try as she might, Petra could not discover anything more about the couple, despite the fact that her mother knew many of the couple's friends and had been in many discussions with them after the accident. She left them clearing the cups and debating second marriages—with no thought to Petra being in a second marriage. She was motivated to follow through on Leana's colleague, whom her Dad had discussed. Unfortunately he couldn't remember her name. Furthermore, he didn't know her; he had simply heard about the conversation from someone else, and he could not remember who that someone else was. She understood that it was the police's lot to ferret out data from unknown sources told to people with no memories.

She called Beauregard and relayed her day's work, including her parents' conversation. He checked the file and said that there was a short interview with her colleagues at work after the accident, but the report said that one woman, named Lillian Jakes, was tearful throughout. He told Petra to head out there and talk to her, being as discreet as she could. He also said that he had already received the detectives' report from Ash, and so he had directed him to follow up at the club regarding the waiter who'd left so quickly. Beauregard had requested that Ash use the photo from the construction site for the alleged Nick Latorska for a potential match.

Petra was tired, probably from all the gluten-free cookies she'd eaten at her parents' house, and so she stopped her car at the famous Hoffington Park, where all the child murders had taken place. It seemed such a restful place for the inexplicable deaths of children. She stepped out of her car and tried some yoga stretches. Feeling better, she was about to enter her car when a familiar face walked by: Gar Lonergan. She couldn't see a way to avoid him; he was waving to her. Beauregard would not like this accidental meeting.

"Hi, Petra. How's married life going?"

She quickly talked about the adjustment in schedules and other innocuous tidbits, finally saying that she had to run because Beauregard was waiting for her. She hoped she wasn't too abrupt. It didn't feel right. It was not her norm for conversation—too little and no fun. Gar simply didn't look like a killer to her.

Petra entered Leana's former employer's firm and was impressed with the offices' ambiance. She knew that she shouldn't have been surprised with the quality of the setting; Leana would ensure that any space she spent time in was at the very least tasteful. Petra asked if she could speak with Lillian Jakes. She was lucky: Lillian was available. Petra gave her name but did not say she was from the police.

Petra was escorted to Lillian's office. She identified herself and provided the same story given to other potential witnesses about trying to close the accident case. Lillian did not question the lateness of the case closing but did ask her, "Do the police really believe it was an accident? I mean, I can't imagine Leana being careless in her driving. Leana drove like a pro and was always the designated driver when the gals in the office went for their bimonthly Friday after-work gathering at Theodore's Bar in Springfield. I mean, she was the best driver. She paid attention to details. Although a little speedy, her reflexes were the best. I've always been suspicious that this was not an accident. Is that why you're really here?"

Petra decided very quickly that all subtlety should be thrown out the door. God was speaking, she was certain. First was the inadvertent meeting with Gar, and now Lillian was ready to spill her guts on her feelings. She was going to go for it, and she hoped Beauregard would understand. "Lillian, I am interested in any reason you think that someone would want to harm her. It's very important before we close this case that we have all the facts. My captain did look at a report from you about someone perhaps stalking Leana. Could you give me some details?"

Lillian was expositive on her relationship with Leana and shared her feelings. "I may be Leana's closest friend, probably because I generally don't gossip. I'm talking to you because I don't feel good about what I know. I need to get it off my chest. I couldn't talk to Gar because I didn't want to be disloyal to Leana's memory. It probably sounds silly now, but I've never been certain that there weren't some problems in Leana's past."

Lillian went on to repeat the story of the car repeatedly going by the office in the weeks before Leana's death, as well as the repeated phone calls. She leaned toward the idea that these events, by themselves, may not be so important given Leana's ability to suck up desire in most men within twenty years of her age—in both directions.

"I mean, there really wasn't an opportunity for other women to attract attention when Leana was in the room. It unnerved a lot of women. Leana once said to me that a lot of attention was not the same as well-intended attention. I thought that was profound. So she was not easily put off by stupidity. But just before her death, Leana was awfully tense; every day she seemed nervous. I asked her about it, and she put me off until the Friday before her accident. We were at the bar, and she said that I must keep my eyes open for anyone coming into the office and asking about her when she was not there. That happened a lot, and so I questioned how I would be able to do it. She said, 'Not anyone from this area. If someone comes in saying he's from out of town and wants to engage us with a situation that looks too good to be true, or if someone comes in, wants information, and says that he's an old friend or a relative, contact me immediately and don't give him any info.'"

Lillian said, "The problem is that there was an older man dressed to the nines who wanted the firm to represent him and connect him to the area. He was representing big talent and was basically representing a national booking agency that would be working with the new gambling casino coming into Springfield in 2018. He looked like a CEO, like on television. Well, I was naturally excited and gave him information about all the firm's agents."

She explained, "I pushed Leana and myself because we often worked together on big-revenue producers."

She reported that Leana had a lot more experience in pricing for national agencies. Lillian told Leana that upon reviewing it, she realized that he was most interested in Leana and her background. He didn't call back, and so she never mentioned it to Leana until that night. He'd left his card, and she gave it to Leana.

Petra asked for a more detailed description, but the man described was not a fit for Latorska. The name he gave her was J. Ripor, and she was told to call him Jay. Lillian could not give more details.

Before she left, Petra reassured Lillian that if any of this checked out, they would be back. "You were a good friend, Lillian. You've done everything you could for your friend. Don't worry; it was just a terrible accident."

# 28

# Potential Defense Investigation

FINDING CARLY CALDERON'S LOCATION and phone number took some Sherlockian work, but after two days of searching, Steve discovered her identity under another name. Computers were great for discovering the whereabouts of people whom one know a lot about, such as social security number, real name, former work, and former home addresses.

In this case, success resulted in his connection to Leana when she was an intern in a public relations firm in New York City, where she later found her first post-university employment. He was told that there was a female colleague of hers who had graduated from the College of New Rochelle. The two were tight and were roommates at the firm's apartment. The gal's name was Carol Sampson. Somewhere in his brain, Steve discerned that Carol maybe shortened to Carly, and when he questioned human resources at the firm, his insight was confirmed. He could get no further help from the firm, but he felt lucky that he was given that information based on a legacy from Mary Lou Prior for her friend.

Given that info, Steve assumed that she was maintaining accounts from New York City and therefore may have been married in the city. He searched marriage records from his commercial investigative database; it was probably worth the annual sum he paid for its high speed and multiple database access. Carly had married a registered engineer named Brian Calderon. She'd had a baby girl before the marriage and then married Brian about six months after the baby was born. He deduced that Brian was probably the father. She now had five children in total and lived in Brooklyn. He found her address and decided that she would never open up in a phone call, and so he watched her house for a couple of days. She lived in a large brownstone in a ritzy area with a nice-looking older gentleman. He saw that she took care of a couple of babies sometimes, probably her grandchildren and probably twins. He waited until they were picked up at three in the afternoon before he rang the bell, knowing that her husband had come home the previous two days after six in the evening.

She opened the door, and her brown eyes glazed over immediately. He could see that she was hip to an unusual visitor. Probably she'd been trained by Leana, or perhaps by life, to be astute in dealing with strangers.

"Mrs. Calderon, May I come in? I am here to discuss Leana Lonergan, or Mary Lou Prior." He read to her from her letter that they found in the post office box.

She let him in and brought him into a minimalist decorated living room filled with plants at one end of the room and abstract art over the ten-foot wall at the other end. It was pleasant, and the furniture, although sparse, was expensive but comfortable. She asked him to be patient while she made coffee; she would need a cup after her stint at babysitting her twin grandchildren.

Carly returned in a few moments with a tray of goodies and some really good but strong coffee—just the way he liked it. He liked her immediately, but did not forget for a moment the reason he was sitting here with this nice, good-looking lady. She was the first to speak.

"I knew someday I would have to answer questions about Mary Lou, and it would be after she had died. You know that she felt she would not die a natural death. She told me many times that her destiny was not that she would live out her DNA's planned years. Am I in any kind of trouble for keeping her secrets? I mean, I haven't knowingly done anything wrong, other than to keep information from husbands, business associates, and other family."

Steve stated, "I'm working with another attorney, and basically I'm working for her. We are investigating her death. So one way to think about it is that we agree with Mary Lou: she didn't live out what was to be her natural life span. But please start at the beginning. We have all kinds of documentation, but it's not perfectly connected. We know all the ones she married, and that all but the last husband has died. We know that she had only stepchildren, of which just four seemed to have any meaning for her. We know that she became quite wealthy from legacies, her work record, and her investments. We want to know about her, Carly—her enemies and her friends. That means your relationship with her."

Carly cried. "She was the best friend I ever had. I was probably one of her few friends. She just had to trust you, you understand. You had to be loyal to her, and it was worth it because she was always loyal in return.

"Our early year together—well, more like a year and a half—was great. When Mary-Lou was an intern with the firm, she fell in love with one of the senior managers in the firm, and I didn't blame her because all the girls were in love with him. However, he only chose the best to—pardon my French—screw around with. He was fooling around, whereas Mary Lou was in love.

"He ended the affair. She seemed to take it well, but I know it hurt her badly. She told me that no man would ever be able to get to her again, and that she would be in any future relationship only for the advantages it offered. She also never talked about Jack Leary, the manager she had the affair with, except with repressed anger."

During Carly and Mary Lou's time together, they noshed. They discovered New York City and partied. "Mary Lou was the best companion and was always able to get into all the clubs. I had the most fun in my life during the time I spent with her."

Then Mary Lou went off with Georgie Haylor to San Francisco. Carly was surprised; she didn't see them as a finely matched couple.

She understood that Georgie had a drug habit because she saw him connecting at a bar one night in the Village. She mentioned it to Mary Lou, who said that a lot of young men dabbled in light drugs. Mary Lou said that she saw that practice among guys at college; but then she said they'd get over it.

Carly said, "I didn't like him, but Mary Lou was normally better at judging people than I was. I wasn't about to tell Mary Lou that the man she was in love with looked like a smooth jerk to me. Scratch that remark, Steve. I don't think Mary Lou was in love with Georgie. He was handsome, wealthy, and from a good family. She was in love with that. And he wanted Mary Lou. He certainly chased her."

After Mary Lou left, Carly fell in love with a guy who was also good looking and from a well-known and wealthy family. "Maybe it was something in the city water at that time, because there was a remarkable similarity between the two men. The difference is that I got in trouble, and Mr. Importance didn't want to marry me. I couldn't go to my parents. They would kill me and make me marry my high school boyfriend, who was carrying a torch for me. I called Mary Lou in California for advice."

Carly teared up again. She said that the day she called was a few days after Georgie had died. And on the day before he'd died, Mary Lou had had an abortion. Carly simply couldn't compute why someone who was married would have an abortion.

"Well, I couldn't believe it. I knew enough not to ask her; I'd have to wait for her to tell me why. Here I was wondering if I, a good Catholic girl, should get an abortion—and even if I wanted to, how could I get a safe abortion? Abortions were becoming available at that time, but I was not ready to share my pregnancy with anyone, and I couldn't trust anyone in my circle of friends about that kind of thing. Mary Lou said that she regretted her abortion, although she had no regrets about Georgie dying. I think that maybe Georgie died of a drug overdose. There was something suspicious about his death. The papers reported cardiac disease. I never believed that. And then Mary Lou saved me."

Mary Lou had sent Carly ten thousand dollars, which in 1972 was a great deal of money—enough to carry her through her pregnancy and pay for the baby. But more important, she retained a New York City attorney for Carly, who contacted the reluctant young man and his family and suggested that they pay lifelong child support or give Carly a large settlement. The attorney told Carly that she was never to talk to her boyfriend again. All conversation was to be with the attorney.

"I told Mary Lou that I didn't want him in my kid's life, and she told me not to worry; he would never want to be in that child's life. Despite that, she made certain that he would not be. If he came near the child, I was to report it to the attorney."

Within a month after her conversation, Carly received a fifty-thousand-dollar child care settlement, which was a windfall. Carly couldn't believe the turnaround in her financial health. She offered to repay Mary Lou the amount she had sent her, but the offer was refused. After that, for a while Carly only received Christmas cards from Mary Lou with cryptic notes of affection for Carly's baby, Angela.

Carly stated that she first met her husband when she was three months pregnant. She had left the public relations firm. She said that she couldn't face her colleagues' questions when her pregnancy would become apparent. She went to the marketing department of a research and engineering firm located on Fifth Avenue. Brian was an engineer in the firm. She said that he was now a partner, reporting Brian's success with great pride. Brian liked her immediately, but she was decidedly off men at that time.

"Funny thing, Steve! When you're not looking, you meet the right one. He never let a week go by without bringing me a coffee, or a pastry, or a new invitation to dinner. I would have normally believed it was funny and enjoyed the attention, but I knew that soon he would want nothing to do with me."

Carly was wrong. When she started to show, he cornered her one day and said, "Unless you hate men—and my vibes say you don't—your pregnancy is not a turn-off. Will you have dinner with me Friday? Just think about it. Don't say no immediately."

She eventually said yes, and a relationship started. He offered to marry her two weeks before the baby was born. She said that a marriage should not be about giving a baby a name; it should be about them. He moved in two months after the baby was born, after she'd faced her family's difficult acceptance of her situation.

As she told Steve, "I had faced my responsibilities, knew I could survive without help, and knew I was extraordinarily lucky to have Brian in my life. Angela thinks that Brian is her dad; he's the only dad she knows. At least, I think that. More than any of the children, Angela is devoted to Brian. I never told her, but Angela is a researcher and checks everything out, so maybe she knows more, but she wouldn't hurt our feelings by telling us."

Carly explained, "Secrets often bite you in the ass." She told Steve that she and Brian never celebrated their anniversary because they didn't know what date to use. The kids questioned them often and thought their avoidance was strange. Their son Devon told the other kids that Angela must have been an early baby, maybe born at five or six months. "Of all the kids, Devon has a smart mouth."

Steve encouraged Carly to continue with Mary Lou's life, and she did. Mary Lou had changed her name to Leana, and Carly agreed that Leana was more sophisticated and better suited her lifestyle. Leana asked Carly to get her mail from a post office box in Brooklyn after the death of her second husband. She explained that she didn't know where she would be next, and continuity in an address for her legal and investment contacts was important.

"She was willing to pay me an annual stipend for collecting her mail, opening it, logging it, calling her with the summary, and forwarding it to a post office box she would give me. I would also be reimbursed for postage and for the cost of the box in Brooklyn. The pay was good for the little work I did; it was all under the table. That was the only condition she had. She wanted no trail. I took it, but Brian made me save 50 percent of the fee just in case there were problems. After about five years, we didn't worry about it anymore."

Steve reminded Carly that he knew she'd actually had an office at one time and then changed to another office. Carly was clearly bothered that he had that information and replied, "How did you find out about the offices? After the death of her third husband, Leana became extremely secretive, almost paranoid. It became our new way of operating. I received expenses for a very small, one-room office in a high-rise—you know, a turn-key operation. She didn't want my children to get curious about my papers as they grew older. She said I needed to keep all records away from my home. It made sense.

"The work was the same, except for a few differences. The volume of mail was greater. Her investments were out of sight from my frame of reference, and she would get an occasional threatening letter. Those bothered me. They didn't bother her."

Steve asked what happened to all her mail and was told that in January of each year, Carly would normally tell Leana what to save from the previous year; the rest was to be shredded. He asked what was in the threatening letters, and Carly said they were all similar: "I know what you did. You will eventually pay. I'm waiting."

Carly said that the letters came only twice a year for quite a few years, but after she left Chicago, another type of threatening letter arrived. It called her a murderer. That was when Leana moved Carly's office and changed the post office box.

"I was disturbed because the move informed me that Leana was worried—not usual for Leana, who was always in full control. I asked if this letter writer was dangerous, and her response was that the man was a ghost from her past and wanted money, and that although he was a thug, he was not dangerous. She simply didn't want him to get any information.

"The office was not leased in my name. It was leased in a Delaware corporation name Lou-Lea, Inc., and had an EIN number. Neither mine nor her social security number was ever used. My husband, Brian, was impressed with Leana's attention to detail, and but for that, he probably would have stopped the questionable though lucrative arrangement. I have been paid a hundred thousand dollars a year plus expenses for the last twenty years. I really did not need the money at that time because Brian worked his way up financially, but I liked having my own money. Leana said that women need to be independent; not even the perfect husband can give peace of mind to a woman like financially independence is able to do."

Carly said she slowly began to realize just how many husbands Leana had lost. Leana never talked about most of them; Carly simply knew from legal correspondence sent to Leana with different last names. She received legacies from trusts and estates with Leana listed as the surviving spouse. The only husbands after Georgie—and she never discussed Georgie—that Leana acknowledged were her second husband, Harry, and her last husband, Gar. A few months before her death, she said, "I picked right only twice. I don't have a good average, and when you think that I probably know more about people more quickly than 99 percent of women, I'm flunking at picking the right man. In both of those good cases, they chose me. Maybe that's the secret, Carly. Remember, Brian chose you, not the other way around. Kind of screws around with the feminist theory that we should always have choice, don't you think?"

Steve searched Carly's memory on the history of all Leana's correspondence. He questioned if there was anything new in the post office box since Leana's death that she had not sent forward to the western Massachusetts post office box. Carly said, "No. In fact, I closed the box about a year after her death. You know that she left me a bank account—well, not in a formal way. She opened a bank account in my name and would have me make deposits to it from her trust; each deposit was authorized by an attorney. However, several months before her death, she deposited half a million dollars in my account. I knew then she had a problem.

"When she called next, I asked her about the deposit. She said, 'Don't use it until I die. I want to avoid causing you a problem when I die; this way no questions will ever be asked of you.'"

Carly had told her that she shouldn't talk like that, and Leana had responded with, "Not to worry, Carly. Planning is part of a life well lived. Don't you watch television?"

Steve spent another couple of hours with Carly. He believed every word she said. She knew nothing about the Hasidic community in Brooklyn, only that she would see them on the street at times. She said that she normally could not tell when Leana was happy or not, but in retrospect she could always feel her stress shortly before her husbands' deaths. Not that Leana ever discussed it.

Carly asked Steve, "Was Leana involved in her husbands' deaths? I just have to ask you that. I mean, that's a lot of men to die who weren't in their eighties."

Steve answered as cryptically as he could. "We'll never know."

# 29

# Who Could Have Killed Her?

NORBIE AND STEVE LOOKED at their respective notes and scratched their heads. Norbie said there were so many possibilities that he wasn't sure how to begin, and so he did what he always did: start with possible motives. The most common motives were included in the seven deadly sins: pride, greed, lust, envy, gluttony, wrath, and sloth. "We can rule out gluttony, I think. Let's look at the others. Certainly greed is a big one, but it doesn't help us in this case. Everyone would look at our client first because he benefitted most from her death.

"Maybe greed could point to others such as her brother, Timothy. But he is not greedy. He has lots of money, is well employed, and doesn't look for anything from anyone. Greed could also cast an eye on Gar's kids. After all, Leana would get a piece of Gar's pie if he died before her. They didn't know about her money; maybe they were just worried about his money. That won't help us. Gar would go to jail to protect his kid, just like my Russian client who said she was a serial killer to cover for her twelve-year-old daughter who was the actual killer. I'm not getting into another situation like that, Steve. Gar's kids are good kids. Besides, this was a planned killing, and most good people who kill do so in the moment, as self-defense or rage."

Steve broke in. "I agree, Norbie. Timothy isn't a killer, but because I don't know Gar's kids, I can't let go of that possibility. Let's look at sloth. There were a lot of lazy sloths hanging about her husbands. Maybe they're too lazy to work and tried to hit her up for money, and she told them to pound sand. If they were really angry, then revenge would look good. On the other hand, killing her in the way she died took planning and effort and a cash investment in renting the trucks, so I rule them out."

Norbie pulled out the lists of people the two hadn't liked when they were doing their history on Leana, and he reviewed her letter in which she gave instructions on whom to look to in the event of her untimely death. She had ruled out Don Turtolo but had said that her stepbrother Jason hated her.

Norbie said aloud, "Other than that poem she wrote when she first went with her adoptive parents, there's no mention of her stepbrother. We should follow up on that. Let's look at Jeffrey Hunt's investigative reports."

They found in the reports that Leana and Timothy's adoptive mother, Ernestine, left 55 percent of the residual of her modest estate to her natural son, Jason Prior of California. The remaining residual was to Leana after Timothy received a condo, bills were paid, and Leana received money for college.

Norbie reluctantly said, "I hope this isn't one of those cases where Jason hated his parents adopting other kids. Sometimes it happens. Leana certainly believed that Jason was a pain in the ass and may be trouble for them."

They both reviewed Hunt's investigative reports and thought that he must charge by the word. There was voluminous material on every item. Finally, they got to some details on Jason. It turned out he had become a residential developer in California, had done quite well, had three grown children and two grandchildren, and was widowed. The report said, "By all accounts, Jason is a difficult man about money. He is known in every court in the area, arguing over contract provisions that he puts in the contracts and that backfire on the unwary. It appears he has made a lot of money pushing people around. Not generally considered a nice man."

"Steve, why would Leana worry about Jason? He lives on the other side of the country and is in his seventies. Why would he harm her now, at this late stage of their lives? He's fifteen years older than her. What could make her worry that he would or could kill her? We should check his criminal history. Now, let's see if we can discover who among the associates of her many marriages would most want her dead."

Norbie worked for several hours, directing Steve. He attempted to collate only what was thought important in pointing to Leana's killer. In the review, he searched for her list of associations she didn't trust. She was specific in her distrust of anyone in the Haylor family other than her former sister-in-law Martha, which left only Mrs. Haylor, George's mother, who was by now pretty old.

Mary Lou also suggested that her associates in Savannah, not including her friend Myra, but specifically including Myra's husband, Mishel, were suspect. She suspected people in Chicago, California, New York City, and New Hampshire. Based on the list, Norbie concluded that the New Hampshire crowd was less likely culprits because Leana's ex-husband's business corporation went to the appropriate heirs.

Hunt's investigation covered Mishel Kortiac and described him as a small-time hanger-on with few skills. He was lucky enough to marry Myra, who was by all accounts a workaholic who had no idea what her husband was up to.

Mishel was a widower who'd married Myra about six months after his wife had died in an auto accident. He had just cashed in two hundred thousand dollars face life insurance policy, which had been doubled by her death from accident. He'd probably cried on Myra's shoulder, and she'd thought that he was a good choice for a husband. Hunt reported him as a major womanizer. Leana wouldn't have liked him. But why would he kill Leana? Was he blackmailing her? Was she going to tell Myra? Did he know something about the death of this Chissie, Leana's dead husband? They don't know enough about him or the other people in the other cities.

Norbie said, "I think we've done enough searching for now, and I know that the police probably know as much as we know—enough to explain why they haven't interviewed Gar yet. We have alternative theories. We have no proof. I need to speak with Gar. Maybe it is time to come clean with the police."

# 30

# A Visit Home, 2014

LEANA HAD HAD ENOUGH of the letters. It was one thing when they were sent to Lake Placid and then forwarded to her postal box, but now she was getting them at home. The sender or senders missed out on Memphis, but then letters came to Savannah, and Chissie opened one while she was gone from the house.

She was later greeted with, "Fess up, Leana. What kind of shit do you have in your past?" She put him off, but Chissie never let anything go. He thought that he might have an edge on her he could bargain with, which was problematic because they had been having difficulties.

The threatening letters again started in Wolfeboro, completely skipping New York City. How that happened, she didn't know. She had changed postal boxes, and maybe that had confused the writer. More likely, he had trouble bribing some postal worker in the big apple.

The particular individual from her past she was focusing on today was a problem. He had been annoying when she was young, and she couldn't imagine what he would be like today. Maybe he wasn't the only one behind the letters; she could think of a few others who could have written those words. Well, now was the time. It was time for her to go home, although to be truthful she never wanted to see this place ever again.

It was also time for her to review the record of the fire. What did the authorities think happened? Maybe all her worries were unfounded; she might find answers to relieve that reoccurring nightmare.

She started with the fire department records. The fire was so long ago. There were now three fire stations covering the area that once was covered in the 1950s by one station. She was sent to the station that stored pre-1970 records. Nothing that old was on digital storage. The department was moving backward and had digitalized back to January 1988. She had to wait thirty minutes for a young, handsome fire department intern to locate the box for her house fire. There were actually six boxes of records, plus evidence boxes. The intern told her that this must have been some fire.

Leana spent about two hours reviewing the records of the fire. There were inspectors, engineers, police reports, and reviews. She realized pretty early that they would never be able to say that the fire was anything but accidental. Also, it was clear that if the fire was set, there were a diversity of culprits. She went over the details of what the evidence showed. The summary was that Mr. Court tripped and knocked over the candle, and ignition of lighter fluid on the table was enough to start a rigorous blaze. *Sounds reasonable to me,* she thought. She and Timothy could rest easy now.

Leana next visited her early childhood address and was not surprised to see an ugly duplex built on the site. "Ugly was, ugly is," she said aloud to herself. Two doors down was the Butler home, but it had been rehabbed. The mailbox said Butler on it. She tried to remember how many siblings Burt Butler had and could only remember a much older sister. She needed more information, and because it was later in the day, she knew that she would have to wait until the next day to look at voting records at town hall.

*Okay, time to go the lazy route.* She spied five doors down, a newer and well-kept ranch house with a woman older than Leana by at least a decade, gardening. Covering her platinum hair with a designer ball cap, Leana walked up the street. She introduced herself as a member of the historic commission assessing homes in the neighborhood for their eligibility for façade grants.

The neighbor, who identified herself as Lydia Wade, was quite excited about a free façade, although she was certain that her newer built house would not qualify. Leana ask her how old her home was, and Lydia said it was one year newer than the duplex; hers was fifty years old, and the duplex was about fifty-one years old. Leana told her that anything fifty years or older old would qualify as historic. Leana took a sheet of paper from her bag and asked Lydia to tell her about the needs of the houses on her side of the street, which was the side chosen for the potential façade grants.

Lydia had a field day telling Leana about income, social, educational, and kindness levels of her neighbors. Leana was most interested in learning about Burt Butler, the son of Mary Lou's neighbor Mrs. Butler—the family who lived next door to her when she was called Mary Lou. The old bat had told the investigators all kinds of horrible things about her family. Leana thought, *They may have been true, but the old gossip was telling my and Timothy's story. She had no right to do that—it's our story.*

Lydia relayed that Burt, the son, lived in the family Butler home, was not overly friendly, took care of his property, worked for the US Postal Service, and was a genius at maintenance. In fact, just about everyone in the neighborhood paid for his skills a few times a year.

Leana asked for his contact info, saying that she had some maintenance jobs at her condo that needed work. Lydia pulled her cell phone and wanted to send the contact to her, but Leana said that she was in the process of getting a new phone, so she would write it down. It took another fifteen minutes to extract herself gracefully from the conversational Lydia.

While driving away, she decided to visit the Priors' home, her first real home with caring parents. She remembered how she'd felt when they'd first moved there. She was waiting for the temper tantrums, the drinking, the obscene actions, and the put-downs on Timothy. They never happened, unless Jason was home and the Priors were in the other rooms of the house. Jason was a born bully, and Leana knew all about bullies. The children couldn't squeal to the Priors about their older son; they may not have believed them. Besides, Timothy and she never would squeal anyway. Squealing simply let one in for more trouble. They had learned early that only they could be trusted to take care of themselves. Jason was a tortured soul, and that truly surprised Leana. How could one be a bully when one was raised by two such loving, good parents?

It was fortunate that Jason was fifteen years older than Leana. He was out of the house a few years after college, and in the next several years he had his own family. She wondered if California had treated him well. She had heard that he had done well financially. There was one thing she most assuredly knew, and that was his family life must have been stressful. She had heard he had three children. Jason, in addition to bullying, had no patience and was not kind. If she believed that prayers would have been helpful, she would have prayed for his children. Instead, she simply hoped that they could stay the course until they could leave their father.

Now she was heading back to Gar, a truly decent man—but decent men could hurt without knowing they were hurting. *Not the time to think of that,* she thought. *I have to do something about Burt. I'll gamble that my instincts about the letters are right. First I'll compose a letter to him without a name, posting it from Hartford.*

While she was making a hard, unexpected left turn, her subconscious kicked in with a very good thought. *Why not send a similar letter to all my past difficult personal encounters? Perhaps fishing the waters will turn up something.*

Leana measured every possible result for unexpected returns from the sent letters. She knew that she was playing with fire, but these letters had put a crimp in her life before, and she wasn't about to let that happen again. Some of the recipients of her potential letter were criminally oriented, and a cryptic letter from an unknown source may not be new to them. Burt was evil, but more in a sneaky and bullying way. He'd like to have her under his thumb, and as long as one didn't live with him, one was safe from violence. *Maybe that isn't true. Maybe it was true of the little boy I knew, but not of the man he has become.* His employment with the postal service screamed out his ability to discover her locations. The others she considered as possible senders were more sophisticated with other means of locating her.

While thinking of the means to locate her, she understood that a search by her social security number would find each employer. That was always a risk—one she was willing to assume. But how the sender was able to get her post office box number was more problematic for her. It wouldn't matter where she ran to; the sender had inside knowledge.

Burt Butler, the bully from her childhood, worked for the postal office, which in her mind was indicative of a possible access to her postal information. Perhaps he had associates in Lake Placid who could see mail sent out by Timothy to a post office box. She thought of some other possibilities. She found herself furious and overheated—not good for her. In the past, she had acted too quickly from uncontrolled rage. She hoped that she had learned a lesson from those actions.

She thought of that idiot car mechanic in Chicago and wondered. Then she thought about a few other former contacts. She didn't worry about Don Turtolo, but he did open the flow of information about her back to Chicago, and that was not a good thing for her. She was sorry that she had been unable to keep her relationship with Myra Kortiac. That loss was truly regretful, but Misha Kortiac was an untrustworthy male whore who would sell his mother for a dollar. He was also pretty smart, which made him more dangerous. She needed to weed out who was stalking her, and it may be more than one devious individual.

She was now in front of the Priors' old house and was enveloped with an overwhelming sense of safety and calm. Ernestine and Lester had given Timothy and Leana comfort they had never known before, and she would be forever grateful to them. The house must have good people in it now. It was as well cared for as she remembered. Lester was always fixing up his homes. He often said, "You can often tell if residents in a home are happy. If they're taking care of the property, it's the first good sign."

Leana thought, *Lester never understood the wealthy, who had someone else take care of their property but who were themselves bastards to the people with whom they lived. One concept has nothing to do with the other.*

She envisioned Timothy and her early lives with the Priors, and she teared up. The only worm in that life had been Jason. In fact, she had often thought that the Priors had adopted her and Timothy because in their hearts, they were disappointed in their biological son. She remembered overhearing arguments with him during his trips home from California—arguments always about money. Jason always needed money for some project, and Lester argued with him about gambling.

The Priors had never adopted the other foster children despite their long stays with them. She had met them all, and they were good people. Nostalgia overtook Leana again, and she allowed herself a good cry. Finally she said to herself, "Close that door." She did so and headed home to Gar.

# 31

# MCU Reviews and Reviews Data

THE DEPARTMENT'S FAVORITE NON-AREA resident district court judge was sitting when Mason filed for the warrants. The judge was easily satisfied with the department's reasons why. Perhaps Mason could reserve the element of surprise. Mason suggested that it would be helpful if the warrants were kept under wraps; the judge wiggled his index finger and said, "Of course, as always." Mason figured that this judge wouldn't be gossiping about the warrants, but there was no certainty that some court personnel wouldn't view the warrants, and there went any surprise. Mason was almost immediately ashamed of that thought. *Most of those folks are professional and can keep their mouths shut.*

Armed with the warrants, Mason left immediately to open the postal box. *Surprise, surprise!* He discovered that the postal box had been closed just a week before.

He called Beauregard, who said, "Damn that Norbie Cull. You're not going to find anything. If he closed the box, then he's probably moved everything else. If we don't serve the other warrants we have, then the squad will later suffer scrutiny that I don't want. If we do serve them, we'll get nothing. Hell. Mason, get a couple of uniforms and try for the computer. Definitely search the house. Try to be inconspicuous. Tell the uniforms to shut their mouths and park their squad car where it can't easily be seen. The neighbors will think there's been a break-in, and we'll get a hundred bogus calls. Gar's got about five acres there, and the house is pretty secluded. Should be okay.

"Call me when you're ready, and I'll call Gar to inform him the search is about to happen. Norbie Cull should be there about five minutes after you're there. Tell Gar that he may come in and talk with me at any time. If anything, we'll start the ball rolling. We're going to solve this case."

Petra walked into the ongoing process of another of Beauregard's reviews of case data and knew immediately that she was now faced with looking at details and attempting to work forward. She remembered her philosophy professor, who had taught her logic and said over and over, "You can't go from the particular to the universal." Well, he was never a cop; that was all they ever did. One detail at a time connected to the next detail, and maybe a picture could be formed. *I have to admit that sometimes it seems that picture was chosen ahead of time, and then there is a selection of details used that would maybe draw that picture. Not with the Captain. No, he didn't work like that.*

"Well, Captain, what are we looking for today?" she asked.

His vague answer was, "I'm moving data into columns—you know, interviews, scene evidence, records, personal information per records and per interview, pictures ..."

Beauregard stopped talking, looked at Petra, and banged his head with his right hand. "What the fuck? Am I losing it? Pictures, pictures, pictures. We need pictures, Petra! We need pictures of everyone."

They started with photos in the files. Unfortunately, there was a dearth of photos. Beauregard said, "We have the photo of Nick Latorski, who is probably not Nick Latorska. We don't have a photo of Leana's stepbrother, Jason, or a photo of Myra Kortiac's husband. Petra, you and Jim interviewed Peter Fraine, Fred Fraine's brother. Does this guy resemble him at all?"

Her answer was, "Not at all, Captain. Let me look at Latorski's photo again. You see, he's trying to look tough here, but that's a really high-end haircut he has. Tough guys don't have such a coiffeur. Maybe he's not the hood type; maybe he's a dude type, as described by the pharmacist from Wolfeboro. Can we get a photo of her stepbrother, Jason, Captain? We haven't researched him at all."

Beauregard said, "Great idea." Then he told Petra to call California for the brother's driving photo, and also Georgia for Misha Kortiac's driving photo. He then said to Petra, "Mason was supposed to request a national data search for this photo. Ask Millie if anything came through for him. Also, bring that squirrel Chip in to see if he can identify the photo from his connections in Chicago. When Mason returns, he can see whether Sid Silverstein has ever seen this guy. I'm going to visit the country club to look at photos for the party Leana attended on the night of her accident. Maybe they'll capture a shot of her talking to Latorska, if he was there."

Beauregard hit the club at lunch hour and, despite not being a member, was given police reception, which meant a nice seat in the bar section. He attempted to explain that he needed to see the manager on business and was not here for lunch. He knew that the staff was aware of his position and was attempting to keep good public relations for the club with the police. He was saved by the day manager, who begged him to join him for lunch. He told the manager his mission. The manager explained that getting the photos for that night would take about half an hour for his event planner, Bea, to find. They could have lunch while they waited.

Beauregard enjoyed the special of the day, his favorite eight ounces of the best beef burger with cheese, onions, chili, pickles, lettuce, and tomato. He added steak sauce and chomped away, assuaging his guilt with fried sweet potatoes instead of regular french fries. Mona would be furious with him if she ever discovered his deviation from his diet. Hopefully she wouldn't find out, but he wondered why he didn't feel at all guilty about lying to her about his dietary habits away from home.

The day manager had chosen a Cobb salad with chicken instead of ham and a side of chicken soup. He said to Beauregard, "You can eat that without any stomach distress? You're damn lucky." Beauregard nodded, but even the nod was a lie. He would suffer some backup after this lunch.

After dessert, Beauregard, the manager, and the event planner reviewed approximately one hundred photos taken during the event in question. Together, they sorted pictures, including staff, and then attempted to find waiters working that evening, specifically one talking to Leana. Bea was the most helpful in identifying staff; she had worked for the club for over five years and knew all the regulars. She quickly found four photos with the waiter in question, whose name was Bob Farrow. Two photos included Leana leaning toward him and pointing a finger in what appeared to be anger. Two of the photos were in profile, and one photo clearly showed his face. The face was not Latorska's face, which was disappointing.

With the most subtlety he could muster, Beauregard requested the pictures. His stated reason was that the police would need a complete file to close the case. The manager was pleased to oblige, and before Beauregard was able to ask for more information on Bob Farrow, the manager offered to send in the staff member who had had the most contact with the waiter to be interviewed by the police; he'd also send by e-mail the digitalized photo. Beauregard thought, *Must be Christmas, cause I just got some presents.*

Back at the station, Beauregard was antsy. He feared that this Latorska, or whoever he was, may be a hired hood. If so, he worried that if and when they found him, and if he was a professional, they may never be successful in discovering the murder for hire payer, let alone prosecuting him or her. He thought, *It could be a her, maybe. And who the hell is this waiter Bob Farrow? Another stalker?*

An hour later, a staff member from the club named Lois was in the interview room and was happily chatting about the waiter Bob Farrow and what she knew about him. She said that he was older and not bad looking, but he had a hard look; she thought that he was looking over every woman member. She wondered at first whether he was one of those older guys looking for a wealthy woman, like she saw on television. When she saw him cornering Leana several times, she laughed, knowing that Leana could have almost any man in the place. Then she asked him why he was interested in a woman clearly in her late fifties. He laughed and said that he thought he knew her, and anyway, she was pretty hot. He wasn't perfect at working all the tables, and Lois let him know. His response was, "I only do this when I have to. I'm more of a big-time mover."

Lois laughed at him, and the waiter was annoyed. After that, he avoided talking to her. It took Beauregard about fifteen minutes to finish this chat with Lois, who finally left saying, "I'm so excited. To think that I have been of assistance to the West Side Major Crimes Unit!"

Millie brought Beauregard some administrative papers for his signature and a message for Mason from an agent at the Commonwealth Fusion Center requesting a return call. She informed Mason of the request, and he said he would not be back at the station until after five. He asked if Beauregard would make the call. Not a problem for Beauregard, who was looking for a step forward in this quest for the real name of this punk Latorska.

He spoke with the FBI agent in charge, and after a discussion on the specifics on the Leana Lonergan case and her possible history as a serial murderer, the agent was more than cooperative. This Latorska guy's real names were many, including Jon Von Leder, Leonard Daly, Lawrence Brennan, and Dylan Murphy. His birth name, Gerald O'Leary, was rarely used except on spotty, legitimate employment.

Gerald had a long rap sheet of charges, but only a couple stuck. One gave him two years in a local jail in New Jersey for embezzlement. He was well-known in the New Jersey and New York areas and was thought to be a hired gun for small jobs. Some thought that he did a couple of low-level killings in Las Vegas and Florida. These were killings of men who were about to talk to the feds.

The agent was very interested in discussing the case with Beauregard and his team, and he would visit West Side the next afternoon. Beauregard noticed that he didn't ask—he simply assumed, and as was customary, Major Crimes would have to accommodate the

FBI or else the mayor or the chief would be on the phone reaming them out. Beauregard was not happy with the FBI moving in on this case, but he had no control over that. He also realized that he alone had let the fox into the henhouse.

Beauregard asked the agent if he could wait a day or two before visiting because the team was busy with work that could not be put off. The agent agreed, and Beauregard promised God he'd attend mass on Sunday in thanks. Before the agent signed off, Beauregard requested a search on another photo. He wondered whether it was this Gerald O'Leary's associate. Beauregard said that there was some talk that they had been seen together, and for future legal issues related to the case, the MCU was interested in ruling out a connection between the two. The agent told him to send it on over; a search shouldn't take too long. To Beauregard's mind, that was the first time in his history with the agency that the FBI said something would be easy.

An hour later, the FBI agent identified the second picture as a man from Hamilton, New York, named Alex Fortesman. He was a sixty-year-old retired accountant with no record. Beauregard deliberated and could not see a logical connection between the two men. He said to himself, *New York is a big state, and Hamilton is not generally known as a town that's home to wise guys. I don't see O'Leary and Fortesman in the same business. What on earth would bring them to West Side on the same night with interest in the same woman? Maybe I could let this Fortesman go if he hadn't disappeared the same night that Leana died. This guy Fortesman is sixty. Maybe he's the same J. Ripor who was stalking Leana at work.*

Beauregard grabbed Petra's notes to remind himself of Ripor's description. *Somehow, other than their both being older men, I can't see Ripor working as a waiter from Lillian's profile on him. It's time to get Petra to make a visit to Leana's workplace again with the waiter's picture, to see if it's Ripor. I'll text it to her now. It shouldn't take long for an answer.*

Petra, true to her nickname of Bolt, was visiting with Lillian within ten minutes of the captain's call. To her disappointment, Lillian said the photo was not J. Ripor; in fact she couldn't even imagine J. Ripor as a waiter. She said, "Yes, they may be around the same age, within ten years, but the similarity ends there." Petra called the news in to Beauregard, who then asked Petra to return to the station.

When Petra arrived, she was surprised to see Beauregard in the conference room with Norbie Cull. He left the room for a few minutes and updated her on the known history of the waiter, whose real name was Alex Fortesman. He instructed her to call the local force up there, reminding her that Hamilton was a college town, home of Colgate University, where everyone knew everyone. "You tell the sheriff up there that Fortesman is a very important witness to a murder case, and you request that he is not to be advised of the police interest in him. When you get hold of him, Bolt, get me to take the call, okay?"

Petra had no trouble connecting with the county sheriff, who personally knew Fortesman; they golfed together and were members of a sporting club. The sheriff was surprised that Fortesman had been in western Massachusetts at all.

She quickly handed the phone to Beauregard, who introduced himself, and they bantered for a bit.

The sheriff said, "Alex is a hometown boy. He doesn't travel except to hunting and fishing shows, and I know about any shows myself he attended this year. Often I go with him. When was Alex supposed to be there? He's been around here all year."

Beauregard didn't give the sheriff a date but said sometime in the last half of 2015. The sheriff couldn't remember that far back but did report that Alex was a loyal and stand-up man who would do anything for his friends.

Beauregard was impatient, knowing that he was needed in the conference room, what with Norbie Cull being an attorney known for only visiting when something was really important. Just as he was thinking in frustration about eating the last donut from breakfast in the kitchen, the sheriff ended the call.

When the call ended, Beauregard received information from Mason, who said, "I just got a cell call from the Fusion Center. Our guy Latorski, real name Gerald O'Leary, has been identified as a DOA found buried in a construction site in Las Vegas. He died from a .38 fragmented bullet to his head in February 2016. His fingerprints were removed from the body. The picture we sent out was noticed, and the Vegas police just matched it to the body. How the hell are we going to find out who hired him for the Leana hit?"

Beauregard asked Bolt to call the Las Vegas department and see what they had in the file. She posed several questions. "Maybe there's a cell phone or other materials that will assist. Did he have a rental car that was later found? Often in a police matter, the rental agency will keep or turn over to the police stuff found in the car. I'll get right on it, Captain."

Beauregard said, "There's no dice on the waiter! He's a stand-up guy, according to the details the sheriff's profile gave on Alex Fortesman.'

Beauregard wrote a list of specifics she was to ask the Vegas police. "It is Las Vegas, after all. This hired killer has a history in Vegas and probably gambles. See if the department out there will get us pictures or videos of O'Leary with associates, maybe at the tables. If he did the hit on Leana, he would have to meet with someone, especially if nothing shows on a cell phone. If he used a cell phone, it would have been a throwaway. He'd have to get payment. Try to find his bank records."

# 32

# Beauregard and Norbie Confer

Beauregard ignored Norbie Cull's thanks for seeing him on such short notice, and particularly for seeing him alone. Beauregard asked, "How can I help, Norbie? Are you here for a client or is it personal?"

Norbie answered, "Both."

Beauregard did not respond, thus forcing Norbie to make the first move. Beauregard thought, *I never bid against myself. Besides, how the hell is he going to start this conversation without saying too much—unless he knows much of what I know? Christ, he probably does. Whenever Attorney Noberto Cull is on the other side of things, this place leaks information like a sieve leaks water.*

Beauregard noticed from Norbie's demeanor that he was playing no games. He expected Norbie to be a straight shooter, but he also expected that Norbie would be protecting his client best by telling the truth. Well, maybe he would only tell most of the truth and leave some things out, like all good lawyers. Beauregard also thought defense attorneys never saw a reason to assist the police in any attempts they may make in suspecting their clients.

Beauregard realized that Norbie was thinking and waited for him to come back to the table.

Norbie looked at Beauregard, himself thinking, *I've stopped thinking about Gar as a friend. Now that I'm talking to the police, he's my client. I don't even know when my brain does this, but it does it automatically in all cases where I represent someone who is close to me. God damn it, Gar is a friend and a good man.*

Norbie said, "Beauregard, my client believes, as I do, that he has information that could possibly assist the police in their investigation of Leana's accident. He's been begging me for some time to share with you some of the information he thinks would be helpful to you. I'm here today to do just that."

Beauregard slowly answered with a smile. "Would your client be Gar Lonergan? And what the hell took you so long to come to me, Norbie? I'm interested—very interested." Beauregard suddenly had to excuse himself when he saw Petra waving at him.

Norbie noticed Beauregard's quick exit, which was not how he normally operated. He completed conferences and then took care of business. Now, Norbie was certain that there was a very active investigation into Leana's death—and that he may be just in time to avoid some very nasty publicity.

Norbie knew that he had enough information to forestall an immediate arrest of Gar, and maybe enough to point the police in another direction. That very morning, he and Steve had reviewed Jeffrey Hunt's complete investigation file, which was made available to them. That in itself was unusual because the investigator had given up the file without it being requested.

Jeffrey had said, "I think that with Jim Locke now in the office, it'd be best if my client retained any work papers I developed before Jim joined the firm. Gar told me to give them all to you." Both he and Steve knew there must be something in the work papers that Jeffrey, and probably Jim, thought was best for Gar's lawyers to get before the police.

The work papers would have been a treasure trove for the police and somewhat helpful in supporting Gar's innocence. There were two areas about which Norbie had no previous information. In investigating the fire that had killed Leana's parents, Jeffrey discovered a neighbor named Burt Butler who stilled lived in his childhood home. When Burt had been contacted, he had been absolutely venomous about Leana. Furthermore, he had seen her shortly before her death. Jeffrey Find's notes summed up an interview with Burt complaining that Leana had sent unsigned, threatening notes to him. He knew it was her because she mentioned in the note his talking trash about her brother Timothy. How she had heard about his talking trash was the question Burt would not answer, but he did talk trash about Timothy to Jeffrey. Jeffrey assumed that the trash talk was included in the notes Burt sent to Leana.

Jeffrey had a partial tape of his interview with Burt, where Burt was heard saying, "Timothy was always a weirdo, even when he was five years old, but he could do anything. I simply suggested that Timothy lit the fire and that people should know about it."

Jeffrey had generally questioned Burt about why it was important to examine that issue over fifty years later.

Burt's answer was, "Mary Lou is loaded, whereas I have to work every day. I was nice to those two when no one was nice to that trashy family. She should have been pleased to pay me a small stipend to keep my mouth shut. She's a bitch and deserves to die. She says I sent her many letters, but that was a lie. I only sent a few over the years. When I told her I'd only sent a couple of letters, she said, 'You're a fuckin' liar, you creep.'

"Imagine, calling me a creep. She was absolutely certain that I had sent the notes just because I work at the post office and could discover her addresses. I think she has lots of enemies and that there were many other letters from people who were also hurt by her. She can't stand anyone saying one bad thing about her precious Timothy. Even when they were kids, you could never get between the two. Poor little Timothy. He's supposed to be autistic, but I'm telling you he was the smartest kid in school. He's living the dream. And me? I have to kill myself working every day just for a lousy pension. She owes me, and I wanted her to pay one way or another."

The next area of investigation that had been unknown to Norbie was Leana's active relationship with her stepbrother, Jason. When Jeffrey Hunt had been investigating Mary Lou's childhood, he'd had conversations with the firm that took care of Timothy Prior, Leana's brother's legal affairs. The attorney was the son of the original lawyer who'd handled Ernestine Prior's estate.

Attorney Bronsen Jr. was quite willing to speak with Jeffrey Hunt about Leana and the family. He did not know Leana well, but he frequently saw Timothy; they were in the same lodge together. He viewed Timothy as distant but very kind when he got to know someone. He said, "Timothy supports many causes financially in this community, and Alice, his girlfriend, does community support. Together they are awesome, and I love being with them."

The interview notes stated that Jason visited the area several times. Each time, he tried to get Leana's address. Attorney Bronsen gave it to him the first time, but Leana called him on it and changed her address. Bronsen Jr. never gave the address to Jason the next time he asked. And Jason did ask. When his request was denied, he asked Timothy, who also told him no.

Norbie decided to give information that could direct the police in another direction. He didn't believe that he was required to give the source of his information if it could compromise Gar. After all, Gar was yet to be named as a person of interest. Instead, he said that he had information, and at this time he was willing to share the info but not the source. Later, if required, he would share the source.

Beauregard listened as Norbie relayed some of Leana's history, carefully pointing out that Leana was concerned about a list of people from her past, whom she felt would have an interest in possibly hurting her. He gave the list and added some information about each one, enough to make them interesting to the police. At least, he hoped that they would be interested in anyone but his client.

Beauregard listened and took some notes. Finally, he looked up and said, "Norbie, would it be helpful—you know, make you more forthcoming—if I tell you that I know that Gar was not involved in any way in Leana's accident?"

Norbie asked, "Why and how are you so certain, Captain? You must know, then, that it wasn't an accident and who did it. Do you know who did it?"

Beauregard answered, "We know who caused the accident. We don't know who hired him to cause the accident. We don't believe it is Gar, but you have to understand that we can't totally rule him out at this point. You have done a great job in listing alternative theories for the unknown subject, many of which we already are aware of. But the devil's in the details, and I believe you have a lot more detail. We know a lot. It looks like you know a lot. Together, we maybe would have the majority of the details. Think about being more helpful. I could always charge Gar as an accessory and get more detail with discovery. Doing that, of course, would involve a protracted process, and Gar would suffer, particularly if he's innocent. And there are a lot of good reasons to believe at this point that he's innocent."

Beauregard received a call on his cell phone, which again was an unusual interruption. He left the room to take the call, excusing himself.

Because Beauregard excused himself from the conference room, he gave Norbie some time to consider what was best for his client and what was so important for Beauregard to leave their meeting.

Norbie thought through this situation that he had orchestrated. *Beauregard knows that Gar didn't kill Leana, but he wants all the info we have. If I give him most of it, I also give him reason to look more closely at Gar, and I can't do that. I also cannot lie, but I can give him my best guess and some info, telling him that I can't put my client at risk. I'll tell him it's the best I can do. Worse case, he calls my bluff. Best case, I send him in a good direction, giving us all some time. Who do I really think killed her? There are so many possibilities when a serial murderer has done her work—and I truly think that Leana was a serial murderer. The issue is that I'm beginning to see her motives. What does that make me, that I'm able to see reasons for a serial murderer murdering?*

Beauregard let Norbie cool his heels for a good twenty minutes.

There was no strategic purpose in this delay. He was simply attempting to get a grasp on what looked to him like a major roadblock. When he returned, he apologized for inconveniencing Norbie.

Beauregard said, "Who do you think, among the many who hated, loved, wanted revenge, or wanted money from Leana, would have the most compelling reason to kill her? And who among that group would have the resources to find and pay a contract killer?"

Norbie grinned and slyly responded. "Now I have to do your work for you, Beauregard? All that work, and I won't even get a nice pension like you. But in the spirit of camaraderie, and attorney and police relations, I'll try to answer you. In my experience, any client I've represented or even heard about who hired or attempted to hire a contract killer found it a difficult task. You simply are unable to trust an amateur, and for our purposes, an amateur would leave a connection to your contract killer. If it's a professional contract killer, then I'd look for someone in crime, the syndicate, or the gambling industry. Is the contract killer a local?"

Beauregard wouldn't normally wish to share too much information with Norbie, but he had great respect for Norbie's intellect and ethics, and so he went ahead with his fishing plan. "There is a dead contract killer who we think killed Leana. He originated from the New York and New Jersey areas. He was found in Las Vegas, and his fingerprints were cut off. His estimated time of death was in early 2016. So either the person who hired him eliminated him, or someone who loved Leana killed her killer. That last one could implicate your client. So maybe you want to tell me your client's travel plans in the first six months of 2016. I know he was traveling for about eighteen months or so, but where?"

Gar said, "Barking up the wrong tree, Beauregard. Gar couldn't even imagine cutting off the fingertips on a body. No, this must have been done by a pro or an angling wannabe. You know that. What's in the contractor's background? You must know something about him and his whereabouts. Let me answer your first question about who would be the most likely to want Leana dead based on this scenario.

Lots to choose from—for example, the players in New York and New Jersey come first to mind. But then other than revenge, what is their motive? They suffered no notoriety from Leana, and she never took any big money from them. She had funds, but there was no way they would benefit from her funds. So I rule them out. They kill for money or revenge, or to show publicly that they haven't been taken advantage of. Nope, not them. Leana once shared with someone that she didn't trust Misha Kortiac from Georgia, her friend Myra's husband, but he's a lowlife and is not sophisticated—or better yet, careful enough—to arrange a contract killing.

"Leana also suggested that Burt, the postal worker from her childhood I just told you about, and her stepbrother were problematic. Both speak to a personal angle. Neither benefitted financially from her death. Is either one capable of hiring a contract killer and then killing him? Believe me, Burt sounds like a sneaky little blackmailer, but not someone who would ever put himself at risk. He'd be easy to check out. I don't know much about Jason Prior. Leana hated him, but he's got to be in his later seventies by now. He's waited a long time to get revenge, if that was his motive."

Beauregard then questioned whether Norbie had considered any involvement from any of the families and friends of Leana's former dead husbands. He mentioned in particular Mrs. Haylor and her daughter from New Jersey, as well as Aaron Goldberg's associates and family. He also suggested the Chicago family and the Wolfeboro family as potentials.

"No, Beauregard. Mrs. Haylor is pretty wealthy, but she doesn't have the ability to connect to the contractor you describe. Her daughter, from what I understand, carried no grudge against Leana. The mattress people in Chicago are financially driven and plainly didn't mourn Senior. I don't know enough about the Fraine family in Wolfeboro; unless Leana really pissed someone off up there, I'd eliminate them. I think this has personal anger behind it. I don't know why I think it, but my gut tells me to go in that direction."

Beauregard said, "What about this Jack Leahy in New York City?

Leana had a fling with him, and he dumped her. She had a history of losing husbands, and it seems more than plausible that she helped some of them die. This Leahy had an unfortunate death. He was married into a very connected family. What about his family?"

Beauregard saw the look of surprise on Norbie's face, and Norbie immediately denied any knowledge of Jack Leahy but promised to look into the relationship. Beauregard understood that Norbie would think from this information that there was another potential person of interest other than Gar; further, it was someone maybe far more likely than Gar to hire a contract killer.

A few moments later, the two professionals agreed to consider what was discussed today and to update each other if new information was received. Both had reservations. Both believed that *consider* was the operative word.

# 33

# New Evidence Emerges

THE MAJOR CRIMES UNIT was busy. Beauregard and the MCU detectives were conferencing while waiting for calls detailing the life of Gerald O'Leary. Beauregard summarized his conversation with Norbie without saying that Norbie was the source, although they knew who the source was.

Ash, confused, asked, "Captain, how are you able to get information from the defense attorney of the husband of the victim while we have search warrants on his home? Everyone here knows that this is a comfortable lovefest between the two of you. Doesn't compute with me, but then, I've not been at this a long time. You must respect and trust Norbie Cull. Never saw this in my police materials. Then again, I guess if you're good with it, I'm good with it."

On hearing Ash's reservation, Mason said, "The captain knows what he's doing. Not to worry!"

There was a spread of papers on the conference table. Most were related to the accident details' match to evidence of the construction truck used. Millie brought in some faxes and some printed info from the Las Vegas police e-mails.

Now that the police knew that the body belonged to O'Leary, they put together details garnered from personnel employed at the hotel he last stayed in under one of his known aliases, Leonard Daly. O'Leary used the Daly name when he came to Vegas, which he often did. The police had a report on him when he disappeared from his hotel room without notice, where he left a satchel there holding one hundred fifty thousand dollars in small bills. The police had been holding the bag in evidence since O'Leary's disappearance.

Millie set a video up of O'Leary at the tables in several venues. Of particular interest was the video of him speaking with a tall, older, and refined man in his midseventies in the Planet Hollywood Casino poker room. The casino's video captured the two deep in conversation in the poker room and later caught them conversing in the next room, in the Heart Bar.

The older man handed a valise to O'Leary when he left. That was five days before Leana's death. Further, O'Leary then returned to New York City on a private gambling shuttle. Later in early 2016, O'Leary left from New York to Vegas on another private gambling shuttle. On that visit, O'Leary played poker nonstop and lost seventy-five thousand dollars. O'Leary was a regular poker player and generally played well, but like any regular player, he would also lose. After this loss, he wasn't seen again; there were no additional photos of O'Leary on that visit. He had a rental car that was found in the garage of the casino. How he got to the construction site five miles away was unknown.

O'Leary was a known gambler, and five different casinos had some history on him. He would occasionally lose up to twenty grand a visit; normally he'd come back and recover most of it. This time, his loss was bigger. He was known to visit the strip about three or four times a year, rarely with a woman. He had been seen associating with some lower-level hoods in the past. He was not a professional gambler, more of a decent card player with big ideas.

Petra immediately asked, "Captain, could that older gentleman possibly match J. Ripor, Leana's stalker at her work? I could have Lillian look at this video. It's a bit grainy, but I think it's worth reviewing. I was just with her, and she is willing to help us."

Beauregard said, "Bolt, before you leave, have Millie request from the Vegas police contact any information they have on the older gentleman."

Mason and Ash discussed how quickly they could get financial records on O'Leary, if any existed. If O'Leary had a bag of one hundred fifty thousand dollars in his room, maybe he was his own bank. "Do we have a last known address on him in New York or New Jersey? Someone paid him to kill Leana; there must be a trail," remarked Ash.

Beauregard said, "Have you guys ever heard the name Ripor before? I mean, it almost has an exotic flair, maybe from India, but he looks like white-bread American to me." Mason agreed.

Ash started laughing. "We've been had. I remember reading in some crime magazines how criminals choose their fake names. Many start by twisting their own names around. He gave his name to that Lillian as J. Ripor. Give me a minute to play with it." They watched as Ash scrambled the letters in the J. Ripor name eight or nine times, finally writing in large letters, "J. PRIOR."

Beauregard swore under his breath and said, "I can't fuckin' believe it; In front of us all the time. Good work, Ash. But why was her stepbrother stalking her? Did he hire O'Leary? Could he hate her that much after fifty years? Would that repressed hate be enough to have him act out, to hire someone to kill her? Even if he hated his sister and hired O'Leary, he doesn't look like the kind of guy to get his hands dirty. It takes a lot to cut out someone's fingertips. Did we ever get a photo of Jason Prior? Mason, call that lawyer in Lake Placid and see if he has an address on Prior. If we have his address, we can get a registry photo. Meanwhile, Ash and I will review the timeline on his visit to Leana's workplace. Also, do we have photos of Timothy and a good picture of Fortesman? If not, I want them."

Beauregard left MCU to relieve his headache. Mona would kill him for getting stressed. That was what brought on his headaches: his blood pressure would spike. He always knew when he was stressed, and her instructions were that when he was stressed, he was to walk out of a situation and do an inconsequential errand. She thought that doing so may help him stop his mind from going round in circles.

Better yet, she said, "Go to church and pray." He laughed at that advice. *There are no freakin' churches left open on weekdays. Even the churches aren't safe today.*

Mona was right again: after ten minutes at the mall in Holyoke, his headache was gone. Maybe it was the Starbucks coffee that helped, although he drank decaf under Mona's orders; to be fair, his doctor also suggested he do so.

Beauregard walked the mall for about twenty minutes. He would later tell Mona that he had found time to walk. She'd be surprised and happy. He thought, *A happy wife is when hubby takes her advice.* He'd improved upon the other familiar phrase about a happy wife. Then his newly uncluttered mind thought, *Fortesman, the nice guy from Hamilton, New York. Hamilton is not too distant from the city or from Lake Placid. What role did he play*? He jogged to his car, which was no small feat for Beauregard, who was carrying twenty extra pounds of cop donuts.

He returned to the unit. The place was buzzing and his cell phone was ringing when he returned. The phone call was from Petra. No need to answer the call, because she was right in front of him with her back to him. He whispered, "Petra, I'm right here."

She turned and was about to tell him not to scare her again, but she was too excited. "Captain, you just won't believe this. Jason was found dead at his home in the Pebble Beach area in Crescent City, California, in December 2016. His head was smashed in with a piece of coffee table driftwood. The police there think it looks like an attempted robbery, but there was no evidence of a break-in. He was murdered in the living room. He lives about a lot or two from the beach, but the land is shaped with trees to hide the driveway. There are no witnesses noted around the time of the murder, and they couldn't get fingerprints off the driftwood."

Beauregard banged his fist on the nearest surface, Ash's desk. Silence prevailed in the room at this unusual emotional reaction from the normally quite balanced Beauregard.

Brave Petra spoke first. "Look, I can't wait this out. This is too much.

Coincidence? Like hell. I'm a cop—I don't believe in fairy tales. Let's look at what we think we know. We've found our hired killer, and he's been murdered. He is a known connection to Leana and her stepbrother, Jason—and then Jason is found murdered in his home supposedly by an intruder with no evidence of a forced break-in. Doesn't it seem awfully convenient to you? It does to me. Maybe someone else is involved in this murder. Maybe Leana's other stalker, Fortesman."

Mason and Ash agreed to disagree on whether this was an example of coincidence, which as all cops knew was always suspect. Ash finally came around to agreeing with Mason, saying, "There are no coincidences around a murder case. All is connected, even in an apparent disconnect!" Ash replied that Mason's saying made no sense at all.

Beauregard's demeanor changed. His facial expression changed in a distorted, slow-motion version of a smile. He was thinking, *Finally, two and two make four. Finally, I see the light!*

Beauregard started barking orders. He wanted lifestyle info on Jason Prior from Pebble Beach and Las Vegas, as well as a history on his Lake Placid visits. "All three, you hear? Listen to me. Why the hell should he want to kill Mary Lou, or Leana? I mean, what the hell kind of anger could move him at this time in his life? Did his life suck after all this time? You said his wife died. When did she die? Are his children in trouble? Was he a big gambler? Why hasn't Vegas investigated him in relation to O'Leary's death? All I'm doing here is finding why dead murderers were murdered—first Leana, then O'Leary, and now Prior. Why can't I have a normal serial murder case?"

Mason laughingly said, "Captain, there's no normal when you're dealing with psychopaths."

Everyone was on overtime tonight until 8:00 p.m. to give California, with its different time zone, someone present at the office available to receive the information when it came through. Beauregard left to join Mona at home. She had put her foot down a few years ago about dinner with the kids three times a week at 6:30. No excuses unless someone was at risk. There was no screwing around with Mona.

# 34

# The Devil's in the Details

"I don't know why you bother coming home for dinner, Rudy. You've been lost in thought for the last forty minutes, and what's really telling is you haven't eaten half of your dinner. Why do I bother? I just don't understand why you can't be here in the moment. You wouldn't let the kids get away with this."

Beauregard was slightly annoyed. *I try my best, and it's not good enough. I should have stayed single. But then, look at the kids, and Mona. Instead of barking at them, my wonderful family, I'll just slice into this meatloaf. Mona makes the best meatloaf, and I was ignoring it. What the hell—she is right again.*

"Mona, what would make you sustain anger against a quasi-sibling after fifty years, given that you haven't had much contact with the person over that period?" Mona tried to get more information, but Beauregard wanted her perspective on that situation with no further details.

"Well, Beauregard, there are three things always at play in difficult family situations: absurd expectations about what the family and its members owe someone, individual personality types, and how life has treated the person after he or she has left the family home. If any two of them are working out of the norm, there could be long-term anger and blame on some element in the childhood, especially if the person felt no love or a loss of love in childhood. Does that explanation help you?"

Beauregard answered, "Yes, maybe. But could that anger motivate you to stalk the sibling and murder her?"

Mona was thoughtful for a minute and finally responded, "Repression of anger without any resolution could, I believe, fuel some pretty negative action. Murder in my mind, however, is a nasty, far out reaction to repressed anger. To reach that point, I would think that the person would have displayed some serious violence previously. Violence fuels more violence. Look over his or her history. I guarantee you, Beauregard, you'll find acting out in there. That's why you just can't stop children with the concept of 'behave or timeout.' You also have to figure out why the child is acting out. It's important to not let the anger go underground. You know, Beauregard, it's kind of like Civil War. First the rebellion occurs in the underground, sometimes for years, and then government buildings are being bombed."

Beauregard asked Mona what she was doing the next day, and whether she would like to take an auto trip to upper state New York. Mona's mouth dropped as she thought, *Could this be my Beauregard wanting to take a trip on a weekday? No, it must be about police business. But I'm still happy at the thought.* She decided to make it easy on him. "You must have something really important to do, for you to travel on a weekday. Care to tell me about it? I'm happy to accompany you, especially if it means a nice dinner at the end of the day."

Mona could see from his face that he was relieved she wasn't making a lot of fuss about the surprise trip. Beauregard didn't like confrontation at home, and for good reason: he knew that in a personal argument, Mona would always end up the winner. He shared the purpose of the trip. "Mona, I have to talk to a man, a witness, and I must talk to him in person. I understand that he stays pretty much in one place, and so I've decided to track him down without telling him I'm coming. I will inform the local sheriff when I get there, but I don't want to give him time to think about his personal loyalties first.

I think that my murder case is really three murder cases, and I think it's solved. Ash, Petra, and Mason can collect all the information we're waiting for tomorrow while we're gone. By the way, who will watch the kids?"

Mona paused before saying, "Do you have any idea how old the kids are? They all have sports tomorrow, won't get home before five, and can cook far better than either of us. The worst that will happen is they'll shortchange their studying and play games. You have no worries, Rudy."

Beauregard agreed and then said they'd leave by seven in the morning.

The trip to Hamilton, New York, was an easy ride—all highway. After a light lunch in a small restaurant, Beauregard called the sheriff and told him he was headed over to Alex Fortesman's home. Beauregard had spoken with the sheriff's office earlier and was simply confirming his arrival in town. Beauregard also had Fortesman's home address and a list of his three hangouts, only one of which would be open early in the day. He thought, *It's a crapshoot, but maybe it's a way to bring some closure. There's something there right in front of me, and I'm pretty sure I know what it is.*

They pulled up to an older, small colonial home with a large barn in back. Offsetting the austerity of the house was a small white fence and a row of wild roses growing greedily for the season along the perimeter on the front and side. The effect was of time unchanged. Mona immediately liked the house and told Beauregard that this man would be a truthful witness. "Nobody could care so meticulously for this old home and not be a truthful person."

Mona stayed in the car per their agreement while Beauregard knocked on the door. An older man with a weathered but nice face answered. He was the waiter at the West Side Country Club on the night of Leana's accident.

Beauregard identified himself, and before he could say any additional words, Alex Fortesman said, "Please come in. I've been expecting you. The sheriff just called. Don't be upset; it's a small community, and we take care of each other. I told the sheriff that I haven't done anything wrong and that I have no problems talking with the police about what, if anything, I know."

They moved through the standard colonial front hall, past the parlor, and into a large kitchen. Alex had set out thick china cups for three. He said that normally cops traveled in pairs and added, "I thought I saw a woman in the car. Please invite her in."

Beauregard explained that she was simply traveling with him and was comfortable staying in the vehicle, especially considering the nice weather.

Alex poured coffee into the two heavy mugs, offered some muffins, and waited for Beauregard to speak.

"Alex, it seems unusual for a man of your age, who is not a waiter, to drive to western Massachusetts solely to work for a couple of days as wait staff in the West Side Country Club. Our information has you interested in Leana Lonergan, who was murdered within hours after speaking with you. I'm interested in your purpose."

Alex's face colored. He stood up and started pacing around the large country-style table. Finally he spoke. "I thought she died in an accident. I was relieved when I heard that she was in a car crash. Captain, I didn't kill her. I couldn't kill anyone unless I were being attacked, or for the defense of our country. I hunt, yes, but my dad and grandfather have always hunted, and I only hunt for my or my friends' needs. Believe me, I know nothing about this."

Sighing loudly, Beauregard reiterated, "Alex, why were you stalking Leana? What relationship did you have with her? Was it money? Were you sending her letters for blackmail? Come on. Why would you work as a waiter when it's not your profession? You must have some story. If not, then you and I have a big problem."

Alex was hesitant at first, stumbling a bit. "I have a friend, and his sister said that she was being bothered by someone from her past. He wouldn't tell me who it was, but he gave me a picture of the guy. He asked me if I would be willing to do some reconnaissance in western Massachusetts—you know, just go, stay a while, and look around.

He knew that I was Special Forces in the service years ago and that I don't talk trash to anyone or about anyone. He didn't want me to do anything except discover whether the guy was in the area; if so, I was to warn his sister. I was to tell her that her brother had sent me. He knew what town she lived in, but that's all. I thought at the time that he should know his sister's address. He explained that their early childhood, before he came to live in New York State, taught them to share very little. He was earnest. Let me explain that I think that he's on the spectrum—you know, autistic. He's also kind of brilliant and a really quiet guy. I'd stake my life on him."

Beauregard thought, *You may have to stake your normal life on him.* "Alex, how long did you stay in the area? Where did you stay? Did you see the man in the picture while you were there?"

Alex took a picture from under the placemat on the kitchen table. It was a photo of Jason Prior. He nodded. "I saw him go into her workplace one day when she was not there. I'd found out where she lived, but it was impossible to monitor her home without being seen. I figured if someone was stalking her, he'd have the same problem I had. Her workplace seemed to me to be the best place to watch undercover. You know, there's a big parking area for the building in front, and her office is in the glass area in front. I could see everyone entering or exiting through the main door. The problem is that her brother didn't want me to be seen talking to her privately. I thought maybe she had a jealous husband or something. After I saw the guy in the picture, I followed him; He was staying at the Hilton Garden Inn in Springfield. I then followed the sister and realized that she regularly went to the country club. I thought that it would be easy to get a job there, wait for her to come to play golf, and approach her with a business reason. I've done it before for the government; I know it works. However, the only jobs open at the club were as wait staff because it was toward the end of the season. I applied, and they were thrilled to have someone older than twenty-one with experience. I didn't tell them my experience was forty years before and in a hash-slinging place. I worked only a couple of nights before the club had a big bash, and then there she was: one beautiful, tough lady."

"Well, go on. This isn't a stage show, Alex—it's an information interview. What did the lady say when you told her about the man in the picture stalking her workplace?"

"Hell, she knew already. She was really angry that her brother had asked me to come. She said that she could take care of herself, but if I wanted to help, then I should take care of her brother. She said, "It will be necessary, if anything were to happen to me. He will need support from a friend. He has Alice, but he needs someone who's been around to protect him." I guess she could see that I'm good at that—taking care of folks."

Beauregard asked detailed questions on the timeline: where Alex had stayed, what car he used to go there, and whether he had used his own name. He recalled Alex's experience in undercover and found the accessing of a name, social security number, and driver's license of a former client who had recently died; it was an easy deed for him. The accessed name was Bob Farrow, and he would be a bit younger than Alex if he were alive. Alex said, "I thought no one would ever check. I don't know how you found me. You're pretty good, Captain."

Beauregard said, "Let's confirm that Timothy Prior from Lake Placid asked you to warn Leana. Is that right?" Alex confirmed it. Beauregard then asked, "Did you know that someone killed Jason Prior recently, in his home in California?"

Alex looked as if Beauregard had dropped a bomb, but he only said, "When, Captain? When did he die? You don't think I had anything to do with that, do you? I want to know when he died. I didn't even know where he lived. I simply went to West Side to confirm that he was stalking Leana."

Beauregard wasn't about to confirm the date. Instead, he asked several questions about where Alex had been in the first half of 2016 and whether he knew Timothy Prior's travel plans in 2015 and 2016. For the first time, Beauregard felt that Alex was being evasive. He said that he would have to check his computer, and as far as Timothy was concerned, he didn't know his schedule but was certain that he rarely traveled. He then asked, "Captain, do I need an attorney?"

After about twenty more minutes of rather unsatisfactory conversation, Beauregard left to return to his car. He called the sheriff and asked him to keep an eye on his witness.

Mona and Beauregard started the drive home, and then they got off route and drove to Stockbridge to dine in the historic Red Lion Inn. The day was a success for each of them for very different reasons.

# 35

# What Suffices for Justice?

THE DETECTIVES STARTED THEIR collation of data feeling more refreshed than they were the evening before. Beauregard had already briefed them on his trip. Mason said with excitement, "It's almost Christmas, and what do we get? A rather disappointing Christmas gift, if you ask me. We've three murders and yet no murderer to arrest. Who did the last one? Probably some nobody. Probably is a nobody whom we'll never find."

Ash and Petra agreed in part but pointed out to Mason that they were all part of putting a criminal justice puzzle together, and wasn't that really important work? Heads nodded.

Beauregard answered, "It's our job to know what happened and hold culpable those who commit major crimes. The problem is in holding someone culpable when we have suspicions but no proof. So again, let's look at all we have and pretend that none of the murderers are dead. Pretend the murderers are going to trial."

Beauregard reviewed with them the new information the unit received from Crescent City and Las Vegas that profiled Jason as a greedy, successful entrepreneur with a grand lifestyle. He had a ferocious temper, and the police were called to his home many times for domestic problems involving his wife and his three sons. All his sons left the family after graduation from college and were never known to return, not even for a visit. Not one attended his funeral. His wife had died three years before, but she had been a recluse for fifteen years prior to her death. He'd had a housekeeper from Honduras when his wife was alive. There was no address for her, and no one had seen her since the wife's funeral. Jason was a known gambler who got into some trouble in one of the Las Vegas casinos for creating a disturbance after his losing in a big way.

Jason's date book notes his stay in one of the smaller Las Vegas hotels at the time of O'Leary's death. His computer records documented rental of a car for the duration of his stay, which was unusual for his stays in Vegas. The police searched Jason's home and found a note, presumably from O'Leary, telling him to meet him with the money, or else there would be a call to the police.

The Vegas police checked with the rental car agency and did a forensic detail on the car. Forensics found dried small blood and skin tissue remains that matched O'Leary's. If Jason Prior were alive, the police would have had probable cause to arrest him. But of course, he was not alive. And the repressed anger! What horrible circumstance did he experience to motivate him to kill Mary Lou after all these years? How much repressed anger would there be to inspire Jason to kill after all these years? Those were questions that were probably not going to be answered to anyone's satisfaction.

The detectives agreed that the West Side Police Department would not find it easy to pursue Jason Prior's murderer. They would have difficulty pursuing Leana's questionable activities. All their information screamed, "Closed case, no case, not enough evidence, killer is already dead."

Mason asked, "Captain, where do we go from here? What can we do with what we know? Who killed Jason Prior, and do we care? Even if we do care, what can we do?"

Beauregard spoke firmly, "It is a conundrum." He normally did not use fifty-cent words, and so they waited, knowing there was more to come.

After a few minutes, Beauregard said in a slow almost exaggerated manner, "First thing, congratulations to you all for your work. We have solved two murders, have located a serial murderer, and understand five or six of her murders. Can we close any of these murders in an official way? No. Justice was done in a vigilante manner, but all the murderers received capital punishment. What is left is the last murder. Even if we are certain of a suspect who might have been responsible, the Crescent City Police do not share our interest because they have no evidence. We have no alternative, as police officers, but to accept their decision unless we discover evidence." They all nodded in agreement.

Beauregard noticed the expression of the faces of his detectives: dissatisfaction with the criminal justice system and its limitations.

Ash was the first to speak. "Even if we can't do anything, I need to know why Jason felt compelled to murder Leana."

A mini revolt seemed imminent. Beauregard stopped them with a gesture of silence. "I agree, but the only direction we have, the only one who knows anything about Leana's early years with Jason, is Timothy Prior, and we have not had good luck talking to him. Timothy has earned respect from everyone near him, and because of that and his condition, he has emotional bodyguards in his girlfriend Alice and friend Alex Fortesman."

Petra said, "Captain, the one thing I have learned in a couple of psyche classes and in discussions with Jim is that the majority of autistics are almost incapable of lying. They generally don't develop the artifices for manipulating that we find in the general population. Timothy won't lie to us if we are able to speak with him alone."

Beauregard then asked, "Who among us would be the best one to speak with him? We can't use a psychologist outside of the department. We'd have to explain the billing for a case that's not a case."

After much discussion, it was decided that either Ash or Petra would be more easily accepted by Timothy and Alice. By all accounts, Timothy trusted his adoptive mother, and so maybe Petra's gender could be an advantage. Then again, they thought that Timothy might relate to Ash because of their common interest in classical music performance.

Beauregard said, "I think that Ash, you and I will go. I must be certain that Timothy is all that he seems. We should attempt to see Timothy at work. Alice would not be with him to intervene, and neither would Alex Fortesman."

Beauregard informed the trio of detectives that he would have a quiet meeting with Norbie and his client. It was time to let them off the hook. "We've accomplished something important: we've been successful in protecting the innocent from charges in this case, and that's always a good thing."

# 36

# Protecting the Almost but Not Innocent Victim

GAR AND NORBIE DISPLAYED some discomfort upon entering the MCU conference room. Norbie had questioned Beauregard when he'd received the invitation; supposedly it was an invitation to listen, not to talk. Norbie explained this to his client, saying, "When the police ask you to come to the station, there is always risk. Shut up, Gar. If you are asked a question, wait for me to tell you to answer it, and answer in the most limited way. You're an innocent, and that means you are the easiest one for them to get to talk too much."

Beauregard told a long story about the detectives' work at putting together evidence. Gar was upset to learn that the police believed that Leana's stepbrother had ordered the hit. His reaction was dramatic. "What the hell kind of adoptive home was this? Take those two kids after their horrible early life and put them in a family with a brother fifteen years older who hated them? What was he, twenty-three years old when the kids went to live with the family? How much could they have annoyed them? At twenty-three, kids have a life and normally don't give a damn about younger siblings. Didn't the parents have a bunch of foster kids before? Leana had too much going for her to end up the way she did. There must have been crazy stuff going on in that home."

Beauregard noticed that Norbie was frustrated. *Norbie knows there's no controlling the mouth of an honest and emotional victim.* He was concerned that Norbie was about to stop the conference, and so he interrupted. "I couldn't agree with you more, Gar. There are big secrets there, and I'm taking your suggestion about the other foster kids who actually had much more experience with him than Leana and Timothy. It's worth a shot to see what they thought of Jason. They would have known him when he was young."

Beauregard reminded both Gar and Norbie that there was no need for any further information related to Leana to be made public. Her death would not be called a murder; there was no value or future in calling it anything other than an accident. The case was closed as far as the department was concerned, and he hoped that Gar would do his best to contain his anger; it would only erode his reputation, as well as that of his family, to publicly discuss any details of the case. Norbie seemed quite happy with the result. Gar insisted that the captain please inform him of any new information about Leana, Jason, and Timothy. He said, "For all her actions, I still care for her and believe she was a victim too."

Not too long afterward, Beauregard and Mason left for a trip to Connecticut. Mason had located and made a list of five of the foster children living locally who were all in their sixties and early seventies. All five had lived for years north of Hartford. Mason had prioritized the list by location, and all were retired. They hoped to find a few at home.

Six hours later, the two detectives returned and actively discussed the results of their day's interviews. Ernestine and Lester's foster children were all law-abiding adults who agreed on several common themes from their time with the Priors. Ernestine and Lester were wonderful, caring, religious, and kind parents to them, even when they themselves were out of line. The Priors supplied a strong moral code as a backdrop for their care, which served these former foster children well. It did nothing for their natural son, Jason. They described him as a bully who wanted everything for himself. He was also described as manipulative and a sneak, one who did everything to torture the children when the parents were not around. One man said that Jason would steal from him when his own natural aunt took him out for the day and bought him a new sweater. He said that the sweater was too small for Jason, but Jason took it out of spite and got rid of it somehow. Each had a similar story. None knew Leana and Timothy well. They met the adopted children when they visited Mom and Dad. In the stories of Jason's abusive behavior, which ran the gamut of ten years, Beauregard saw the makings of a disturbed personality. He thought, *Doesn't sound like he has any empathy or guilt. Added to that, they said he could be charming to his parents and to outsiders. Where have I see that before?*

On the next day in Lake Placid, Beauregard and Ash walked into Sentinel Accountants, LLP, and asked to see Timothy Prior. When asked about their business, they said it was personal. They were brought into a conference room. Timothy joined them, shook their hands, and didn't make eye contact.

Timothy asked them, "How may I be of service?"

Ash started the conversation. "Timothy! Gar, your sister's husband, is having a very difficult time accepting her death and wondered if you could talk to us about her. It's important to him to know more about her childhood with the Priors."

The two detectives could see that when Ash mentioned the Priors, Timothy relaxed a little. Beauregard asked if he could talk about them and whether Ernestine and Lester were good parents to Timothy and Mary Lou.

Timothy's manner in speaking was automatic but not robotic. It took coaching to get him to expound with more than a few sentences in answer to any question. He apparently saw no need to say more than, "They were good to us. They gave us what they had. We went to church every week, and sometimes more than that. Our parents taught us about God and what's the right thing to do, and we did good as much as we could. Mary Lou and I always tried to do good."

Ash asked if he would tell them about the times they couldn't do good, repeating his exact words. Timothy looked away from them but finally said, "Whenever our brother Jason was around, it was hard to be good. He didn't like us but didn't want Mom and Dad to know. He was awful mean to us, and he was old enough to know better. He was always going after Mary Lou, trying to touch her, but she was too fast for him. Once I tripped him to give her time to get away. When he came after me, I started screaming, and Mom rescued me. You know I used to scream all the time when I was frightened, but Mom taught me how to control it, mostly."

Ash thought, *Something just doesn't compute. Timothy is trying to be honest, but at the same time he is very guarded. He is giving us limited information. Autistics are normally honest. His mom certainly instilled discipline in him.* Ash also noticed that Timothy was constantly playing with a piece of cord, and when he talked about Jason, his twisting of the cord accelerated—in fact, it broke in half.

Beauregard also noticed the ritual with the cord and asked Timothy, "Do you like Jason now?"

Timothy answered, "It doesn't matter now. Jason is dead. I can't talk any more to you. Please leave." He left them alone in the conference room.

The detectives left the accounting firm's offices. Ash was the first to speak. "Captain, how the hell did he know that Jason was dead? Maybe the family lawyer got notice of his death. I'll call while you drive. Do you think Timothy could be involved?"

His question reminded Beauregard of something, and he told Ash that Alex Fortesman was informed by the captain that Jason had been killed. Alex appeared taken aback by this information, and as a friend he would tell Timothy the news.

"I'm not sure we've learned much, Ash."

The next day, Beauregard called a meeting of the detectives in the MCU conference room. He presented a report written for Chief Coyne. The report essentially stated that the accident that killed Leana Lonergan was probably not an accident but a hit on Leana Lonergan by a known killer from New York who had been found murdered in Las Vegas. There was strong evidence from the Las Vegas police that the person who had hired the hitman was Leana's stepbrother, Jason Prior, who was later murdered in a break-in at his home by an unknown perpetrator. There was no evidence at that break-in crime scene and no known person of interest at this time. Therefore the MCU suggested closing the accident and murder case of Leana Lonergan.

Mason was the first to react. "So we go no further with this Timothy guy. I read your report on Fortesman and Ash's on Timothy. I don't know how Timothy did it, but he sure as hell looks good to me for it. And we have a motive: Mary Lou spurned Jason. All the information we got back about Jason shows his life had become a shit show. His wife's death, after what may have been fifteen years of an abnormal domestic life for him, could have added fuel to the fire. You know some of these guys just have to blame someone. As far as Timothy is concerned, I give him a pass. Jason was evil to him and killed his sister, who was his protector. How did Timothy kill Jason? Was it a meeting, and Jason so inflamed him that Timothy hit him maybe in self-defense with the piece of driftwood? Or did Timothy plan it? I don't know. He didn't bring a weapon with him. I for one don't think I care if he murdered Jason."

Petra liked Timothy but said, "I think he's good for it, Captain. It looks like he never actually lied to us, but Ash's report says that he stopped the conversation when he realized he was in trouble. He certainly knows right from wrong. That means from the perspective of the criminal justice system, he's triable for his actions."

Ash jumped in. "Like all systems, there are flaws. The only way we prove this case is to get Timothy to confess, and my gut tells me that he's waiting to confess, if his girlfriend Alice and his friend Alex don't get him to lawyer up first."

Beauregard tapped the report with his finger and said, "Case closed. It's no longer our business. I believe that Leana and Timothy were complicit in the fire that killed their parents and brother. I've no way of proving that, and from all accounts, those people deserved to be punished—and they were. I have no way of proving that Leana was a serial murderer, but I know it's true. It looks as if our serial murderer was murdered as punishment for having more money and a better lifestyle than Jason, and for having rejected Jason when she was young. Her murderer, O'Leary, and his murderer, Jason Prior, received punishment."

Beauregard continued. "Now, there comes the question of Timothy. Why would he murder now? You know there is a concept that autistic children often have rage before reason, for which they must be taught methods of examining their rage and then controlling it, reasoning it out. When Timothy was a child, I understand any uncontrolled rage he had from living with such abusive parents. I also understand his uncontrollable rage when he learned that the one light in his life, Mary Lou, was murdered—and he knew who was responsible for murdering her. What I don't understand is how that rage went on unrelentingly for a time before Jason was murdered. I think that perhaps he was uncertain that Jason was really the culprit. Perhaps he went to see him and tried to have a discussion. There would be no discussion with Jason about Mary Lou. The actual murder does not look planned, but it was most likely done in one moment out of rage. I'm willing to let that be."

# Acknowledgments

To Joe, my husband, for his unquestionable loyalty, kindness, and love.

To my children: Kerstin, Joey, Raipher, and Julian, the lights of my life.

To my grandchildren: Dream, Endure, and Prevail!

I am grateful for all technical assistance I received from my good friends:

Police Matters:
Retired Springfield Massachusetts Chief of Police Paula Meara
Massachusetts State Police Officer John Ferrara

Attorneys:
Charles E. Dolan
Joseph A. Pellegrino, Sr. (ret. Justice, Massachusetts Trial Courts)
Raipher D. Pellegrino

And to my editors: I thank you for your support and counsel.

To all above: All errors on implementation are solely mine.

# Care to Review My Book? (or "Honest Reviews Don't Kill")

Now that you've read the story to the end, I'd love to know what you think of it – and read your honest review about the book on Amazon, Goodreads or another major online book site where it is featured.

Thank you for your interest in my books!
**Kathleen**

# More Books by K. B. Pellegrino

**Kathleen B. Pellegrino** – Author & Storyteller

**EVIL EXISTS IN WEST SIDE TRILOGY:**

Sunnyside Road Paradise Dissembling (Liferich Publishing)

Mary Lou – Oh What Did She Do? (Liferich Publishing)

Brothers of Another Mother – All for one -- Always? Expected to be published 2019

You can find K.B. Pellegrino's books on all major online Book Stores, such as Amazon, Barnes & Noble, kobo, I Books Store, SCRIBD, as well as on her website at: KBPellegrino.com/books

# Preview: "Brothers of Another Mother — All for one — Always?"

If you want to get a taste for Kathleen's upcoming book, **download a free Chapter** of the Trilogy's book #3 "Brothers of Another Mother – All for One—Always? at KBPellegrino.com/brothers –of-another-mother-free

# BONUS

*"I am grateful for every reader who picks up my books to read them. I'd like to give something back that you might find interesting."*

***—Kathleen***

To access **freebies** like book Giveaways, Free Books or Free Chapters of published and upcoming books, and more, visit:
kbpellegrino.com/bonus

CPSIA information can be obtained
at www.ICGtesting.com
Printed in the USA
BVHW041914070319
542068BV00011B/249/P

9 781489 718815